"Every time I'm around you, Tessa, I seem to get drenched."

"That's the risk you take when you're my friend," she lightly replied.

She realized she'd said something significant because of the way he turned to her, his expression thoughtful, his eyes intent on hers.

"Are we that? Friends?" he asked her, his voice radiating a vulnerability that tugged at her heart. "I know I haven't exactly made your job at the hospital easy."

"Well, I always did appreciate a challenge," she quipped.

He looked uncertain, so she touched a hand reassuringly on his ____ ____ we're friends, No____

He ha____ ____ ____ th her, the emoti____ ____ ____ nted to his gui____ ____ ____ ed she had the courage ____ ____ ____...

Dear Reader,

Here, at the end of my Findlay Roads series, I faced the hardest story to tell. How do you take characters who have suffered so much, grieved so long, and give them a happy ending worthy of their struggle and the series as a whole?

So I talked to people and listened to what they'd gone through. Not just with childhood cancer, but with grief, loss and hope. Then I faced my own crisis when my father suffered a critical accident. I learned no one is exempt from tragedy, but you find your strength when faced with the worst.

For Noah and Tessa, their grief is different but equally real. He is mourning the loss of his daughter and wife, while Tessa struggles with infertility. I am so grateful to the people named in the acknowledgments, as well as others who freely shared their personal stories with me. They helped me find these characters' voices.

If you're facing a challenge of your own, know that you are not alone. Don't keep your struggles to yourself. Reach out, talk to people, share your story. That's how you'll find your way through—one minute at a time, then one hour, then one day. No storm lasts forever. May you find hope at the end of your struggle, just as Noah and Tessa did.

As always, if you'd like to share your own story with me, I would love to hear from you. You can contact me through my website at cerellasechrist.com, online via Facebook or Twitter, or by mail at PO Box 614, Red Lion, PA 17356.

Cerella Sechrist

HEARTWARMING

Tessa's Gift

—

Cerella Sechrist

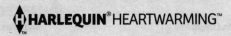

Recycling programs
for this product may
not exist in your area.

ISBN-13: 978-1-335-51055-6

Tessa's Gift

Printed in U.S.A.

Cerella Sechrist lives in York, Pennsylvania, with two precocious pugs, Darcy and Charlotte, named after Jane Austen characters. Inspired by her childhood love of stories, she was ten years old when she decided she wanted to become an author. A former barista, Cerella could spend hours discussing coffee origins and flavor profiles. She's been known to post too many pug photos on both Instagram and Pinterest. You can see for yourself by finding her online at cerellasechrist.com.

Books by Cerella Sechrist

Harlequin Heartwarming

Gentle Persuasion
The Paris Connection

A Findlay Roads Story

Harper's Wish
A Song for Rory
The Way Back to Erin

Visit the Author Profile page
at Harlequin.com for more titles.

Dedicated to my nieces, Emily and Ellis. You are the daughters of my heart, and you make every day an adventure. I love you both so much.

Acknowledgments

Special thanks to...

Tracy Bedell-Hoke and her daughter, Elizabeth, for sharing their family's experience with childhood cancer and answering my questions, no matter the time of day.

Zachary and Jackie Loder for being so open about their struggles with early-onset menopause and infertility.

Dr. Bradley Phiel and Linda Kimes from Heston Veterinary Medical Center for assistance with animal therapy questions.

Linda Seitz and her therapy dog, Viva, for details on animal therapy, especially in a hospital setting, and for graciously agreeing to appear as characters in the story.

Lisa Lawmaster Hess for our weekly writing sessions, which include brainstorming, encouragement and caffeine.

Every single person who offered their support and prayers as I finished up this book in the midst of my dad's accident. Thank you.

CHAPTER ONE

TESSA WORTH BENT over to finish clipping the leash to the pole. Before she could stand, her canine companion gave a hearty shake of his head, and she jerked back from the spray of slobber.

"Ugh."

She wiped a strand from her chin as she straightened. "Rufus, we've been through this," she chastised the dog. "Flinging drool on the ladies is no way to win hearts."

The English bulldog looked up at her with doleful eyes.

"Don't even start with me, mister," she said, then gave a quick glance around to be sure no one was witnessing her one-sided conversation with the dog. "Those bedroom eyes may have worked for you when you were a stray, but they won't get you anywhere with me."

Rufus huffed, and another gob of drool

landed on her sneakers. She groaned and swiped her shoe on the back of her leggings.

"Okay, listen. Just let me get some tea, and I'll bring you one of those muffins you like."

Rufus whimpered.

"No, not the bran-and-apple ones. The blueberry. Your favorite."

Rufus licked his chops, leaving a strand of slobber dangling from his nose.

"Oh, buddy. We really need to do something about that."

Rufus parked his behind on the sidewalk, unconcerned.

Overcome with affection, Tessa knelt down to scratch him behind the ears. He groaned with pleasure, and she was reminded once again how looks could be deceiving. During her time working at the local animal shelter, she had watched Rufus be bypassed for adoption again and again in favor of the younger or cuter pets.

When she'd left the shelter for her new job as a marketing and PR coordinator for a nearby hospital, she'd realized she couldn't leave Rufus behind. After all, they had something in common—she knew what it was to feel like she didn't quite measure up. She'd adopted him on her last day working at the shelter a little over two weeks ago. She hadn't regretted that decision for a second, despite the drool issue.

"I'll be back in a few minutes. Sit tight."

Rufus sneezed, which she took for a sign of agreement, and then Tessa stepped inside the Lighthouse Café.

The Lighthouse was a long-standing fixture of the Findlay Roads community. She'd gone there as a child, during summer visits to her grandmother's cottage before she'd moved to the town permanently after college. Back then, it had been a diner, complete with blue vinyl booths and geometric-patterned countertops.

Since it had been converted to a café, however, it had undergone extensive renovations to give it a much more modern and trendy vibe. With the tourist boom that had occurred in the town over the last several years, the café had become a favorite not only of locals but of out-of-towners. It helped that local son and famous country music star, Sawyer Landry, occasionally stopped in to play a couple of sets when he was in town.

Tessa walked inside the café and stepped up to the counter to place her order.

"Hey, Tessa," greeted the barista behind the bar.

"Hi, Liam," she replied. "Can I get a mint green tea latte to go, please?"

"Sure." Liam began punching her order into the system. "How's that new job going?"

"Good," she replied as she tugged her wallet out of her hoodie pocket. She didn't carry a purse when she took Rufus on his morning walk. It was challenging enough trying to wrangle a fifty-pound bulldog. She needed both hands free for the attempt. "Pretty good. I've only been there a few weeks and I've mostly been getting the lay of the land, but now I'm finally starting to dig into my actual duties a little more."

After almost two years working at the animal clinic, Tessa was enjoying the challenge of a new position. She'd worked for years as a pediatric nurse but stepped away from it after she'd bailed on her own wedding... and all the complicated emotions that went with that.

"That's $3.59," Liam said.

"Oh, I nearly forgot. Can you add a blueberry muffin?"

Liam arched a knowing eyebrow. "You're spoiling that mutt, Tessa."

Tessa assumed an affronted expression. "I have no idea what you're talking about. That muffin is for me."

Liam laughed as he punched her order into the system. "Sure, Tessa, sure. You know I can see him from here, don't you?"

Tessa turned in the direction Liam pointed, noting that Rufus was sitting patiently where she'd left him, his hooded eyes watching the café door with interest.

"He was found abandoned by the side of the road. He deserves to be spoiled a little bit."

Liam held up his hands in a gesture of surrender. "I'm just saying, you spend more money on that dog than on yourself."

Tessa shrugged. "He's worth it."

Liam shook his head as he took the ten-dollar bill she handed over. She didn't expect others to understand. She certainly hadn't been surprised by most of her family's reaction when she'd brought Rufus to the last family dinner.

Her sister Harper and her husband, Connor, as well as Connor's daughter, Molly, had made cooing noises over Rufus as if he were a newborn puppy. Her other sister, Paige, had been somewhat less supportive, asking why she'd chosen such an ugly dog to adopt. Tessa had made all the appropriate defenses about Rufus's character and disposition, but in the end, the family had assumed her choice was just part of what she'd once heard Paige refer to as Tessa's "pre-midlife crisis," a term that caused Tessa to flinch, though she hadn't let her sister know she'd heard her.

Just because she'd left her fiancé at the altar and then quit her well-paying job as a pediatric nurse in favor of minimum wage at the local animal shelter didn't mean she was going through a crisis. Well, Paige's assessment maybe did make sense. But only because her family didn't know the whole story behind her choices.

And that wasn't something she was planning to share anytime soon. If ever.

Tessa wished Liam a good day and then stepped to the end of the counter to wait for her order. She cast a quick glance outside to check on Rufus and then swiveled her gaze around the room, always interested to see the new faces in town.

She'd inherited her grandmother's cottage years before, and since then Findlay Roads had truly become home, more than the suburbs of Washington, DC, where she'd grown up. If only Nana could see how the town had grown. Much of it retained the same quaint, Chesapeake Bay charm Tessa remembered from her childhood. But there were plenty of new houses, shops and restaurants to cater to the tourist influx. Not to mention the Delphine, the sprawling luxury resort her own father had built to capitalize on the investment boom.

She noticed a couple in the corner and idly speculated whether they had come to the café to meet with a Realtor and visit some local properties. Real estate in the area had skyrocketed. The cottage she lived in was easily worth a fortune compared to what her grandparents had paid for it so many years ago.

She waved at a few familiar faces, including a girl she used to work with at the pediatrician's office. She hoped Allison wouldn't come over. While she had always been friendly with her coworkers, encounters with them now tended to be awkward since they, like her family, didn't understand why she had up and left her job so unexpectedly.

She shifted her attention back to the bar, and her eyes fell on another new face. He was handsome but almost seemed to have a brooding aura as he studied his phone. His dark brown hair was trimmed short, and he was dressed in dark slacks, a heather-blue shirt and a plain gray blazer. Simple but sophisticated. She entertained herself by speculating on what sort of business he had in town. Was he looking to move here, as she'd imagined the young couple were? Or was he simply a businessman passing through? Perhaps an entrepreneur looking to invest in one of the local businesses. Maybe he had a secret job with the CIA, and he'd come to Findlay Roads searching for an international thief. She nearly laughed at the notion, though his handsome appearance did put her a little in mind of an actor from a spy thriller.

"Tessa, your order's up."

She pulled herself out of her reverie and reached for her tea latte and the brown paper bag holding Rufus's muffin. From the corner of her eye, she noticed her CIA agent was still intent on his phone. He hadn't even glanced up.

"Spoiling that dog of yours again?" asked Shannon, the barista at the bar.

Tessa made a face as she grabbed the paper bag. "You guys are way too interested in what I feed my dog."

Shannon chuckled. "Nah, it's not that. We're just glad to see you coming around again."

Tessa couldn't argue with that. When she'd worked as a pediatric nurse, the Lighthouse Café had been part of her morning routine. She'd stop in for tea and a pastry before she headed to the clinic. But when she'd quit the doctor's office and had to tighten up her budget, daily trips to the coffee shop had fallen from routine to a treat. It was only now, with her new job at the hospital, that she'd picked the habit back up. Plus, the café was on her walking route with Rufus. And he did like their muffins.

"Thanks," she said. "It's…nice to be back."

Shannon eyed her for a moment, and Tessa tensed, fearing she'd ask more questions. But Shannon just nodded and grinned, and Tessa gathered her tea and muffin and turned to go.

"Hey, Tess."

She paused at the door as Liam said her name.

"Tell Rufus the next one's on the house."

Tessa raised her tea latte in thanks and pushed out the door. Rufus was on his feet the second he saw her, his tiny nub of a tail wagging a greeting.

"You wouldn't believe the grief I endure for you," she teased him. She bent down, balancing her carryout cup in one hand and trying to juggle the paper bag on one arm so she could open it. She pulled out the muffin as Rufus jumped up and chomped the muffin out of her palm. Tessa tottered, thrown off-balance. Hot tea sloshed out of the cup's lid, splattering across her hand. Scalded, she gasped as she jerked to her feet, bumping against something solid while Rufus greedily chewed on the muffin. She registered cursing behind her as she regained her balance and frowned down at her dog.

"Rufus! That was rude!" But Rufus took this admonition in stride as he licked the crumbs from his jowls.

Tessa turned, an apology on her lips. The CIA agent was dabbing at a large coffee stain on his shirt. She glanced down and saw his cup on the ground, dark liquid chugging from the lid. Rufus, finished with the muffin, had taken it upon himself to begin lapping up the liquid. "I am so, so sorry," she apologized to the man.

He fixed her with a glare. "You really ought to watch what you're doing," he said, his tone deep but frosty.

"I'm sorry, it was my dog…" She trailed off with a quick glance at Rufus.

"Then you should watch what your dog is doing," he returned.

Tessa frowned. "Let me buy you another coffee," she offered.

He checked his watch. She noted it had a mechanical timeface with a leather wrist strap. Under different circumstances, Tessa might have found it charming. She had never understood the digital watch thing, but even her dad wore one these days. She preferred a more traditional look.

"I don't have time for another coffee."

His words drew her attention back to the agent. He balled up the napkins he'd been using to clean his shirt and edged around her to toss them in a nearby trash bin. Rufus, who had finished his breakfast, suddenly took note of the man and gave a low growl. The guy paused midstep at the warning. Tessa stared at Rufus in surprise. During all the months she'd known him, she'd never heard him growl.

"I'm sorry, he's not usually like this," she said.

Rufus let out a nonthreatening bark as if

to apologize, but the stranger only arched an eyebrow.

"Sorry if I don't share your assessment. He looks like he belongs in the pound."

Tessa felt a ripple of irritation. She was sorry she'd ruined the man's shirt but did he have to insult Rufus?

"At least let me pay to dry-clean your shirt," she offered, still trying to make amends.

He huffed. "I'm already running late."

"Here." She picked up the brown paper bag from the ground, tearing off a piece that hadn't been splattered by coffee. "Do you have a pen on you?"

He grunted but pulled a pen out of his jacket pocket. "That's not necessary," he said, even as he handed it over.

Tessa scribbled her name and phone number on the bag. "Sorry to cause your morning to get off to a rough start, but it's like the saying goes, 'It's never too late to start your day over.'" She passed the pen and paper back. "When you get the dry-cleaning bill, let me know, and I'll send you the money."

He stuffed the items into his pocket and pushed past her without another word. She watched as he stepped across the street and got into a pickup truck, which was slightly incongruous with his sophisticated demeanor. She sighed.

"Well, Rufus, we better head back home so I can change or I'm going to be late for work, too."

Rufus belched in response.

DR. NOAH BRENNAN still wasn't very comfortable in his office. Ever since he'd started working at Chesapeake View Children's Hospital six months ago, he'd been unable to personalize the space. His last office had been filled with personal touches. Fingerpaint drawings, framed photos, the Post-it notes that Julia had stuck onto his iPad every morning. He'd filled the room with memories and reminders. But all of those mementoes were boxed away now, collecting dust in a storage locker.

He'd never been embarrassed by the emptiness until today, when he'd walked in and found Ana Morales, the hospital's director of development, eyeing the bare walls and desk.

Inwardly, he cursed. "Ana. I didn't know you were waiting for me. I apologize for running behind this morning."

It was that woman at the coffee shop with

her unruly dog. He fingered the scrap of paper in his pocket where she'd scribbled her name and phone number. Tessa Worth. He had little patience for careless individuals. Carelessness was how people ended up in the emergency room—something he'd witnessed firsthand during his residency.

If it hadn't been for Tessa Worth, he might have had time to settle into his morning routine before being faced with this unexpected visit.

Ana, fortunately, waved a hand to dismiss his apology. "You spend every waking minute at this hospital. There's no need to apologize."

She crossed to the desk and took a seat in front of it, tucking a strand of black hair threaded with gray, behind her ear. Her olive skin was lined with only a handful of wrinkles, and her brown eyes were astute. He fidgeted uncomfortably and avoided her gaze by stepping behind the desk and taking a seat.

Ana was the reason he was working at Chesapeake View. She'd been the hospital administrator at his previous job before becoming the director of development here. Ana knew his background, knew how he'd wanted a fresh start, so she'd recommended him to the hospital's board. Noah's reputation as a physician and the accolades he'd received over the years had sealed the deal for them.

But since coming to work at Chesapeake, Noah had gone out of his way to avoid Ana. She was still a reminder of his losses, and that made it difficult to be around her. She seemed to sense his dilemma and didn't seek him out other than when necessary. The fact that she'd come looking for him today made him curious and on edge. Maybe it had something to do with the way his morning had started off with the coffee shop woman. Things tended to go downhill when his day began poorly.

But what had she said when she had offered to pay for his dry cleaning? *It's never too late to start your day over.*

It sounded so much like one of Julia's old sayings, before their lives had taken a turn for the worse, that he'd nearly flinched. The thought of his dead wife shook him. Would the ghosts he'd tried to leave behind never stop haunting him?

"What can I do for you, Ana?" he asked, trying to take his mind off his memories.

Ana straightened and gazed at him directly. Noah frowned. Whatever had brought Ana to his office, she meant business.

"How are you doing?" she asked.

It was an innocent enough question, but he knew what lay behind it. "How are you *surviving*?" was perhaps a more accurate way to phrase it. But he didn't want to talk about his feelings. It was much easier and less painful to simply wall them off. If he focused on his loss, he'd never be able to do his job.

"I'm fine, thanks, Ana. How about you?"

She eyed him as he turned the question around, but thankfully, she chose not to press. After another minute of watching him, she came to the reason for her visit.

"Noah, as you know, the hospital recently brought a marketing and public relations coordinator on staff to assist me."

Noah recalled some mention of a new coordinator, but he didn't pay much attention to the world beyond his hospital floor. He wanted to keep his focus on what mattered most—his patients.

Ana paused, watching him carefully. "We've talked before about bringing more awareness to the hospital and the pediatric oncology department specifically—*your* department."

Noah's eyebrows knit together. He was fully aware that part of his duties was to help promote his department. His reputation was part of what had won him this position in the first place, and the board had told him they expected him to actively participate in all publicity campaigns. But in the last six months, he'd managed to remain uninvolved in such efforts, which was the way he wanted to keep it.

"Ana, I've told you before. I'm a doctor, not a public relations ploy."

A spark of determination entered Ana's eyes. Noah had always respected her, but now, her flinty gaze made him wonder just who would win if he was forced to go head-to-head with her.

"Dr. Brennan," she began, and Noah tried not to flinch. He recognized that by addressing him so formally, she was making it clear she was serious. "So far I've tried to be sensitive to your situation."

Noah flushed with suppressed anger. "I don't need your pity, Ana."

She leaned forward. "It's not pity to give someone time and space to mourn."

He looked away. "I don't need time and space. I need to be free to do my work."

Ana sighed. "Your work includes bringing attention to the hospital and its programs, along with fund-raising to support those programs. You're one of the top pediatric oncologists in the country, and that benefits the hospital tremendously, but it's also important to broadcast those successes."

Noah stiffened. "My job is to save children's lives," he corrected.

"Which is something you do with great skill," she returned, "but it's not all that is expected of you. The board would like you to be more actively involved in promotional efforts."

Noah blinked. "The board is more interested in me playing a part for the public than helping the children on this floor fight for their lives?"

Ana's expression hardened. "Self-righteousness is not an attractive trait, Doctor, even on you."

He didn't reply. It wasn't self-righteousness. He had no claim to righteousness of any kind. If a doctor couldn't save the very patient who had mattered most, what right did he have to act blameless?

Still, he had no desire to use—and in fact, was very much against using—his skills or reputation to support a sales pitch for the hospital.

"Noah, I need you to work with this new PR coordinator. Trust me, she's trying to help these children as much as you are. More funding will allow for better technology, updated equipment, and a host of other things that will only give the kids an edge in fighting cancer and other diseases."

Noah clenched his jaw, chastened by her words. He'd never begrudge the children the opportunity for more resources. What he resented was the hospital trying to use him, to leverage his skills and status when both of those things were clearly overrated.

"Promise me that you'll be nice to this coordinator."

He raised his head. "I am always professional with staff," he pointed out.

Ana arched an eyebrow. "I didn't say I wanted you to be *professional*, I said I wanted you to be *nice*."

"I am nice," he protested.

Ana looked skeptical. "Well, let's just take it one step at a time, shall we?"

Noah appreciated Ana's position, but he

wasn't going to make any promises. He wasn't the easiest person to work with, and his attitude often put people off, which was just fine with him. It was better for others, and for him, if they didn't get too close. And he didn't intend to make an exception for this new coordinator, no matter how sweetly Ana asked.

CHAPTER TWO

CHESAPEAKE VIEW'S ONCOLOGY ward was actually a bright, welcoming place. The walls were painted a buttery yellow, and butterflies with vibrant wings in jeweled tones of red, green, blue and orange were stenciled onto the walls. As Tessa stepped off the elevator, she faced the reception desk, made of blond wood and accented by the teal counter. The lights were housed in globes of pastel colors, emitting a soft, radiant glow. There was a waiting area with blue overstuffed chairs and sofas, along with a large, flat-screen TV running an endless loop of cartoons. A glass mosaic dominated one wall depicting a garden with butterflies amid the flowers.

Though the environment was cheery, Tessa prepared herself for a fight. She'd been warned that Dr. Noah Brennan could be difficult, but if she was going to do her job well, she'd need him on her side.

Tessa took her new job seriously. Her position as a marketing and PR coordinator was a newly created role, and her contract was only for a year. The hospital's board of directors was looking to raise funds and boost awareness of their programs, specifically in the pediatric oncology unit. If she was able to leverage Dr. Brennan's reputation and accolades to bring more attention to the hospital, the board had hinted her contract would be extended.

And she desperately wanted this job to continue. While she'd enjoyed working at the animal clinic, her small salary there hadn't been enough to pay for the upkeep of her grandmother's cottage.

Plus, this job was a blessing, allowing her to keep her hand in pediatrics, which had once been her passion, without requiring her to work directly with patients. She missed the daily interaction with children she'd had as a pediatric nurse, but her heart ached too much now to be around them day in and day out.

She adored kids. She always had. Becoming a mother was something she'd looked forward to her entire life, or at least until a couple of years ago. Since then, she'd made a concerted effort to avoid children. Now, she only prayed she could excel at this job so she could find her way past the heartache of the last two years.

She checked the time on her phone and nibbled at her lip in worry. Her boss was nowhere in sight. She had been scheduled to meet Ana Morales here fifteen minutes ago. The episode at the coffee shop that morning had cost her time, though, and she was running late. While Ana was a fairly flexible person, Tessa knew that arriving late, especially when she was finally going to meet the hospital's most prestigious doctor, wasn't the way to keep this job.

Fearing maybe Ana had come and gone without her, Tessa moved toward the nurses' station to see if Ana was hopefully running behind herself. She was relieved when she spotted Miranda, one of the nurses. Miranda confirmed that Ana was already there and waiting for her in Dr. Brennan's office. She pointed the way down the hall, and Tessa set off at a brisk pace, hoping she hadn't missed anything too important. As she walked, she remembered her conversation the week before, when Ana had described the hospital's chief pediatric oncologist.

"Noah is one of the best in the country, if

not the world," Ana had said. "He's brilliant when it comes to treating childhood cancers. He came on board six months ago. He was looking for a— Well, a change of scenery, I suppose you could say."

Tessa remembered sensing there was something Ana wasn't telling her about Dr. Brennan, but Ana had continued speaking before she could ask any questions.

"We've tracked the success of other hospitals' PR campaigns, and using someone gifted and well-known as the face of the campaign has yielded tremendous results. We are hoping to replicate that kind of success here. That's where you come in."

Tessa had read between the lines; whether she kept her job or not rested on the success of this venture with Dr. Brennan.

And now she was finally going to meet the man. She reached the door with Dr. Brennan's name on it and swallowed, feeling a wave of nerves as she prepared to meet the doctor she'd be working closely with in the months to come.

She tapped on the door and waited until she heard a muffled call for admittance. Pushing it open, she stepped inside, her gaze first falling on Ana. She smiled a greeting at her boss.

"I'm so sorry I'm late, Ana, but I got tied up—" As she was speaking, her gaze automatically shifted to the man standing on the other side of the desk. She drew up short as she recognized him.

It appeared the man from the coffee shop wasn't a CIA agent at all.

He was a doctor.

NOAH BLINKED IN surprise at the woman who had just stepped into his office. She looked equally stunned.

"Noah, this is—"

"Tessa Worth," he interrupted Ana and then immediately winced. Tessa would probably think it strange that he had noted her name on the scrap of paper she'd given him.

"Oh, good, you two have met already," Ana said. "Well done, Tessa, on diving right in."

His eyes were locked on the woman standing just inside the doorway, and he couldn't seem to tear them away. She looked as surprised as he felt, her cheeks coloring at Ana's praise, but she also hadn't spoken up. He wondered if she was waiting to hear how he would respond to this awkward situation. After another breath, he forced himself to look away from her and back at Ana.

"Ms. Worth and I met informally this morning."

Ana frowned but didn't question the explanation. "Well. Tessa is our new marketing and PR coordinator for the hospital."

He nearly groaned aloud. *This* was the woman he was supposed to work so closely with? Based on their earlier encounter, he was even less thrilled than he'd been when Ana had explained the directive to him.

"Oh, well then. Tessa, Dr. Brennan is the head of our pediatric oncology ward."

Tessa seemed to have gathered her composure as she stepped forward and raised a hand. "I'm pleased to meet you, Dr. Brennan."

He ignored her hand, stubbornly keeping his arms folded across his chest.

Ana cleared her throat, and as he caught her eye, he noted the scowl on her features. He reluctantly dropped his arms and shook Tessa's hand. He couldn't help noticing the softness of her skin, her fingers pleasantly cool within his. He broke the handshake as quickly as he could.

"I'd like for Tessa to shadow you today to get a better understanding of your role here at the hospital."

Noah and Tessa both began to protest at the same time.

"I don't think that's warranted—"

"I'm sure Dr. Brennan has a lot to do—"

Ana's expression silenced them both. "Let's keep in mind what these PR campaigns are really about. It's not about me, or either of you, or even the hospital. It is about raising money for these children. Getting them more care, better care and the very best tools to help them get well. So whatever issues you are dealing with should be set aside for the sake of this initiative. We are here to save lives."

Noah frowned. He had to hand it to her—Ana had the guilt speech down pat. How could either of them protest when she put it like that? For the length of several heartbeats, no one said anything.

To his irritation, it was Tessa who broke it.

"I'd be happy to shadow you today, Dr. Brennan, if you don't mind."

Of course he minded. Not that he would say so now after Ana's tidy little reprimand.

"That would be fine," he replied, his voice

tight. Ana picked up on his annoyance and shot him a warning look.

He ignored it. He appreciated the need for fund-raisers, and Ana was right—these children deserved every weapon the hospital could supply them in their fight against cancer. But Noah's job was on the front lines, fighting with and for these kids. It wasn't to be in the spotlight, promoting the hospital's work. It only distracted him from his true purpose.

"Well then, if there's nothing more you two need from me, I'll leave you to get better acquainted."

Noah felt a moment's panic, and he could tell, from Tessa Worth's wide eyes, that she was experiencing the same emotion.

"Maybe I should come back later, give Dr. Brennan time to…do…whatever he usually does in the morning," she finished, shifting her weight from one foot to the other.

"Later *would* be better—" He jumped on this opportunity to delay the inevitable.

"Don't be ridiculous. The whole point is for Tessa to get an understanding of your day," Ana said to him. "I trust you two will figure it out."

Before either one could protest further,

Ana stepped around Tessa and out the door, leaving them alone.

He suppressed a sigh as he said, "Well, let's get started, then."

As TESSA FOLLOWED Noah on his rounds, he realized she'd gotten to know far more people in a couple of weeks than he had in six months. She greeted all the staff on the floor by name, asking after their spouses, their children and their pets. One of the nurses reminded her she was supposed to email them a recipe, and Tessa complied by instantly sending it out from her phone.

The more he saw how quickly they warmed to her, the more irritated he became. Who was this woman to show up and ruin his day, starting at the coffee shop and now here, in his own hospital?

It only made him more determined not to like her, especially the times they accidentally came into contact—when their arms brushed, or she leaned toward him to ask a question. She was bright and attentive, which only made his efforts to ignore her all the more difficult.

He updated her briefly on the next patient, Kyle Miller, trying his best not to notice how long her lashes were as her brown eyes focused intently on his. Clearing his throat, he turned and walked into Kyle's room. Kyle was ten and had been battling leukemia since his diagnosis five weeks ago.

"Hello, Dr. Brennan."

Kyle's mother, Sheila, greeted him warily. It was a tone he was used to hearing. He knew she'd want answers, so he focused on Kyle and put Tessa out of his head as he brought up the boy's chart on the iPad Noah held in his hand.

Tessa shifted beside him, and when he remained absorbed in Kyle's chart, she took it upon herself to tell the family who she was. As she chatted with the parents, he scrolled through Kyle's latest test results, trying not to listen but finding it impossible.

"You like model ships?" she commented, and from the corner of his eye, Noah saw she was referring to the wooden craft Kyle had obviously been assembling.

"Yeah," Kyle shyly confirmed. "This was a gift from my grandpa. He came to visit me yesterday."

"That's great," Tessa said, and he marveled at how genuine she sounded. "It looks pretty hard to assemble, though. Is your dad helping you put it together?"

Kyle's father, Matt, laughed. "I can't even glue together popsicle sticks, so I'm no help."

Noah flicked his eyes up just long enough to see that the entire family seemed to be slightly more at ease as Tessa spoke to them. He continued reviewing the boy's chart. The test results looked promising, and he felt a measure of relief. Kyle might be turning the corner before long.

"My dad once tried to put together a model airplane," Tessa was saying. "I think he ended up using it for kindling one winter."

There was more laughter, and something about the sound set Noah on edge.

"Kyle's numbers are improving," he said, interrupting the conversation. "This means the treatments are working. We'll continue on this course."

The mood shifted, and Noah felt the family's momentary joy dissipate as swiftly as blowing out a match.

"For how long?" Sheila asked.

"We'll continue the chemotherapy for a couple more months. The numbers in the next few weeks will determine how long the treatment progresses."

"So...that's good?" Matt asked.

"For now," Noah said as he looked back at the iPad. "As I said, we'll just have to wait and see."

Someone cleared their throat, but he ignored it. Then, a second time. Noah glanced up and realized it had been Tessa who made the sound. She was staring at him, her eyes conveying some sort of message he couldn't read. He stared back at her, uncertain why she was looking at him in that way. After a few awkward moments, she turned back to Kyle and his parents.

"I'm sure what Dr. Brennan means is that this is good news. The treatments are working. That's why we will continue doing what we're doing, in order to help Kyle obtain full remission from the disease."

Noah frowned. "I can't make any promises to that end."

Tessa's head whipped around, and she gave him that sharp gaze once more. He noticed that Kyle's parents were glancing back and forth between him and Tessa. He didn't much like it.

"Does that mean I'm not going to get better?" Kyle piped up.

"I'm going to do everything in my power

to make sure that you do," Noah stated, his tone firm.

"Dr. Brennan, could I have a private word with you?" Tessa asked, her tone sweet but unyielding.

Noah made an effort not to let his irritation show. What in the world did she want now?

"Of course," he agreed, attempting to sound reasonable. Tessa turned to the family.

"Would you excuse us for a moment?"

She stood and headed from the room as he hurried to keep pace with her clipped strides. She didn't stop walking until they were out in the hall and several feet away from the room, well out of earshot from Kyle and his parents.

"What are you doing?" she demanded.

"I don't understand the question," he said.

"Those people are facing the most horrific scenario they can imagine, the possible death of their son, and you are treating them no differently than if their child has a common cold!"

Noah blinked once, then twice, before his anger began to rise.

"Excuse me?"

"You heard me," she muttered in a low

tone, keeping her voice down. Noah was vaguely aware that they were standing in an alcove of the hallway—not in direct sight and hearing of others but close enough for someone to observe their exchange.

"Can you remind me again, Ms. Worth, what it was you were hired to do here?"

She opened her mouth to speak, but he cut her off.

"Marketing. Fund-raising. Publicity. Goodwill. Not diagnosis. Not medicine. Certainly not cancer treatment. That is *my* job," he reminded.

Her eyes were shining with rage, deepening them to a beautiful caramel brown. But he was angry, too, and determined not to be distracted.

"That's not the only part of your job," she countered. "You're also supposed to support these people, treat them with compassion."

"I'm compassionate," he argued and then cringed at the defensiveness of his tone. He did not need to prove himself to this woman.

"Not from what I can see," she fired back, and the passion of her words stirred something deep inside him. When was the last time he'd encountered such fervor? When was the last time he had ever felt such fire in himself? Not for years. Not since before Ginny had started experiencing symptoms… He shifted the watch on his wrist, righting it so the face stared up at him.

"That little boy is terrified," she continued. "So are his parents. And you did nothing to reassure them."

He tensed. Passion was one thing, but he would not let her presume to know his job. "I don't make false promises," he replied, his voice cold in contrast to the heat in hers. "Hope does more harm than the cancer itself."

She opened her mouth, presumably to contradict him, but he forged ahead, rattled by her judgment of him and his methods.

"Do you know what hope is, Ms. Worth? It's a disease. It leads you along, blinds you to reality and leaves you unprepared for death. When you cling to hope, it eats away at you, one minute at a time, a more silent killer than the leukemia ever will be. Because it destroys you without evidence. It misdirects, making you think there is a chance that life will one day be the same, that you can go back to normal. But there is no normal life anymore. There is no chance of that."

Noah wasn't sure at what point in his

speech he'd stopped referring to his patients and began speaking of himself, but he kept going, a flood of angry words that he could not seem to stop. It had been so long since he'd allowed himself to get angry, to rail against the forces beyond his control. But this woman and her sudden intrusion into his day had worn away at the defenses he normally kept in place.

"You can do everything right—treatments, protocols, rules—but all it takes is one mistake, a single slipup, and the disease rushes in, more ravenous than before. And where is hope when that happens? It abandons you." He clenched his hands around the tablet he still held, trying to keep his fingers from shaking with rage. "Do not mistake compassion with false guarantees. I do not lie to my patients. They should be prepared for every scenario."

A memory of Ginny surfaced, in the last days before the disease had taken her, her face chalky, purplish-red bruises beneath her faded green eyes. She had looked at him, almost accusingly. He had promised her she would get better, that she'd be running and playing again before she knew it.

Within the month, she was dead.

His voice was hoarse with the effort of keeping back the tears and resisting a grief so deep and sharp that it felt as if his heart had been pierced. "Hope is fine for fairy tales, but it has no place here, in these halls," he rasped out.

And then he turned away, oblivious to the stares he sensed around them, and headed for his office, where he could close the door and remind himself that he was no longer hope's victim. Because fate had already taken everything that mattered to him, and now, there was nothing left for it to claim.

CHAPTER THREE

RUFUS STRAINED ON his leash as Tessa rang the doorbell of her parents' Findlay Roads home. Though her mom and dad had a penthouse apartment in Washington, DC, they had purchased a second home in town a couple of years ago. Her father divided his time between the Delphine, the local resort he owned, and his financial investment firm in the city.

Tessa liked having more family nearby. For years after her grandmother died, she was the only one who called Findlay Roads home. But then after her sister Harper lost her job as a restaurant critic, she'd moved in with Tessa until she got back on her feet. Now, Harper was happily married to local restaurateur Connor Callahan, and had adopted Connor's daughter, Molly. She and Connor had recently celebrated the birth of their first child together. Little Grace was a beautiful combination of Connor's green eyes and Harper's blond hair, and Tessa was every bit as enamored with her as she was with her other two nieces.

Tessa's parents still spent a lot of their time in the city, but now that they owned this house, they were making more and more trips to Findlay Roads. Only her oldest sister, Paige, and her husband and daughter still lived exclusively in DC. Tessa was hoping that might change at some point. For one thing, she was extremely close to her niece Zoe, Paige's daughter, and she'd love the opportunity to see the six-year-old more often.

Rufus whined impatiently. "Rufus, behave," she warned him. She probably should have left Rufus at home. But she couldn't stand the thought of making him stay by himself after she'd spent the whole day away at work. Not to mention that after spending so many hours with Dr. Noah Brennan, she needed Rufus to lower her stress level.

Then again, she knew she couldn't rely on Rufus alone. In the past two years, she'd shut too many other humans out. It was easy to love animals because they didn't wound like humans did. But over the last few months, Tessa had realized how isolated she'd become, how she'd begun to justify shutting people out of her life. She didn't want to become that person. She didn't want to turn into someone like Noah Brennan. She shuddered at the memory of their day together, and his bitter words.

Do you know what hope is? It's a disease.

It made her curious. What had happened to Noah Brennan to make him so jaded?

In any case, she was glad she'd decided to bring Rufus along. Zoe and Molly loved having a dog to play with during these family gatherings. And while Tessa would never admit it aloud, she sort of liked ruffling Paige's feathers with the dog. Paige had always been kind of stuck-up. Tessa loved her, but sometimes she wished Paige wasn't quite such a snob. She hoped Rufus would loosen Paige up a little bit.

It didn't look promising, though. Paige kept a good distance from the dog at all times.

The door opened, and her mother stood on the threshold.

"Tessa, darling, come in." Her mother leaned forward to place a kiss on her youngest daughter's cheek as Rufus tried to slip inside. He only got past the doorway before his leash came up short, pulling Tessa past her mother and inside with him.

"Oh, you've brought Rufus!" Her mother bent down to politely pat his ears, and Rufus grunted a greeting.

She knew her mother found her choice of canine companion odd, but at least she didn't criticize him like Paige did.

"Everyone else is in the dining room. We were just waiting for you before we started."

"Sorry if I'm late. I had to swing home and pick up Rufus after work."

"Oh, that's no trouble, darling. You know we keep ourselves entertained. How was your day?"

Tessa recognized the hesitation in her mother's tone. Her family was relieved that she had left her job at the animal shelter for something more distinguished. But they were still baffled because she hadn't told them the real reason behind her radical decisions from the year before. They'd given up asking since she'd stubbornly refused to share any details. But she knew they worried about her. They were all hopeful this new job was the light at the end of the proverbial tunnel. She didn't quite see it that way. Her life, her hopes for the future, would never be what they once were. But she, too, was hopeful for some kind of new beginning.

"Do you think we should lock Rufus on the patio while we eat?" her mother suggested. But the question came too late. Molly and Zoe had caught sight of him and were emitting girlish squeals of delight as they descended on him.

Rufus woofed and wagged his tail at the attention. Tessa had to smile as the girls knelt down to scratch his ears. He flopped onto the floor and rolled onto his back, inviting them to scratch his belly.

The rest of the family greeted her, but she couldn't help noticing how Paige eyed Rufus's presence with pursed lips.

"Tessa, we weren't aware you'd be bringing the dog."

Tessa shrugged. "He was home alone all day. I didn't feel it was fair to leave him while I came over here."

"Well, perhaps he's not the right pet for you, then. After all, with this new job, you're bound to be working some late hours. How is it going?"

"Slow down, Paige." Their father, Allan, held up a hand. "Give her a chance to sit down first."

Tessa was relieved for the intervention. She unclipped Rufus's leash as the girls continued to pet him, pausing to offer them both a kiss on the head.

"Zoe," Paige chastised, "that's enough playing with the dog."

Zoe reluctantly stood. She sneezed and wiped the back of her hand across her nose.

"Now go wash your hands. No wonder you can't get rid of that cold with all the germs you pick up."

"I'll go with her," Tessa offered. "I should clean up anyway." She took her niece's hand, unconcerned about the germs, and led the way to the bathroom. They took turns at the sink as Tessa asked questions about her day. Zoe sneezed again as they finished up.

Tessa's medical training kicked into gear, and she felt her niece's forehead. "Let me check your lymph nodes, munchkin." She felt around Zoe's neck, noting her lymph nodes were slightly enlarged. "You've had this cold on and off for a few weeks now, haven't you?"

Zoe shrugged. "Mom says I need to wash my hands more."

"Well, that certainly can't hurt," Tessa

agreed. "Has your mom or dad taken you to the doctor?"

Zoe nodded. "They gave me annie botics."

"Antibiotics?"

"Yeah. Annie biotics."

Tessa smiled. "Okay, then. I hope you start feeling better soon, kiddo."

She took her niece's hand again as they made their way back to the dining room. Dinner proceeded as it usually did. She, Harper and Connor talked about mutual friends in town, along with how the restaurant was doing. Her mom chimed into their conversation occasionally while Paige and her husband, Weston, discussed current events and business with their dad.

Molly and Tessa's mom chatted about school and summer plans, but Tessa couldn't help noticing that Zoe remained relatively quiet, only poking at her food instead of eating it. No one else seemed to pick up on Zoe's strange mood, but then again, Tessa had always had a special bond where Zoe was concerned.

At one point during the meal, she was able to stretch her leg under the table and knock Zoe's foot with her own. The six-year-old looked up, startled, and met Tessa's gaze.

Tessa winked, and Zoe grinned. She experienced some relief at the sight. Zoe had lost one of her baby teeth a month ago, and there was still a small hole where her adult tooth hadn't quite filled in yet.

Tessa leaned back as she finished the last bite of her dinner, feeling full and a little sleepy after the long day. Rufus had loyally curled up next to her chair, and she reached down to pat him as a reward for his quiet behavior during the meal. As she straightened, Connor stood and cleared his throat.

Around the table, everyone's attention shifted to him.

"I made something special for dessert since today, Grace turns three months old."

Tessa felt a tug in her chest. Her eyes fell to Harper, who was cradling her infant daughter in her arms. A stab of jealousy struck her directly in the stomach, decimating any desire for dessert, no matter what delicious dish Connor had cooked up.

"And I just wanted to take this opportunity to say how thankful I am to be part of this family. As you know, my mom died when I was still a lad, and my father's been gone for several years now…" Connor trailed off, his Irish accent more pronounced as his voice filled with emotion. Harper used her free hand to reach out and grab Connor's.

"Aye, well." He sniffed. "I am a very blessed man." He looked down at Harper with a smile that was achingly sweet. "I have a loving, supportive wife. And I never thought I could be so lucky as to have *two* gorgeous daughters." He winked at Molly before his eyes came to rest on Grace, who slept like an angel in her mother's arms.

"So before I bring out dessert, I just wanted to offer up an Irish blessing." He reached for his glass and raised it. The rest of the family followed suit, except for Zoe, who yawned and leaned against Tessa's side.

"May your troubles be less," Connor said, "and your blessings be more, and nothing but happiness come through your door."

The rest of the family voiced their agreement with these words and drank to little Grace and all the blessings of family.

And while Tessa sipped from her water glass right along with them, she couldn't help feeling removed from her family's joy. Because how could she share in their happiness when the one thing she'd always wanted— a biological child of her own—could never be hers?

Noah scanned the common area of the assisted care facility for his father-in-law. He found him by the window, staring out at the courtyard. Noah felt a moment of hope that his father-in-law was aware of the beauty of the day. But as he approached, his wishful thinking dissipated. There was no awareness in the other man's eyes. Only a blank, unseeing stare.

"Hey, John," he greeted, dropping a hand onto the other man's shoulder and squeezing by way of greeting. "How are you today?"

John said nothing. Not that Noah had expected him to. The stroke had rendered him catatonic.

"It's a beautiful day," Noah said. "Why don't we go outside?"

Since John could neither agree nor protest, Noah took hold of the wheelchair and navigated the older man into the courtyard. When they were outside, he made sure to tuck the blanket tightly around John's hips. The spring weather was pleasant, bright with sunshine and only a very mild breeze, but Noah knew how quickly his father-in-law could become cold. He pushed him around the concrete walkway until they reached the opposite side of the courtyard, where a bench awaited. He parked John beside it and sat down.

"I see the daffodils are blooming," he remarked. "I know those have always been some of your favorites. There are several planted along a walkway at the hospital, and whenever I see them, I think of you." He drew a breath. "You'd love the landscaping there. In fact, you'd probably keep the staff tied up for hours, telling them facts about different flowers. I remember the first time we met, and you kept me out in your garden forever, just talking about plants. I was so petrified to be meeting Julia's parents that I hardly said two words, and you just kept talking about soil acidity and compost techniques." He chuckled softly at the memory.

John kept staring straight ahead, seemingly oblivious to the beauty of the day as well as Noah's conversation. Noah sighed, humor evaporating, and leaned back on the bench.

"Speaking of the hospital—they've brought on some new marketing coordinator. Her name's Tessa. She and I are supposed to work together to elevate the hospital's reputation and my role there." He made a face even though he knew John wouldn't register it. "Can't they see it for the distraction it is? My focus is patients, not publicity. That's what they hired this Tessa woman to do. Let her worry about garnering public awareness and leave me to do my job."

He stood and started to pace. "The first time we met, she made me spill my coffee all over myself. I had to go back home to change, so I was late getting to the hospital. And then she tried to tell me how I should talk to my patients." He shook his head. "In any case, it's not my job to worry about publicity. My patients need my undivided attention. All it takes is one wrong judgment call, one distraction, and it could cost a child their life."

He stopped suddenly, the weight of these words settling around his heart, reminding him of Ginny. He sank back onto the bench. John didn't so much as twitch, and for that, Noah was grateful. He would give anything to restore his father-in-law to awareness, but that was a selfish wish.

He envied John his ability to block out the world and the memories of all they had lost. How pleasant it would be to forget, to be blissfully ignorant of the disease and death that had stolen all that he loved most in this world. And while it might have been nice to speak with the other man once more, Noah thought it was better this way. Let John have his catatonic peace. It was the only thing left to him. At least Noah still had his battle with the disease that had taken his daughter…and, indirectly, his wife. It was a distraction, but it was rarely enough to silence the guilt and grief completely.

"It doesn't happen often," Noah whispered, "but sometimes, I'll get so involved with a patient that I forget. I forget how I lost her. In some ways, I wish it happened more." He closed his eyes, letting the sun warm his face and fighting back tears. "Is that wrong, do you think? That there are moments I just want to forget? Not forget Ginny or Julia, really, but just to have a bit of respite from the grief?"

He opened his eyes. "But I suppose it *is* wrong. My memories are my punishment. I don't deserve to forget, do I? Why should I when I'm still here and they're gone?"

He swallowed. "There are days when I hate Julia for doing what she did. And there are other days when I envy her. I wish I'd been able to find the courage to do the same thing." He paused. "But that's not right. I'm here because I have to make amends. I need to save the others even if I couldn't save Ginny."

The burden of this confession overwhelmed him. It brought no relief to speak it aloud. John's eyes had slipped closed, and Noah wasn't sure if he was asleep or simply resting. It didn't matter. He prayed that John had peace now, even if Noah didn't. That would have to be enough.

THE DAY AFTER Tessa's first interaction with Dr. Noah Brennan, she purposely avoided him. She knew Ana wanted them to work together, but she wasn't up to dealing with the man's disapproval. She used her morning in other ways instead, writing up several grant applications on the hospital's behalf and getting a start on the email campaign she had in the works.

Tessa kept the door to her office closed, and to her relief, Ana didn't pop in to check on her. She liked her new boss, but she didn't need more pressure where the hospital's all-star doctor was concerned. By noon, however, Tessa was ravenous. She'd had no appetite that morning, so she'd skipped her early walk with Rufus and hadn't had her tea latte. Before heading out the door, she'd grabbed a tea bag, and later found a crumbled packet of crackers, two mints and a sealed snack bag of gummy bears that she kept for Zoe and Molly in her purse. It had made for a poor breakfast, and now her stomach was rumbling so loudly she feared the sound of it would draw Ana to her anyway.

By 12:07, she knew she had to give up and venture to the hospital commons. She hoped she wouldn't run into Ana and have to answer questions as to how she and Dr. Brennan were getting on. She grabbed her wallet, peeking her head out of the office before she made a dash for the main lobby of the hospital and then followed the walkway to the atrium that housed the commons cafeteria.

It was peak lunch hour, and the tables were filled with visitors, nurses, doctors and other staff members. Feeling like the new kid at school, Tessa got into the line and waited, scanning the area for free seats. She could always take her lunch back to her office, but it would be far easier to hide out here, with so many people. Tessa had noticed that Ana often worked through her break, so it was probably safer to be out of her office at the moment.

Once she had her chicken Caesar salad and fruit cup, she looked for a place to sit. She perked up when she saw a small table with only one other occupant. She headed in the direction of the vacant seat, hoping the diner would be willing to share their spot. She was nearly upon the table before she recognized the person sitting there.

Dr. Noah Brennan. She stifled a groan. Then again, if she wanted to keep this job, maybe she should make an effort to get to know him a little better. As she was working up the courage to sit, he looked up and met her eye. She forced a smile, the decision made for her. "Mind if I join you?" she asked, gesturing with her head to the empty seat.

His expression didn't change, nor did he respond for what felt like a full minute. But then he dipped his head, and she moved forward to slide into the vacant chair.

"Thank you," she offered. They were both silent for a few minutes.

Tessa picked at her salad, realizing her appetite had disappeared. She felt awkward and miserable and again marveled at Dr. Brennan's utter lack of people skills. How were they going to work together when they couldn't even sit at the same table without the atmosphere becoming uncomfortable?

She put her fork down and shifted to face him.

"I feel like we got off on the wrong foot," she said. "I'm sorry about how I spoke to you yesterday and for what happened at the Lighthouse Café."

He didn't respond, but she noticed something in his posture, an easing of the shoulders, so she took it as a good sign and continued.

"I adopted Rufus—that's my dog—a couple of weeks ago, and I'm still training him." She smiled at the thought of her pet. "Rufus has a good heart, but sometimes he gets a little too excited…especially when food is involved." She chuckled to herself. "You should have seen him at the animal shelter where I worked. He always knew when feeding time was getting close. I swear, that dog has an internal clock. If we were one minute late getting the food to him, he would start barking to remind us."

She smiled at the memory. Rufus had been overlooked because he was a little homely and he seemed gruff. But the truth was, he was the sweetest dog she'd worked with during her time at the clinic. It was why she'd taken him with her when she left.

"You worked at an animal shelter?"

Dr. Brennan's voice was so unexpected that it took a moment for it to register that he'd spoken.

"What? Oh. Yes. I mean, I did. Before I got this job."

He cocked his head, and she felt compelled to justify her experience.

"I worked there for a little less than two years. Before that, I was a pediatric nurse at a physician's office."

Dr. Brennan pushed his plate aside and looked at her. His eyes were a dark gray, "storm-tossed," as she'd read in a novel once. She was struck again, as she'd been in the coffee shop, by how handsome he was.

"That's quite a shift, from pediatrics to pet care," he said.

His gaze was curious, and his interest rattled her.

"Not just pet care," she corrected. "The animal clinic also assists abused animals and finds foster placements. In fact, that's a large part of what they do."

He continued to eye her with curiosity. "Still, what caused you to make a change like that? Unless…it wasn't your choice?" he prompted, arching one eyebrow.

She frowned at his implication.

"It was my choice," she said firmly. "I had a…crisis of faith, I guess you could say."

It was the truth, without revealing the details. He waited a beat, then when she didn't elaborate, he looked away…but not before she witnessed a flash of some emotion in his eyes.

"I see," was all he said.

She poked at her salad again. "Anyway, after I left pediatrics, I took a step back and decided to work with animals. Then I saw this job opening. During college, I spent summers working at my dad's investment firm as a marketing intern. I even worked there after college for a few months until I moved to Findlay Roads. I had the qualifications for this kind of role, so I thought I'd give it a shot. And here I am!" she awkwardly declared, her voice too loud on the last few words.

She speared a piece of lettuce and forced herself to take a bite.

"How about you?" she asked in an attempt to be conversational.

Dr. Brennan's head whipped back in her direction but he said nothing.

"How did you end up here?" she asked.

Instead of replying, he stood and gathered up the remains of his half-eaten lunch. She swallowed, the lettuce sticking in her throat.

"The same as you. I gave it a shot. Here I am."

The clipped reply struck her harder than it should have. She was obviously being dismissed. She felt the sting of rejection. She had only been trying to build a bridge between them, since they had to work together.

She made one more effort to get past whatever dislike Dr. Brennan had for her.

"I'm sorry, did I say something wrong?"

He tossed his wadded-up napkin onto his tray.

"No."

The denial did nothing to reassure her.

"Dr. Brennan, I have apologized for yesterday, but if I have done something else to offend you, I would prefer you tell me. Like it or not, we have to work together, and I think it's best if we make an effort to get along."

He fixed her with a cool stare, but she refused to be cowed by him. She stared right back.

"I'm here to do a job," he said, "and distractions like marketing are detrimental to

the care of my patients. I understand we need
to work together, but you and I don't have to
be best friends in order to do that. We're both
professionals, and I expect we can manage
just fine on that level."

Her cheeks were flaming with embarrassment and anger by the time he was finished.
She had never met anyone so presumptive,
so arrogant. She stood to her feet, as well,
disliking how he still loomed over her.

"I suppose we can," she returned, keeping
her own tone cool, "but I'll remind you that
the very definition of 'working together' im-
plies *cooperation*. I haven't been here long
enough to see how you run your department,
Doctor, but you don't strike me as much of
a team player. So may I remind you that a
medical community is just that—a *community*. We rely on each other, elevate each
other and encourage one another. But especially, we work hand in hand to provide the
best care possible to our patients. You say
marketing is a detriment to your job, but you
can't care for those kids without help from
others. You are not their one and only sav-
ior. Therefore, I'll expect you to be an active
participant in whatever scenario I present
you with."

He blinked, looking surprised. She didn't blame him. She'd shocked herself with that little speech. She wasn't naturally a forceful person. In her family, that was usually Paige. And, if pressed, maybe Harper. But never Tessa. Apparently, Noah Brennan had brought it out of her.

"The next time I see you, Dr. Brennan, I hope you have a very different attitude than the one I've seen thus far."

She picked up her lunch tray, and with one last glance at Noah Brennan's startled expression, she turned on her heel and left.

CHAPTER FOUR

"THANKS, DIANA," Tessa said as she slipped Rufus's monthly flea and tick meds into her purse. She'd stopped in at the clinic after work, using the errand as an excuse to check in with her former coworkers. Her week with Dr. Brennan had been rough, making her miss the simple joy, albeit accompanied by hard work, of dealing with four-legged patients.

Diana came around the counter to kneel down and greet the bulldog. He wiggled his behind in greeting.

"Sure thing, honey. I'm glad you stopped in. We've been wondering how you're doing at that new job of yours."

Diana reached out to drag her famously long nails across Rufus's spine. He groaned with pleasure.

Tessa thought about Dr. Brennan and their most recent altercation. She liked her job, but she wasn't sure about the pediatric oncologist. The man was perplexing, leaving her emotions in a tangle. His self-righteousness was irritating, but she couldn't shake the feeling there was more to him than that. The way he'd spoken about hope... She'd been unable to get the words out of her head.

Do you know what hope is? It's a disease.

The idea made her shudder. Not only because of the heartbreaking defeat it promoted but also because it made her certain Noah Brennan must have suffered something truly devastating in his life. How was she possibly going to deal with him over the course of the next year? And would she ever be able to win him to her side?

"Tessa?"

She snapped to attention.

"What?"

Diana frowned at her. "I asked how the new job was going?"

"Oh. Right." She cleared her throat. "Um, good. I'm working on a bunch of fundraising ideas right now to present to the hospital board."

Diana beamed. "Good for you, honey. We all knew you'd do all right." Diana originally hailed from the South, and despite having lived in Findlay Roads for twenty-plus years, she still carried a slight twang when she spoke.

"Thanks. I appreciate the vote of confidence."

Rufus jumped up on Diana, placing his paws on her knees in a bid for attention. She reached down to scratch behind his ears.

"How are things here at the clinic?" Tessa asked.

Diana made a face. "Well, we're understaffed as usual, sugar. Alexis up and quit without notice last week."

Tessa furrowed her brow. "Really? I thought she loved working here."

Diana waved a hand in dismissal. "She did, but her boyfriend decided he's moving to New Mexico, so she's going with him."

Diana had a penchant for gossip, and she filled the next twenty minutes with details on Alexis's sudden departure, along with several other items of interest. Tessa listened politely but didn't add anything to Diana's dialogue. She'd learned that it was best to just let Diana talk, and eventually she'd run out of things to say.

Fortunately, this happened sooner than expected when a mom and her little boy stepped into the clinic, and Diana was forced to assist them.

The mom began chatting with Diana, but her son honed in on Rufus immediately and asked if he could pet him.

"Sure," Tessa agreed. The boy looked to be around ten, and something about him reminded her of Kyle Miller, one of the hospital's leukemia patients. He had the same smattering of freckles across his nose. "He likes to have his belly rubbed," Tessa suggested, and hearing these words, Rufus obligingly sprawled out on the clinic floor and rolled over.

The boy laughed and knelt down to run his palms up and down Rufus's abdomen.

"What's his name?" he asked.

"Rufus. And I'm Tessa." She joined him on the floor and ran her own fingers over Rufus's fur.

"I'm Jeremy." He was quiet for a minute, but he kept rubbing his hand up and down Rufus. "I had a dog once," he finally offered. "She died."

Tessa clicked her tongue in disappointment. "I'm sorry, Jeremy. That's tough, losing a pet. But I bet another animal would love to come and live with you."

"Yeah," he agreed. Rufus seemed to sense the boy's disappointment. The dog rolled himself back over and stood up on all fours, looking at Jeremy with sad eyes.

Suddenly, Jeremy reached out and wrapped his arms around the dog's neck. Rufus just stood there and let himself be squeezed. It seemed to cheer Jeremy up. After a minute, he released her bulldog and stood back up. He was smiling.

His mother had concluded whatever business she'd come in for and had turned to leave. "Jeremy, are you ready to go?"

"Yeah." He stroked Rufus's back one last time before standing. "See ya later, Rufus."

As he faced the door, his mom looked over her shoulder to mouth a "Thank you" to Tessa.

She nodded and stood. Diana was watching her.

"That was good for Jeremy. He's had it rough the last year."

"Oh?"

"His dad was abusive. Beat the boy up pretty badly before his aunt there alerted the authorities and took him in. She's thinking of getting him another dog. He hasn't said what happened, but I suspect the father got rid of his last pet."

The story tugged at her heart. She had assumed the woman was the boy's mother. "That's awful."

Diana agreed. "Leave it to Rufus to cheer him up, though. There's nothing quite so healing as the love of a dog," she wisely imparted.

Rufus looked up at Tessa then, his soulful eyes wide. It was then that Tessa had an idea. One that would not only benefit the hospital's patients but maybe soften Noah, as well. It wasn't her job to banish his demons—she knew that. But she'd been hired to elevate goodwill and recognition for the hospital. How could she promote a doctor who didn't believe there was hope, especially for himself? She had to help Noah see there was value in promoting his work and the hospital's programs. And Diana had just given her a clue on how to do it.

"Diana, you're brilliant."

The older woman threw her a glance. "Well, thank you, honey. I think you're pretty special, too."

"I've gotta go. Maybe I can swing by this weekend and help you guys out."

She clipped Rufus's leash on and hurried toward the doors.

"That would be great, honey. How about Saturday?" Diana called after her, and Tessa gave her a thumbs-up. But she was already pulling her cell phone from her pocket as she stepped outside, thumbing through the contacts for Ana's number. She knew she should probably wait and speak with her boss in person, but she didn't want to lose a minute on this idea.

NOAH KNEW SOMETHING was amiss from the moment he stepped off the elevator to begin his shift. During the day, the pediatric oncology ward usually had a constant background noise, including the hum of conversation, the beep and buzz of hospital equipment, but also children's chatter and laughter. It never ceased to amaze him, the resiliency of children. Even while they were in a battle for their lives, kids managed to smile, to laugh, to remain upbeat no matter what they faced. That was not to say they weren't afraid. Noah was well acquainted with the fear they experienced daily. But somehow, they managed to find tiny things to be happy about.

Ginny had been the same way. He and

Julia lost their smiles long before she did. They scraped together just enough optimism to keep up a hopeful front for their daughter. But Ginny had seen through them. She was the one who had often worked at holding them together. Even when she was dying, the disease taking over her body by insistent inches, she'd done her best to smile.

"Sing to me, Daddy," she used to say.

She loved "Itsy-Bitsy Spider" even after she had long outgrown it. She liked to see him do the hand motions, and she would laugh when his fingers inevitably tangled together. He swallowed hard at the memory. He would give anything, all that he owned and more, just to hear Ginny laugh one more time.

But today the ward was too quiet. He cocked his head, listening, and there was noise—it was just concentrated to a single area. What in the world was going on?

He checked his phone as he stepped down the hall, drifting toward the sound with a mild curiosity. When the nurses' station came into view, he found it empty. Where had all his staff disappeared to?

A few more steps, and he had his answer. A crowd had formed in the children's playroom area. The room was full of people, and a few were even spilling out into the hall. He experienced a moment's panic. Had something happened to one of his patients? Why hadn't he been called? And why was everyone congregating here?

He began pushing through the crowd, not bothering to apologize. The group shifted around him, and he heard a few people offer greetings, but he ignored them. If one of the kids was in trouble...

He emerged from the edge of the crowd into an open area of the playroom. No one was hurt or in need of care. On the contrary, the group of kids huddled on the floor were all smiling. His gaze shifted to Tessa Worth. She was seated beside the kids, her face beaming. She hadn't seen him, but his heart jerked at the sight of her. How was it that this woman was upending his carefully ordered world at every turn?

He was just about to ask what was going on when he saw... *it*. He blinked, disbelieving. No. She couldn't have... No one had informed him... He narrowed his eyes as the children giggled. But there was no denying what was right in front of him. The dog, a mixed breed resembling a border collie, was wagging her tail and preening with all the attention. How many pets did this woman own? And what made her think it was okay to bring them into *his* hospital?

He cleared his throat. "Ms. Worth." He finally had her attention. "Perhaps I could have a word?"

She smiled, but it looked uneasy.

"Of course," she said. She turned to someone, a woman he didn't recognize. "Linda, if you or Viva need anything, just let one of the nurses know."

The woman nodded and then turned her attention back to the dog. Noah belatedly realized that Linda must be the animal's owner. So apparently the dog did not belong to Tessa after all. It was a minor point, he decided, as he took her arm to steer her through the crowd.

It was a mistake to touch her. He was all too aware of the softness of her skin beneath his palm. It wasn't until they were past the group that he realized how tightly he held her. As if she had suddenly realized it, too, she tugged her arm free.

"What can I do for you, Dr. Brennan?" she asked, a trifle too sweetly.

He didn't want to discuss the situation

in the hall. They were still too near to the crowd, and he didn't relish a repeat of the previous week's performance, when their argument had grown all too heated within full view of the staff and patients.

"I would appreciate it if you'd accompany me to Ana's office," he stated, doing his best to keep his tone professional.

She frowned. "If you like."

He turned and started in the direction of the elevator. He sensed her follow. They were silent as they waited for the elevator, the tension growing with every second that passed. His ire built.

"How long have you had this planned?" he asked as the elevator car arrived.

"What do you mean?" she replied, too lightly.

He stepped inside the elevator, and after a beat, she followed. They rode to the first floor in silence, making their way across the atrium and into the office area. He walked up to Ana's door and with a perfunctory knock, swung it wide.

Ana looked up from where she was seated at her desk, a pen hovering over whatever notes she'd been making. If she was startled by the intrusion, she didn't show it.

"Noah," she greeted and then shifted her attention. "Tessa. How are you both today?"

He didn't waste time with niceties.

"There is a dog in my cancer ward."

Ana blinked.

"A *therapy* dog," Tessa put in. "Like we discussed."

Ana and Tessa shared what he could only describe as "a look" with some sort of secret communication passing between them.

"I wasn't informed about any sort of therapy dogs. Because if I had been, I would have pointed out that studies show there is very little benefit to having animals in a cancer ward. It is possible they might even do more harm than good, by bringing in outside germs—"

"Those studies also admit that the presence of pets lowers cortisol levels and takes the patients' minds off the stressors of their treatment," Tessa cut him off. "I contacted the national Alliance of Therapy Dogs to find a properly trained animal, and they recommended Linda and Viva to us. ATD is well aware of the requirements of medical facilities, and their members are required to go through the necessary clearances in addition to a yearly evaluation—"

"Hold on." He swiveled his gaze back to Ana. "You agreed to this? Without getting my approval?"

Ana arched an eyebrow. "I'll remind you, Dr. Brennan, that I don't need your permission to do my job."

From the corner of his eye, he noticed Tessa's shoulders relax. They tightened again when Ana shifted her gaze to the other woman.

"However, I assumed Tessa consulted with you before I gave her the green light. I was told she informed you of her plans."

"I sent you an email about it," Tessa lamely defended.

"An *email*?" he gritted out.

Noah wondered if she had chosen that communication method solely because he avoided any items in his inbox that weren't directly related to his patients' care. Tessa had probably figured that out by now since he never replied to anything else.

"Well, if I had brought it to you in person, you would have shot it down."

"So you decided to circumvent me altogether?"

"I wasn't circumventing you! Email is the

accepted form of communication for most office correspondence."

"If it doesn't relate directly to my patients—"

"Aha! But see, this email *did* relate directly to your patients. You just chose to ignore it because it had 'publicity' in the subject line."

"Which you knew I would do!"

"If you'd just give Linda and Viva a chance, you'd see how great this could be— not only for your patients but for you, too."

"For *me*? How is having animals on my oncology floor going to help *me*?"

Ana cleared her throat. They turned their attention in her direction and she leaned back in her chair and folded her arms across her chest.

"Tessa has a point. Animal therapy is a great idea. Not only is it beneficial for the children, but it earns us some positive publicity. I was pleased she suggested it."

Noah could practically feel Tessa radiating satisfaction over Ana's praise.

"However." Ana's gaze became steely. "I expect the two of you to work *in unison* on these projects. Tessa, you should have consulted Dr. Brennan and received his input rather than leading me to believe he was on board. Though, granted, I should have known better than to assume you had his buy-in."

"I understand, and I apologize," Tessa said, "but I'd just like to point out how much the children are loving the therapy dog."

"Any child loves a zoo, but I hardly think it's appropriate to host one in an oncology ward," he pointed out.

Ana shot him a warning look. "One dog does not constitute a zoo," she said. "The therapy dog program is a great idea, and I chose to run with it because it is not only beneficial to the patients but the hospital as a whole. I'm sorry that Tessa didn't fully loop you in on the idea, but I'm sure that oversight will not happen again."

Tessa looked suitably chastened. "No. No, it won't," Tessa agreed. "I'll be sure to include Dr. Brennan in all decisions going forward… in person."

Ana nodded her approval, and Noah recognized it was time he also conceded defeat.

For all his stubbornness, he was no match for these two women, especially if they were united. And truthfully, would it be so bad to have therapy dogs occasionally visiting the ward? He remembered early on in Ginny's treatments a hospital staff member had brought a bunny around. Ginny had been delighted. It hadn't changed the outcome of her treatments, and she'd still been stressed about her chemotherapy that day, but for a few minutes, she'd been able to put aside her worry and just be a kid again.

The memory settled some of his anger. Perhaps Ana and Tessa had a point.

"Fine," he bit out. "But any issues that arise are her responsibility—" he pointed to Tessa "—not mine."

"Agreed," Ana said.

He had the sense that Tessa wanted to say something more. But what else was there to be said? She'd won, this round at least.

TESSA SHOULD HAVE felt validated by the discussion in Ana's office, but in truth, she felt awful.

After Noah left the room, Ana had questioned her on how the patients were reacting to the therapy dog, and Tessa shared what a great success the idea had turned out to be. The kids loved it, and the parents were thrilled. The nurses and other staff had found excuses to stop in and pet the dog.

Linda and Viva would be in the hospital

for a few more hours visiting patients' individual rooms, if the families wanted to participate.

Noah was the only one who had responded negatively to the animal's presence. Tessa couldn't say she was surprised by his reaction, but a part of her was disappointed. She'd hoped that Dr. Brennan would exhibit a little humanity, a softening of his hard exterior, and give her a glimpse of the man beneath.

She realized she had lingered too long in Ana's office, musing on Noah Brennan and his jaded view of the world.

"I know Dr. Brennan is a challenge, but I would encourage you to be patient where he is concerned."

Tessa raised her head. "Because he's a brilliant doctor." She said it as a statement of fact, assuming that was what Ana meant. But to her surprise, her boss hesitated.

"That's one reason, admittedly." She frowned, seeming to struggle. "But it's more than that. Noah is not only a good doctor, he's a good man."

Tessa found this an odd remark. "I never meant to imply he isn't," she said. Just because they'd gotten off to a rough start, and he seemed to have a particular dislike for her—or at least, for her role as the marketing and PR coordinator—that didn't make him an uncaring person. It was part of what confused her so much about him.

Noah seemed to care a great deal for his patients, even if he didn't show it to them. He spent many unnecessary hours at the hospital, she'd found, reviewing charts and reading up on the latest cancer treatment research. She believed his explanation that he found all of her efforts to be distractions from what he was meant to be doing: treating children. He was surly and overbearing, but that didn't make him a bad man.

"I know he can be challenging," Ana went on, "but keep in mind that his demands of others pale in comparison to what he demands from himself."

She sensed Ana was trying to tell her something that she couldn't voice aloud, whether for confidentiality reasons or private ones.

"Just try not to take his attitude personally. It's not about you. You're doing a fantastic job, and the therapy dog program is a great idea. Noah will get on board with it, in time."

"Mmm." She didn't want to disagree with

Ana, especially being so new to the job. But she was pretty sure the handsome doctor did have some personal dislike of her. But regardless of how they clashed personally, as he'd said, they were professionals. They could surely find their footing in a working relationship even if they'd never be, as he put it, "best friends."

She only wished she didn't have to fight him every step of the way.

"I'm sure it will work out just fine," she finally offered.

But as she left her boss's office, she couldn't help thinking that there was no way Noah was ever going to believe they were on the same side.

CHAPTER FIVE

AFTER THE DOG INCIDENT, Noah had to concede that Tessa's ideas had merit.

So he decided to experiment, based on Tessa's criticisms, and tried smiling as he spoke to his patients. But he couldn't remember the last time he'd smiled. This observation in and of itself was startling. He could still smile, couldn't he? Maybe he couldn't. Maybe Ginny's and Julia's deaths had stolen his ability to ever do something as simple as smile ever again.

But he had to try. When he entered Madison Ryan's room, he did so with a grin on his face.

By the look on her and her mother's faces, he didn't succeed too well. He caught his reflection in the mirror that sat over the nearby sink and nearly jumped. His smile resembled a creepy leer. He immediately smoothed out his facial features and tried for something more relaxed instead of so ridiculously upbeat. It seemed to make Maddy and her mother more comfortable. He'd have to practice smiling in private, in front of a mirror, before he tried it again with a patient.

He began sharing the latest update on Maddy's condition, offering up blood cell counts and other test results. The news was positive, but Maddy and her mother only stared at him uneasily. Though they seemed to understand this news didn't mean the little girl was cured, he felt the need to add, "I should caution you not to get too excited just yet since we still have a long road ahead."

The pair was silent. He stopped, thinking of Tessa. What would she say about his gloomy outlook for this child? How had he felt, as a parent, when Ginny's doctors delivered such updates? Of course, he'd understood the terminology better than most, given his background. But he remembered that he'd taken every scrap of hope that was offered to him at the time, feeding the will to go on, to keep fighting for his daughter's sake.

He might not believe in hope now. Not anymore. But did he have the right to withhold it from others? Maybe Tessa had a point.

Would it be so bad to give his patients the opportunity to enjoy their successes?

"So…" He cleared his throat. "We still have a battle to fight, but these test results are good news."

He watched as some of the tension eased from Mrs. Ryan's shoulders.

"This is a win," he tried again. "And you should celebrate."

The change was instant. Maddy beamed as her mom leaned down to embrace her. There were tears of happiness in her eyes as she straightened.

"Thank you, Dr. Brennan. I can't tell you how grateful I am for all that you're doing for my little girl."

For a moment, he wanted to correct her, to let her know he didn't deserve such praise. But instead he motioned to the child. "Maddy's the one with the hardest job. And she's doing great at it."

His patient's grin widened even more, and warmth bloomed in his chest. It felt startlingly good to see those smiles, to focus on this win with them. He realized that this victory was much the same as what Tessa was attempting with the dog-therapy program.

He was still averse to the idea of animals in a hospital. The environment should be kept sterile, especially in a cancer ward where the patients' immune systems were already so heavily taxed. But he appreciated what Tessa was trying to do. She wanted to boost the kids' spirits, take their minds off their pain, no matter how briefly.

As Maddy's mother ran her palm over her daughter's patchy hair and murmured words of encouragement, something shifted inside of Noah—something he hadn't felt in a long time. Before he could consider it too closely, he heard someone say his name.

"Dr. Brennan?"

He turned, already sensing her there. Tessa Worth.

"Could I have a moment of your time?" The soft plea in her voice stirred something else in his chest. He nearly offered a sharp reply, but he caught himself. Did she really deserve his scorn? She was only doing her job, after all. Why was he giving her such a hard time? Because it inconvenienced him? Or was it something else?

He didn't really want to consider the answers to some of those questions. But neither did he wish to punish her for doing what she thought was right.

"I can be with you in a couple of minutes. Why don't you wait for me in my office?"

She nodded and before she left, offered a smile to Maddy and her mother. He marveled at how easily she could do it. And her smile was beautiful, warm and welcoming. Everything about her was kind and caring.

He shook himself, frowning at his own distraction.

"Well." He cleared his throat. "Maddy, I'll catch up with you tomorrow, okay?"

She nodded, a lingering grin keeping her face bright and hopeful. On impulse, he held up a hand. Her mouth dropped slightly, and then she beamed as she smacked her palm against his in a high five.

Before he could pull his arm away, her mother grabbed it.

"Dr. Brennan. Thank you." There were tears shining in her eyes.

Both mother and daughter looked as if he'd handed them a gift. It wounded him, as much as it warmed him. He knew the dark place they were living in. He knew what it was to be on their side of this conversation, how desperately he'd clung to every reassurance, how he'd convinced himself that Ginny would win the fight.

The reminder nearly made him issue a warning, cautioning them against hope. Hope blinded a person to reality. He didn't want that for Maddy, nor her mother. But he didn't want to see them weighed down by fear, either. So he forced himself to nod before leaving the room.

SHE WAS STANDING awkwardly in front of his desk when Noah entered his office. As he closed the door behind him, he gestured for her to take a seat. They sat at the same time, he on one side of the desk and she on the other.

"I wanted to apologize," she said without preamble, "for not speaking with you in person about the animal therapy ahead of time."

He opened his mouth to speak, but she rushed on, as if she had to get the words out before he said something that might stop her.

"It was unfair to spring it on you. I mean, yes, I emailed you about it, but I should have been more direct. It was—" she straightened and cleared her throat "—unprofessional of me." She licked her lips. "But I think the program will do a lot of good for the children," she finally said.

"I agree." He enjoyed seeing her eyes widen at his response.

"You...do?"

"Yes." He nodded. "I still don't think it does as much good as you believe it does. But I'm willing to concede that it eases the patients' anxiety, at least for as long as the animal is present."

"Yes. Exactly. They deserve a few minutes of joy, don't you think?"

Of course he wanted his patients to experience happiness, but he wasn't sure how much she understood about the fight against cancer.

"Certainly they deserve it," he replied, "but I'm not sure it's possible, at least not in the way you think it is."

She frowned, but he jumped in before she could come up with an argument.

"I just mean that what these families are experiencing is probably the most frightening battle of their lives. No matter how many puppies you throw at the situation, it doesn't change the reality of what they're up against."

To his surprise, she nodded, though he hardly thought she agreed with him.

"There's something else I'd like to say."

He braced himself as she drew a deep breath.

"I'm sorry for how I spoke to you last week, in the commons. That was inconsiderate of me. I recognize that you're a good doctor, and you didn't deserve my criticism. How you handle your patients is..." She trailed off, and he wondered if she was struggling to find something nice to say.

He held up a hand before she could speak further. "Did Ana put you up to this apology?"

Her lips parted and then closed. "Excuse me?"

"I know Ana is determined you and I maintain a civil working relationship. Did she suggest you apologize?"

Her cheeks flushed to a pretty pink, and her eyes shone. She sputtered for a moment and then let out a sharp *"No!"*

She stood and began pacing. "You just might be the most insufferable human being I have ever met! No, Ana did *not put me up to this*." She did a fair imitation of him as she repeated his words. He found himself amused more than irritated. "I was only trying to...to..."

"Get back on my good side?" He only said it for the reaction he knew it would evoke.

He realized he was forming a bad habit of enjoying getting under her skin.

"You *have* a good side?" she tossed back, and he nearly—but not quite—smiled, without any real effort. It startled him: what had been so difficult with his patients almost came naturally when Tessa Worth was around.

He stood to his feet. "Apology accepted," he said.

She sputtered once more. "I retract my apology," she declared crisply.

"It's too late. I've already accepted it."

Her eyes narrowed, and he marveled at himself. Was he…teasing her? This woman who was such a thorn in his side? He should get her out of his office, as quickly as possible.

"Now, if you'll excuse me, Ms. Worth, I have patients to see."

He thought she might protest—he was stunned to realize that a part of him hoped she would—but she seemed to realize it was a lost cause.

"Thank you, Doctor," she ground out, and he had to give her credit for maintaining her composure.

Although she did slam the door on her way out.

OVER THE NEXT couple of weeks, Tessa found herself both relieved and strangely disappointed that she had no further run-ins with Dr. Brennan. They fell into a routine of working around each other. Tessa spent quite a bit of her time in her office on the first floor, but she also dedicated several hours of her week to visiting the pediatric oncology ward. She wanted to have a clear understanding of the work being done there, and the experiences of the children and their families. She checked with Ana, to ensure she wasn't spending too much time away from her desk, and found that Ana fully endorsed her choice.

She expected Dr. Brennan to protest her intrusion into his ward, but she was surprised to find he said nothing to her at all about it.

But neither did he embrace her presence. He greeted her with a nod whenever he saw her, and occasionally, she sensed him watching her as she interacted with the staff or patients, but he gave no indication he disapproved. Although part of her wished he'd make more of an effort for them to be colleagues, she didn't press her luck.

Gradually, she began to relax, even when she knew he was nearby. She was always aware of his presence, but she no longer anticipated an altercation every time she stepped into his territory. She didn't mistake his silence for acquiescence, but she was at least hopeful they could be professional about their individual roles at the hospital.

The animal therapy program with Linda and Viva became a regular occurrence, and Tessa even sent out a press release to local news crews for some coverage. She was thrilled when one news outlet decided to send a reporter.

Noah grumbled about the news crew's interference. But to his credit, when they arrived and interviewed him for the story, he was polite and professional, even going so far as to thank them for featuring the hospital. Tessa was relieved, and when the story aired that night on the local news, her father called to congratulate her.

It was the first time in a long time that she could remember him being proud of her. Her relationship with her dad had always been different than her sisters'. As the baby of the family, he hadn't held her to the same exacting standards. But she knew he'd been disappointed when she left her fiancé at the altar, quit her job as a nurse, giving no explanations, and went to work at the animal clinic. He'd seen it, as Paige had, as a step down in the world. She knew his encouragement now was because he wanted to see her continue to succeed in her new job at the hospital. There was nothing wrong with that, of course. She only wished he could have expressed the same support when she'd been a lowly staff member at the animal clinic.

While Tessa was proud of the success, her work became more challenging to her personally. She had left pediatrics because it hurt too much to be around children. She'd thought public relations would be easier because she wouldn't be working directly with the kids, but she'd be contributing to their healing just the same. And in some ways, it *was* easier. She didn't have the responsibility of their day-to-day care, as the nurses did. But she was becoming too invested in them, in their struggles and victories.

She couldn't help asking them questions, about their journeys with cancer. Most stories had the same beginning, with the family being blindsided by the diagnosis. It started with seemingly innocent symptoms— persistent coughs, ongoing flu, nosebleeds, bruising, joint pain—until finally everything culminated in a visit to the emergency room or a family doctor that had the foresight to request the appropriate tests. From there, it was a whirlwind of activity—rushing to the children's hospital, the immediate onslaught of treatment and the worry and the waiting...

When Tessa heard these stories, her heart expanded and contracted at the same time. And even though it was ridiculous and wrong, she couldn't help feeling a strange sort of envy. These families were experiencing heartache and tragedy, and she would never wish that for anyone. But as she observed mothers and daughters, fathers and sons, she couldn't help the grief that smothered her. She would never know what it was to hold her own, biological child in such a way, to soothe and reassure them, to feel the solid weight of them in her arms.

But how could she be so selfish, when these families were fighting for a future where they may no longer have that privilege, either?

CHAPTER SIX

TESSA HAD BEEN dreading her first official marketing meeting. It was a small group, which only added to her anxiety. Ana would be there, as would two members of the hospital board. But more important, as the chief doctor for the pediatric oncology department, Dr. Brennan was also slated to attend. Since she'd been tasked with elevating publicity for the children's cancer ward in particular, it only made sense to have the irritable doctor in attendance, but his presence certainly wouldn't make her job easier.

She was acutely aware of all she had to prove in this meeting in order to continue this job once the trial year was up. The meeting meant a late night, which she didn't mind so much, except that the entire day had been dreary, building up to the thunderstorm that had unleashed an hour ago.

Tessa could hear peals of thunder overhead, and the insistent pounding of rain on the windows as she gathered her laptop and the other items for her presentation and headed to the first-floor conference room. The table had already been set up with coffee, water and snacks, though no one was present in the room just yet. She drew a breath as she pulled out her proposed plans and put a copy of the presentation at each place.

A flash of lightning caused her to look toward the window, and when she turned back, she realized Dr. Brennan had entered the room.

"Oh. Hello," she said. She hadn't expected him to appear so soon. In fact, she had suspected he would either attend late or skip the meeting entirely. Unless, of course, Ana had cautioned him otherwise.

"Hi," he greeted as he stepped farther into the room. She eyed the proposals she'd laid out and secretly hoped he didn't reach for one. She could only imagine his reaction to some of her suggestions. To her relief, he ignored them and poured himself a coffee from the carafe instead.

"Would you like a coffee?"

She was startled that he'd offered. She shook her head. "I prefer tea, thank you."

"Oh. I'm sure we have some—" He turned as if to go, but she stopped him.

"No, that's all right. Water will be fine. Thank you, though."

Just when she had pegged Dr. Brennan as thoroughly absorbed in himself and his work, he did something to make her reconsider her preconceived notions about him.

He took a seat at the table, and moments later, Ana and the two members of the hospital board entered the room. The meeting proceeded much as Tessa thought it would. Tessa had already met Don Hess and Maggie Frank, but Ana still took the time to remind them of Tessa's role at the hospital and generously point out all that she had accomplished in her short stint on the job.

As Ana went through her talking points, Tessa slid a glance toward Dr. Brennan. He was checking his phone and sipping on his coffee, apparently tuning most of the conversation out. Tessa hoped that would continue when it came time for her to review her proposal. But when Ana announced that Tessa would be sharing a few of her ideas, Noah put his phone away and turned his full attention on her. This, more than the gazes of the others in the room, set her nerves on edge.

"Um, w-well, if you'll take a look at the proposals I've provided, you'll see, er, various suggestions for benefits and fund-raisers we might be able to accomplish in the n-next year." She cleared her throat, desperately trying to find a foothold of confidence despite feeling Noah's eyes, sharp and observant, on her.

She needed to have faith in her proposal. She'd worked hard on these ideas, and some of them were very good. She took a sip of water, allowing the others time to review her plans. She knew exactly when Noah finished. Watching him surreptitiously from lowered lashes, she saw him flinch, his posture stiffening.

"A gala?" It was Maggie Frank who spoke first. "That's a delightful idea."

Noah glanced up, shooting daggers in her direction. "Galas have been overdone, don't you think?"

Tessa licked her lips. "It would elicit a lot of interest. As you can see from my proposal, my father, Allan Worth, has offered his resort, the Delphine in Findlay Roads, as the venue, free of charge. That will save us considerable expense. And with you as the keynote speaker, Dr. Brennan, I'm sure it would be a great success."

He glared in response. "I have no interest in being featured at such an event."

"Come, Dr. Brennan, the board would be delighted to see you participate," said Don Hess. Hess was a retired oncologist himself, and now that she had both board members in her corner, Tessa grew bolder.

"You underestimate people's interest in you," she said to Noah. "You stare down death on a daily basis. More than that, you do it on behalf of *children*. People would love to hear you speak. If you were the featured guest, we could sell so many tickets. It could potentially be huge for the hospital."

"How can you argue with an endorsement like that?" Dr. Hess asked.

Noah rubbed his palm over his face. It was only then that she noticed how tired he looked. She wondered how many hours he'd put in today. Or if he'd eaten anything. She'd noticed that he rarely took breaks and that he spent far more time inside the hospital than out of it. That was all fine and good, but he had to take care of himself first if he expected to have energy for his patients.

"I'm not a public speaker," he pointed out. "I'm a doctor."

"And as in any position, sometimes we are asked to do things outside of our comfort zone," Ana spoke up. "I think Tessa's suggestion is a good one." As if to reinforce her point, a peal of thunder growled outside.

Noah sighed. "What would I have to do?"

Tessa was surprised he didn't attempt to argue further. "Just…give a speech. Shake some hands. Be your charming self." She tried not to sound too sarcastic. To her further bemusement, he emitted a sound between a scoff and a snort.

"I've been called many things in my life, but I'm not sure 'charming' was ever one of them."

This earned a round of chuckles from everyone in the room except Tessa. His words were self-deprecating, but there was something in them, some hint of self-criticism that kept her from being amused.

"Does that mean you'll do it?" Maggie asked, after the laughter faded.

Noah paused for a long moment before saying, "I'll consider it."

"We can't ask more than that," Dr. Hess said as he stood. "Now, let's wrap things up.

That storm doesn't sound like it's letting up anytime soon, and it's growing late."

They concluded quickly after that with both Dr. Hess and Ms. Frank expressing their satisfaction with Tessa's proposal and their eagerness to see her implement some of her ideas. She thanked them both and bid them good evening, and then turned to look for Noah. She frowned when she noticed he had left the room, without a goodbye. The realization disappointed her. Not that it should have. She was certain Dr. Brennan had far more important things to attend to.

"How do you feel?" Ana asked, drawing her attention.

Tamping down her disappointment, Tessa drew a deep breath and released it. "Pretty good, I think."

Ana squeezed her arm. "You've gotten off to a great start. Believe me, Dr. Hess and Ms. Frank would have spoken up if they didn't like your ideas." Ana gathered her things and slung her bag over her shoulder. "And at some point, you'll have to tell me your secret."

"My secret?"

"With Noah. Dr. Brennan. You're making progress with him."

Tessa frowned. "But he only said he'd consider speaking at the gala."

Ana raised her eyebrows. "Tessa, I've been trying to get that man more involved for ages. I've never once gotten him to 'consider' anything. Trust me, you're definitely doing something right."

And though it shouldn't have mattered so much, Tessa couldn't help feeling a rush of pleasure at Ana's words.

NOAH INWARDLY BERATED himself as he headed for the hospital exit. Why had he agreed to think about Tessa Worth's proposal? He was normally firm on these things. If he gave an inch, she'd take a mile. But he couldn't seem to help himself. There was something about Tessa Worth—her passion as she talked about these publicity projects—that stirred dangerous emotions. Her enthusiasm was nearly infectious. Add to that the fact that the board would expect him to fall in line with whatever wild proposal Ms. Worth suggested, and he didn't have much leverage to refuse. Plus, it didn't help that her wide, hopeful brown eyes weakened his resolve.

But surely he wasn't going to do it. He had greater things to worry about than delivering speeches to guilt people into giving their money. They should follow him around the floor for one day, watch him tell parents their children were in a fight for their lives. They should witness the nurses gather up a child's hair after it had fallen onto the pillow in clumps. They should see a patient's skin turn pale from his or her time in treatment. That would do more to elicit funds than any words he could offer.

As he reached the doors, he welcomed the pounding of the rain. The stormy night matched his mood. He hesitated beneath the eaves of the hospital entrance. The rain was coming down in dark sheets. At least he'd had the foresight to grab an umbrella.

He opened it now and held it over his head as he stepped out into the downpour. He made for his pickup at a fast clip, feeling the rain drive hard against him. If he hadn't had his umbrella, he'd have been soaked in seconds. Even so, he felt the damp clinging to the back of his pants.

The parking lot was even emptier than usual for this time of night. The rain had probably driven most visitors and nonessential staff members home.

He had nearly reached his pickup when he

saw a flash of headlights and heard the sputtering of an engine, audible even over the rain's pounding. He looked in the direction of the stuttering car, and recognized Tessa Worth in the driver's seat, her face set in frustration as she obviously tried to get the engine to turn over. He frowned at the sight and felt a tug of sympathy. Of all the nights to have car trouble, this had to be the worst.

He watched as she tried one more time to get the car to start, heard the engine's weak, gasping attempt to fire up, and then saw Tessa drop her forehead to the steering wheel in defeat.

He started through the rain in her direction. She kept her head lowered, and he felt a strange and sudden urge for her to look up, to see him, to offer him a smile. The intensity of this desire struck him so hard and fast that he nearly stumbled. But Tessa didn't glance up, and it wasn't until he tapped on her window that she jerked to attention.

Her mouth formed an O of surprise at his appearance, and she blinked several times, as if disbelieving of his presence. He pointed at the base of the window. It took her a moment to understand his meaning but then when her car window wouldn't roll down, she cracked the door to allow him to talk to her.

"Car trouble?" he questioned.

Her eyes were huge in her face, and there was a sheen of tears over them. "I'm not sure what's wrong. Maybe it's the battery? I don't know." She had to talk loudly so he could hear her over the drumming of the rain.

"Try it again," he shouted.

She turned the key in the ignition, but the car only sputtered faintly. It might be something as simple as jumping the battery, or perhaps the alternator had gone bad. In any case, it wasn't something to be dealt with on a night like this.

"Let's just leave it," he suggested. She frowned, and he wasn't sure if it was because of his suggestion or perhaps because she hadn't been able to hear what he'd said. "I can drive you home," he shouted to be sure she understood.

He knew that she did because she stared at him. "You want to give me a lift?"

She sounded surprised, and that bothered him. He realized he didn't always come off as the warmest of individuals, but did he really seem like the type of man that would leave a colleague stranded alone on a stormy night in a half empty parking lot?

"Yes, we're both going the same direction, aren't we?" He knew she lived in Findlay Roads. That much had been evident from their encounter at the coffee shop. The town wasn't very big; he wouldn't be going far out of his way to drop Tessa off at home. He looked out into the rain. It showed no signs of abating.

When he turned back, Tessa nodded in agreement. "Okay."

He waited while she grabbed her things and then held the door open for her, angling the umbrella to provide her some shelter as she exited her car. She was already dripping, presumably from walking across the parking lot to her car. She must not have had an umbrella handy.

Rain sluiced down the inside of his jacket and along his back. He was unable to keep them both covered as she got out of the car. Tessa already looked bedraggled from her short time in the storm. He didn't mind a little rainwater if it meant keeping her from getting soaked all over again.

He waited as she locked her car, and then they made a mad dash together through the rain. He opened the passenger side door of his black pickup and waited until she was securely inside before closing it again. He was pretty well drenched himself from trying to keep the umbrella over Tessa's head as they'd run. As he rounded the driver's side, he tossed the umbrella into the back seat. When he shut the driver's side door, the rain pattered against the vehicle but left them cocooned in a bubble of silence within the truck's interior.

"You're soaked," Tessa observed, and he grunted in amusement.

"As if you're one to talk."

She looked down at herself and laughed softly. "Yeah, I guess that's true. But I appreciate you doing your best to keep me dry, even if it was a lost cause."

Her words warmed him, burning off any chill the damp might have created. He started up the car and turned the heat on to help dry them off. Without any other preliminaries, he put the car in gear and pulled out of the parking space.

Tessa was quiet for the first mile or two, though it didn't feel awkward. She was, he realized with a start, someone he could be at ease with in silence. She seemed comfortable, too, and he relaxed, relieved he didn't have to make idle small talk, something he abhorred.

After some time, she ventured to speak, "Thanks for considering my proposal, about speaking at the gala. I know you'd rather be pricked with a thousand needles than go through that. But it would be for a good cause," she reminded.

He scoffed. "At least with the needles it would be poetic justice. I've seen enough children have to be stuck with them over the years." He frowned, thinking of his daughter and how she'd never grown accustomed to them. While Ginny, like most children with leukemia, had had a port placed in her chest for her chemotherapy treatments, she still had to endure the occasional injection. She'd cried every time.

They were silent again for a few minutes.

"You really don't get it, do you?" she spoke again.

He turned his attention from the road just long enough to view her expression. Her hair was damp but drying in the heated air, curling around her jaw. Her expression was shadowed in the dark interior of the pickup, but he could see the shine of her eyes, the curve of her nose and the swell of her lips. She was a beautiful woman. He had known it from the first, when she bumped into him outside the Lighthouse Café. But he'd never quite acknowledged it. He hadn't found a woman beautiful since Julia…

He looked back at the road. He was driving well under the speed limit due to the rain. Or perhaps he wasn't in any great hurry to arrive at his destination.

"I'm not sure I know what you mean," he answered her question.

From the corner of his eye, he saw her shift toward him. He forced himself to keep his eyes on the road.

"You don't get that people…admire you. To those parents, to those kids, you're a hero. You're the one who saved their lives."

He made a face. "The chemo does that. And the kids themselves. They put all of their hearts into battling this disease. And some—" He cut himself off before he said too much. "They fight. They're just kids, but they fight hard. They deserve the recognition. Not me."

"But you can be their voice. You can be the one who speaks on their behalf, brings awareness to what they're going through."

He shook his head. "I'm not worthy of that honor. One hundred percent of my attention needs to be on their care."

Tessa's voice was soft when she replied, nearly drowned out by the rain pounding against the pickup, "Maybe there's some truth in that, but you can't do everything, you know. You can't carry that burden. You can't be held responsible for the things that go wrong, especially if you won't take credit for the things that go right. You should let others shoulder some of that weight with you."

There was an insight in her words that made him uneasy. All the little barricades he kept in place—his gruffness, his resistance to speak on his own behalf, his refusal to become too personal with his patients or staff—were his weapons. These were the ways he punished and protected himself. It alarmed him that Tessa had so easily called him out on the ways he castigated himself. But beyond the shock that he might not be hiding his motives as well as he thought, there was a certain relief. Tessa knew. Or at least, it seemed she suspected a few things. But how much did she know of his past, of his story?

When she spoke again, he found himself tense with anticipation of what she might say next. Her voice was soft, just barely audible amid the engine's hum and the rain's patter. "I understand what it's like to think less of yourself, to feel as though you are responsible for things beyond your control."

He felt her gaze on him in the soft glow from the pickup's clock, and he turned his head briefly to meet her eyes.

"Sometimes," she said softly, "I have this dream where I'm in the middle of the ocean, treading water. And off in the distance, there's a beach."

He looked back toward the road, but he kept listening, intent on what she had to say.

"And I believe that if I just swim hard enough, I can reach it. So I start swimming, but no matter how much I kick, I don't get any closer to the shore." She paused, and he feared she was done speaking. After another moment, however, she spoke again. "My legs grow heavy and my arms get weak. My lungs start burning. I know that beach is there, it's *right there*, and I want to reach it so much…but my body starts shutting down. And there's nothing I can do about it. It will forever be just out of reach."

His heart twisted within him. It occurred to him that Tessa Worth, for all her sweetness and light, understood what it was to carry a heavy burden.

"Sometimes, no matter how hard you swim, you're still stuck in the ocean," she said, her voice still soft. "But I wonder, maybe it's not about reaching the shore. Maybe there's something that the water still has to teach me."

He was moved by her openness and touched that she'd shared such personal thoughts with him. Should he tell her about Ginny and Julia?

It wasn't as if his life was a great secret, but neither did he share it willingly with others. Ana knew, of course, and he was sure rumors and gossip had spread among the hospital staff. DC wasn't that far away, after all, and his ghosts still haunted him. Had Tessa heard about it from Ana or someone else? Or was she really that perceptive on her own?

"Make a left up ahead."

Her voice startled him from his internal deliberation and, thankfully, the moment passed. He did as she instructed and then followed her directions for several streets more until she pointed out a lovely little cottage visible through the rain. He couldn't see a lot of details through the dense downpour, but it looked like it was cozy, on drier days. Or perhaps even more so on nights like tonight.

"Thank you so much for the ride. I really can't tell you how much I appreciate it," she said as he pulled into the driveway.

"It was no problem," he said, still feeling the urge to say more, to keep her with him a little while longer. She made no move to leave the car, though.

After a beat, she said, "I don't know about you, but I'm starved. Do you want to come inside and I'll make you something to eat? As a thank-you?"

He hesitated, very nearly refusing outright, based on precedent. He had to guard himself from the instinct to share more of himself with her. He didn't deserve any kindnesses. And he should be wary where Tessa Worth was concerned. He was drawn to her too much.

But she was right. He was hungry, and the rain had lulled him into a sense of surrealism. Besides, he was curious to know more about Tessa, especially after what she's said during their drive. Was her home as warm and welcoming as her personality? It couldn't exactly hurt, could it? Maybe it would even benefit him. They were colleagues, after all, and he should probably make more of an effort to be a team player.

All of these arguments passed through his head in the blink of an eye before he turned to Tessa and said, "All right. Let me grab the umbrella and get your door for you."

CHAPTER SEVEN

TESSA WAS PRACTICALLY giddy that Noah had
agreed to come inside. She was even more
impressed that he held the car door for her,
then protected her with the umbrella so she
could get inside without being deluged by
the rain. She was still a little soggy as it was,
but Noah was worse. His chivalry had cost
him, and he dripped water as she unlocked
the front door of the cottage and they stepped
inside.

Rufus immediately came running to greet
them, and Tessa stopped short in the entry
with Noah bumping into her from behind.

She'd forgotten about Rufus. Noah's last
encounter with her dog had been less than
pleasant. To make matters worse, Rufus bypassed her and faced off with Noah instead,
offering a low growl that was more curious
than threatening.

"Rufus!" she scolded, but Noah shocked
her as he took it in stride.

"Hello, Rufus," he greeted and held out a hand to be sniffed.

Rufus jumped up to inspect this offering and then let out a huge sneeze that covered Noah's hand with drool. Tessa wished she could push Noah back out the door and start all over.

"I am so sorry!"

Again, Noah surprised her. He wiped his hand on his pant legs as Rufus dropped back to the floor. "Well, I was already pretty wet anyway."

She found herself staring as Noah straightened. "Who are you and what have you done with the real Dr. Brennan?"

"Noah," he corrected her, and she realized that Dr. Brennan—Noah—was apparently full of surprises this evening. "And I don't know what you mean."

She shook her head as she hung up her bag and took Noah's dripping umbrella to air-dry on a hook inside the door.

"Just that whenever I think I have you pegged, you do something totally out of character," she replied.

He followed her farther into the house, and she noticed him looking around with interest. "Gotta keep a girl on her toes," he said.

Her lips parted. Was he actually bantering with her? Rufus pawed at her leg, a reminder that he hadn't been fed yet. But both she and Noah were dripping rainwater onto the floor.

"I'm going to grab you a towel," she offered, "and just change clothes quickly."

Noah glanced down at his attire with a frown. "Sorry, I'm dripping water everywhere."

"No problem," she replied. "You were doing a good deed, after all."

He stared straight into her eyes then. Her stomach leaped at the way he looked at her. She swallowed.

"I'll be right back."

She took the stairs two at a time with Rufus on her heels. She made quick work of changing out of her soggy clothes and into a pair of flannel pajama bottoms and a long-sleeved T-shirt. She dug deep into the closet and found an oversize sweatshirt that Weston had left there two summers ago when he, Paige and Zoe had come for a visit. Rufus whined, reminding her he still hadn't had dinner. She ducked into the bathroom for a towel and then hurried back downstairs, Rufus trotting after her.

Noah was examining her wall of family

photographs in the living room with interest. She stood next to him and handed over the towel, following his gaze from one image to the next.

"That's my family," she said, naming each of them off. "These are my nieces. Harper adopted Molly after she married Connor, and Zoe is six. She's Paige's daughter. I don't have any photos up yet, but Harper gave birth to a baby girl a few months ago. Grace."

Her heart warmed as she looked at the pictures. She walked by them every day, but in moments like these, when she stopped to really view them, she was reminded all over again of how blessed she was by her family.

"Hmm." Noah didn't say much, and she sensed his spirits were flagging somehow.

"Here's a sweatshirt, if you want to at least put on one article of dry clothing," she said, drawing his attention away from the wall. "I'm going to head into the kitchen and make us something to eat."

She pointed out the downstairs bathroom and then went into the kitchen, pausing to scoop some kibble into Rufus's dog bowl. By the time Noah joined her in the kitchen, she had two grilled cheese sandwiches warming in the skillet and soup that she'd poured from a can heating in the microwave.

"Sorry it's not anything special," she apologized as she plated up the grilled cheese. "If my brother-in-law was here, we'd be eating a much fancier version of grilled cheese like Gruyère with caramelized onions on a brioche bun. He owns Callahan's, the restaurant down by the waterfront."

"Callahan's has great food," Noah said, "but this is perfect. Thank you."

They settled at the table and were silent for several minutes while they ate. Tessa liked that she didn't feel the need to fill the silence with Noah. Maybe because she knew he wouldn't appreciate small talk anyway. But as they finished up the last of their impromptu meal, she felt the urge to speak up.

"Thank you for bringing me home."

He shrugged. "Anyone else would have done the same."

She stared at him. Did he really believe that? "No, they wouldn't have. Even though you seem strangely determined not to believe it, you're a good man, Noah Brennan."

She sensed the mood shift the moment the words left her lips. He raised his head, meeting her gaze, his gray eyes intent.

"If the dead could speak, I'm afraid they'd disagree with you."

Tessa blinked, momentarily thrown by this statement. "I don't understand."

Noah stared down at the crumbs remaining on his plate. "My wife, in particular, would find fault with your words."

Tessa opened her mouth and then closed it, silently willing him to continue.

"I had a daughter, you know. Ginny. She was eight when she died of leukemia."

His words struck at the center of her heart. She could never have a child of her own. But to have one and then lose her... She swallowed hard.

"Noah, I had no idea. I'm so sorry."

He gave a short nod and then continued. "I'm a pediatric oncologist. I knew all the current treatments, all the trials. I was familiar with the remission rates. I promised Ginny we would beat it. I promised my wife our daughter would live." He looked up then, meeting her eyes. "I lied." He drew a sharp breath. "For children over the age of five, which Ginny was, the survival rate for acute lymphoblastic leukemia is about ninety-four percent. That leaves a six-percent margin to worry about. Such a small number. But every parent wonders if their child will be part of that six percent. I've always found it ironic that as a pediatric oncologist, it was my daughter who fell into that tiny window."

Tessa reached out, curling her hand around Noah's where it rested on the kitchen table. He stared at where her skin touched his but didn't seem to feel the contact. The watch she'd noticed the first day they'd met pressed into the base of her wrist.

"Julia—my wife—she couldn't forgive me. I broke my promise. I used to think I was healing children, until I realized how arbitrary this disease is. And my wife saw me for what I was—a failure. I couldn't save the one child who mattered most." His voice dropped to a whisper. "I threw myself back into my work, after Ginny died. It was my penance, my attempt to make up for my failure. I spent hours at the hospital, crashing there at night and then getting up to start all over again in the morning. I dreaded being in that house, now that Ginny no longer inhabited it. So I wasn't home on the one-month mark of Ginny's death. I worked as late as possible until I knew I couldn't avoid going home anymore. By the time I got there, it was too late. Julia had emptied a full bottle of antidepressants, mixed with alcohol. If I had just gotten there a little sooner…" He stopped and raised his head. His eyes were lined with tears. "I couldn't save my daughter, and then I failed my wife, too."

Tessa could only stare, heart in her throat. She had suspected that Noah carried some burden. But nothing like this. Never this. It was a cruel twist of fate that a doctor so familiar with childhood cancer should lose his own child to it. And then the added burden of his wife's suicide… Tears flooded her own eyes. How was he still standing, still working, after that?

"That's why I wear this." He used his free hand to tap the watch he wore. "It was a gift, from Ginny. She gave it to me for Father's Day, the year she was diagnosed."

"Noah, I—"

"No, I don't want sympathy. I don't deserve it. I was arrogant, thinking that if any child could beat cancer, it would be mine. And then I was selfish, ignoring my wife's struggle."

"You had your own grief to deal with."

He gave a violent shake of his head, denying this excuse. "That's why," he said. "That's why I don't want to be a keynote speaker or help promote the hospital. Because I'm not who they think I am. I'm not a gifted doctor. I'm just giving kids whatever weapons I have to help them fight this battle. It's not up to me." The depth of his anguish was evident in his voice and in the sad gaze he turned on her. "Don't try to honor me, Tessa. Please don't." His eyes pleaded with her. "I don't deserve it."

"Oh, Noah," she breathed and tightened her grip on his hands. "You are so much worthier than you give yourself credit for. Don't you see how unique you are?"

He blinked, and behind the wash of tears, his eyes were a soft, burnished pewter. "Unique?"

"You can speak for these children, not just as a doctor who helps them fight this battle but as someone who has lived through it. Who else could possibly inform others so perfectly on both sides of the situation—both the medical and the personal? Maybe *that* is what makes you gifted. You are so much more than just a doctor. You are a survivor."

She could see when the words struck home, giving him a new perspective to consider.

"I…suppose there's some truth in that.

Or at least, a means to honor Ginny, after I failed her so completely."

"Noah. It wasn't your fault she died. Or your wife. You cannot believe that's true."

She thought of the dream she had shared with him, and the meaning behind it that she hadn't revealed. Rationally, she knew it wasn't her fault that her body had failed her, denying her the opportunity to be a mother. But she also knew how impossible it could be to persuade one's heart.

"Sometimes life…betrays you." She swallowed hard, thinking of her own struggles these last two years. "It doesn't mean you have to shoulder that burden alone."

She nearly flinched speaking these words aloud. Wasn't that the choice she had made? To carry the weight of her diagnosis on her own shoulders rather than ease its burden by sharing it with someone else?

Noah didn't argue with her, but when she turned her eyes back to his, he was watching her with an intensity that nearly stole her breath away. For a moment, she thought he saw deeper than she'd intended, into the very depths of her own personal heartache. She cleared her throat and looked away, her cheeks burning.

"Tell me about your daughter," she murmured.

Noah smiled and began to speak. They sat at her kitchen table for quite a long time after that. Eventually, the rain eased up until there was only the gentle drip of water from the eaves outside as Tessa and Noah sat inside the cottage and talked, late into the night.

NOAH WOKE THE next morning and realized that for the first time in years, ever since Ginny had been diagnosed with leukemia, he had slept through the night without waking. He felt cleansed somehow. Not absolved, but at least renewed.

He had Tessa Worth to thank for that. His confessions to her had been an unburdening. He still carried a weight, but having shared it, it didn't seem quite so heavy. He appreciated what Tessa had said to him the night before. He didn't feel innocent of Ginny or Julia's deaths, but Tessa had made a good point about finding purpose from his loss.

It was Saturday, and he had a rare day off. He thought about Tessa, wondering if she needed any help getting her car from the hospital. He debated whether he should call her, but what would he say if she picked up? He considered swinging by her house to check on her, but that felt intrusive.

He told himself that his desire to see her was only a result of his confession. Now that she knew his secret, he didn't have to be so guarded around her. Perhaps he could even call her a...friend.

It was a rare gift. He'd drifted out of touch with most of his friends over the last year, and he'd practically cut all ties completely with them once he'd moved to Findlay Roads and began working at Chesapeake.

He was restless, torn between wanting to see Tessa and not knowing how to go about it. He paced the living room for a few moments, an easy enough feat since the room was practically bare. He'd lived in the house for six months, having moved in when he began working at the hospital, but he'd brought little with him to his "fresh start."

It was painful to be around items that were too familiar, that evoked memories. The couch where he and Ginny would snuggle and watch cartoons. The kitchen table where they'd shared meals. The dresser that Julia had always complained about because the drawers would stick. He'd taken none of that with him. He lived with too many ghosts already. But neither had he made an effort to fill up the house after he'd bought it. So now it was an empty skeleton, a shelter but not a home.

He suddenly felt entombed, trapped within the four walls. He needed to get out, to breathe fresh air. He decided to walk to the coffee shop, in part because he associated it with Tessa. He didn't expect to find her there, but the walk would do him good.

The storm last night had cleared off, leaving a day filled with sunshine and warm, clean air. He set out at a brisk pace but then forced himself to slow down so he could appreciate the morning and take the time to observe this town that he'd made his home.

His decision to move to Findlay Roads after all that had occurred hadn't been entirely arbitrary. He needed a clean slate, a way to rebuild his life after loss. He'd read about Chesapeake View's burgeoning pediatric oncology department, realized that it was far enough away from his old life to allow for a new beginning but also close enough to John's caregiving facility that he could continue to check in on his father-in-law on a regular basis. Things fell into place with alarming speed and within a matter of weeks, he'd changed his life.

If only he'd been able to leave his demons behind in DC as easily as he'd left his job. At least the goodbyes had been relatively painless. He suspected his former friends and colleagues were relieved when he'd announced he was moving. No one had known what to say to him anymore. He didn't bother telling them that there was nothing anyone could say. No words healed the kind of wounds he carried.

But even though Findlay Roads had been a choice based on its convenient location, he'd been pleasantly surprised with the town on the Chesapeake Bay. It hadn't become too touristy yet, but he could see a blend of old and new in its streets, brick buildings that had stood for centuries revitalized by modern storefronts and boutiques.

Now, as he strolled the sidewalks of the town he'd chosen as his home, he felt he'd made the right choice in coming here. His ghosts had followed him, and he didn't expect they'd ever leave him. But maybe, if he gave it enough time, he could learn to live with them. And maybe, having a friend like Tessa would be a good first step down that road.

As he approached the coffee shop, Tessa on his mind, he thought he was imagining her there. But then he realized he wasn't day-dreaming. Tessa stood outside the Lighthouse Café, in the same spot she'd been when they first met, clipping Rufus's leash to the rail-ing.

"It seems we had the same idea," he said as he approached her. He was gratified to see her expression light up when she recog-nized him.

"There must be something to that whole 'great minds' thing," she replied.

He bent down to greet Rufus, surprising himself as he did so. He wasn't normally an animal person. He had promised Ginny that she could get a kitten, once she was finished with chemo and in remission. Of course, that day had never come.

But after spending time at Tessa's house last night, he was feeling a bit more generous toward the homely bulldog. Rufus nudged Noah's palm with a cold nose, leaving a trail of slobber in his wake, but Noah brushed it on his pants without concern.

"Did you get your car situation sorted?" he asked as he stood.

"It's being towed to my mechanic's later

this morning," she said as she brushed a loose tendril of hair out of her eyes. Her blond strands were pulled back into a messy bun with several wisps falling free to frame her face. The effect was reckless, but he found it suited her.

"Stopping in for your tea?" he asked with a gesture to the café entrance behind them.

She glanced over her shoulder. "Yeah, plus a muffin for Rufus. He's feeling peckish this morning."

He laughed softly and then caught her staring at him, mouth slightly agape.

"What?"

She shook her head. "Nothing, it's just… I'm not sure I've ever heard you laugh before."

The statement momentarily sobered him. She was right. He hadn't laughed in…he couldn't even remember the last time. He quickly changed the subject.

"So, what plans do you have for today?" As soon as the words left his mouth, he inwardly flinched. He certainly hoped that didn't sound like a come-on. He had no intention of pursuing Tessa Worth in such a way. For one thing, it would be unprofessional, given that they worked together. And for another, he had told himself he would never fall for another woman after Julia. He had failed her. It wouldn't be right to fall in love again. His question was idle curiosity, nothing more. He hoped she understood that.

"Actually, I'm volunteering at the animal clinic today. They're understaffed at the moment, so I figured I'd help out."

"Ah. That's very generous of you."

She eyed him thoughtfully before seeming to come to a decision.

"You should come with me."

He blinked. "I beg your pardon?"

"To the clinic. They could always use another pair of hands. It would do you good to get yours dirty."

He wasn't sure what she was implying and whether or not he should be offended. "I'm not very good with animals," he said.

Rufus, blasted dog, took that moment to whine and put his paw on Noah's shoe, as if in reassurance. Tessa looked from her dog and back up to Noah, her lips quirked with amusement.

"Oh, I think you'd do just fine. Rufus is a very astute judge of character, you know."

Noah glanced down at the dog. "Thanks for nothing, Rufus."

Rufus yawned lazily, unconcerned.

"So, what do you say? Want to join me?"

As unappealing as a day surrounded by animals sounded, he paused to consider the suggestion. After talking with Tessa, he felt the promise of possibilities. He'd cut himself off so thoroughly from others in the time since Julia's and Ginny's deaths. If pressed to name a friend, the closest he could come was his father-in-law, and all his conversations with John were one-sided.

Tessa had made him wonder whether he could be normal again, or at least act like it for stretches of time. When he was with her, he could pretend for a couple of hours. So he looked into Tessa's warm brown eyes and found himself answering, "Sure."

CHAPTER EIGHT

TESSA FOUND IT hard to believe, but the evidence was right in front of her. Noah Brennan was smiling. Granted, he was also being licked aggressively by a seventy-pound golden retriever named Sadie, which should make anyone smile. But given Noah's reluctance with animals, she was both surprised and pleased at how he'd embraced their time at the animal clinic.

As he attempted to wrangle Sadie into the oversize stainless-steel bathtub, Tessa tried giving him a few tips.

"Don't push her, you're never going to get anywhere doing that. Try getting her to walk up the ramp on her own."

Noah pointed at the bottom edge of the ramp that led up to the tub, but Sadie wasn't interested. She turned her head to give Noah a wet kiss on the cheek.

"Ugh. Can we get Sadie a breath mint, please?"

Tessa suppressed the urge to giggle. "We'll try brushing her teeth after this."

Noah wrestled the dog into position. "Come on, girl. Just up and into the bath."

Sadie sat down instead. Noah groaned and straightened.

"I have now decided that dog groomers have the most difficult job in the world," he announced. "We need a raise."

"We're doing this for free," Tessa reminded him.

"Then we are definitely grossly underpaid and should go on strike. Don't you agree, Sadie?"

Sadie stood to her feet, turned and walked up the ramp and into the bath, as easily as if all one had to do was ask. Noah stared, and Tessa couldn't restrain herself anymore. She burst out laughing.

She swallowed back her amusement and said, "Come on, let's get her washed."

They joined forces to lather Sadie with soap and rinse her off. Working hip to hip with Noah Brennan was a novel, and not entirely unpleasant, experience. She saw him at the hospital every day, but they were rarely in such close proximity. Their torsos brushed together frequently as Tessa tried to keep

Sadie still and Noah hosed down the animal's fur. Tessa hoped it was his concentration on his task, and not her nearness, that made him suddenly very quiet.

When they finished with the dog, they both took a hasty step back as Sadie shook herself dry, sending water droplets flying. Though Tessa didn't appreciate getting splattered, the action at least broke any tension that had been building between her and Noah. They both laughed as they wiped water off their faces.

"It seems that every time I'm around you, I'm fated to get drenched," Noah remarked without malice.

"That's the risk you take when you're my friend," she lightly replied.

She realized she'd said something significant when he turned to her, his expression thoughtful, his eyes intent on hers.

"Are we that? Friends?" he asked her, his voice radiating a vulnerability that tugged at her heart. "I know I haven't exactly made your job easy."

"Well, I always did appreciate a challenge," she quipped.

He looked uncertain at her response, so

she touched a hand reassuringly on his arm. "Of course we're friends, Noah."

He had, after all, shared his secret with her, the emotional burden that kept him weighted to his guilt and grief. She only wished she had the courage to do the same.

But her need to keep her own secret didn't mean they weren't friends. After all, she hadn't even told her family the truth behind what had happened two years ago.

Her words seemed to comfort Noah. He looked back to where Sadie was sniffing at the lingering soap bubbles in the bath.

"Okay, what's next?" Noah gamely questioned.

They spent the rest of the morning helping with the animals, grooming three dogs, two cats, a hamster and one very wily ferret before Tessa announced they were finished.

Noah breathed a sigh of relief. "I am not sure how you did this job every day."

She finished rinsing down the grooming tub and blew a hair out of her face. "Oh, it's not so bad. It can be exhausting, but it's very satisfying, too."

"I imagine it is," he said.

She bit her lip, wondering if he felt that way about his own work. Surely saving children's lives was a far more gratifying experience. Or maybe he didn't think that way since every life he helped to save was a reminder of the family he had lost. She felt a stab of sadness for him.

"You know, you never said whether you have any family left or if they live nearby." She broached the subject cautiously, recognizing that he didn't discuss such things freely.

He was quiet only for a moment before replying. "My parents live in Utah. My dad's a professor, and my mom's a nurse. I have a sister in Arizona. She's married to her work. We're not a close family, but they were there for me when…everything happened." He drew a deep breath. "The hard thing is that I was closer to Julia's family than I was to my own. Her mom passed on just before Ginny was diagnosed. And her dad…" He trailed off, going silent for several minutes.

Tessa let the quiet linger. If Noah wanted to speak further, he would. If he didn't, she wouldn't push him. After a time, he continued.

"Julia's dad, John, had a stroke after she…" He cleared his throat. "He's in a home now, not too far from the hospital. I go to see him about once a week or as often as I can."

"That's very kind of you," Tessa said.

He shook his head. "Not really. He lost his wife, his granddaughter and his daughter, and finally, his health. I'm partly responsible for all that. I hope my visits bring him comfort and not pain. Although I can't really tell. He's been catatonic since the stroke." He licked his lips, staring straight ahead.

She studied his profile, overcome with the urge to touch him, to place her palm against the rigid line of his jaw and tell him he was not to blame for all that had occurred.

"The last thing John said to me before the stroke was, 'Don't forget she loved you.'" He looked down at the floor. "I never asked him who he meant. Julia or Ginny."

"Maybe both," Tessa said. "I'm sure they both did love you."

"Maybe," he replied, "but I'm not sure they could forgive me. Especially Julia. Her death was the final punishment, I suppose."

Tessa frowned. Hearing even more of Noah's history made her realize how isolated he must feel. No wonder he threw himself so completely into his work. It made her grateful to have the family that she did.

They might not be perfect, but she knew they loved her, and they were always there for her. She suddenly had an idea.

"My family is getting together for dinner tonight. Why don't you join us?"

He opened his mouth, and she was pretty sure he was about to say no, so she rushed ahead.

"Sometimes it gets a little crazy with my nieces, and even more so if I bring Rufus along, but I think you'd get along great with everyone. Besides, Connor is cooking, so you'd be getting a gourmet meal for free."

His lips tugged upward at this argument, and she felt a strange little fizzy sensation in her stomach at the sight.

"I wouldn't want to impose," he said, but she could sense his resolve weakening.

"Believe me, my family would probably be thrilled if I brought a friend. They've been worried about me for far too long."

She let this last statement slip without considering the questions it would elicit. Sure enough, Noah turned toward her with a curious expression.

"Why are they worried?"

She shrugged, avoiding his gaze. "They

just haven't agreed with some of my life decisions in recent years."

"Such as?"

She sighed. "Well, quitting my job as a pediatric nurse, for one thing, and then coming to work here, at the animal shelter. They saw it as step down in life. Or at least, my parents and my oldest sister did. My other sister is more laid-back about things."

"What do they think of you working at the hospital? You may not be a nurse, but you have a very important job there."

It startled her, to hear him speak of her job as important. While their relationship was improving, she had never expected to hear him concede her role as a marketing and PR coordinator was a worthy endeavor.

"They're thrilled," she said. "But that's only one part of what happened." She drew a deep breath. "I was engaged to be married. I left my fiancé standing at the altar around that same time." She lowered her head, ashamed.

She had never meant to break Burke's heart. But he had recovered quickly enough, and in the end, they'd both realized they weren't meant to be. Their relationship had been casual and sweet, but it wasn't the stuff of great love stories. Besides, she had always suspected he still had some lingering feelings for his childhood friend and former sister-in-law, Erin, and sure enough they were now married.

Meanwhile, she had been so caught up in her own diagnosis that it had been easier than she thought it would be to let him go. She was happy that he had moved on, found love with someone else. And while she didn't miss Burke, she missed that feeling of security, of a future with someone by her side. And she certainly mourned the loss of her hopes for a family one day.

"Oh." She detected the curiosity in that single word. She'd gotten used to the tone. After all, she'd heard it a lot from others in the weeks following her aborted wedding.

Most people hadn't been rude enough to ask outright why she had failed to appear on that special day. And for those who were bold enough to ask, she'd simply replied that the timing wasn't right. But with Noah…she felt safe enough to admit just a little bit more than that. Not the whole secret, but more than she had revealed to most.

"Burke and I got along well. Almost too well. We never had an argument, never disagreed about anything. He was steady, and I loved that about him. But I'm not sure I was *in* love with him. And I had a suspicion he wasn't really in love with me. It turned out I was right. He married someone else, later that year."

It was as much as she was willing to give him at the moment.

"Even if you weren't in love with him, leaving him had to have been painful."

She turned her head, surprised that Noah would pick up on such a thing so quickly.

"Yes. In some ways, it was." She hadn't admitted that to anyone else. When Burke had married Erin, she had insisted it was as it should be. After all, it wasn't Burke she had loved and lost—it was a future that was never meant to be.

"So, what do you say?" she asked in an attempt to turn the conversation around. "Dinner tonight? With my family?"

This time, Noah didn't hesitate. "I'd like that."

NOAH SHOWED UP promptly at 6 p.m. at Tessa's sister's house, as she'd instructed him to do. He held a bottle of wine in his hands, grateful he hadn't forgotten all the social graces.

It had been a long time since he'd visited someone's home for dinner, and he couldn't help being a little nervous. He was acutely aware that he lacked appropriate conversational skills these days. He hadn't cared much for other people's opinions in recent years, but he realized he didn't want to do anything to embarrass Tessa in front of her family. Not that it should matter what anyone thought. He and Tessa were coworkers, perhaps friends, nothing more. He had no inclination toward romance. And even if he did, it wasn't possible. He didn't deserve to find love again, not after how he'd so miserably failed Julia.

Before he could sink too deep into the memories, the door opened, and Tessa stood before him. She had showered and changed since their morning at the animal clinic, as had he. Now she wore her blond hair long and loose, clipped back by two barrettes. It fell softly past her shoulders, over the pale blue sleeveless top that she wore. She was dressed in faded jeans, and he glanced down quickly enough to see her feet were bare. She appeared relaxed and comfortable, and seeing her, he immediately felt better.

"You made it." Her smile was wide and

welcoming, but he heard the relief in her voice. Had she thought he wouldn't show up? "Come inside, I'll introduce you to everyone."

The next twenty minutes were a whirlwind of introductions and greetings. He hoped he'd remember all the names of Tessa's family. There were her parents, Allan and Vivienne Worth, followed by her oldest sister, Paige, and Paige's husband, Weston, along with their little girl, Zoe. Tessa had told him that Paige, Weston and Zoe lived in DC, but they often visited Findlay Roads on the weekends. Then there was the middle sister, Harper, her husband, Connor, who owned Callahan's, the restaurant along the waterfront, and their daughters, Molly and Grace. Grace was the newest addition to the family, a pale-haired, green-eyed angel of an infant. It was Connor who proudly showed off his three-month old baby.

Noah made what he hoped were appropriate congratulations, though he wasn't sure Connor even heard. The other man was too busy staring at his family with a sort of dazed happiness, as if he couldn't believe his luck.

Noah watched as Connor wrapped an arm

around his wife, who had taken Grace in her arms. Connor pressed a kiss to Harper's temple, and she looked up at him with adoration. It was obvious the two were very much in love, and the sight of it caused a sharp pain in his chest. Why was it so difficult to view others' happiness? He didn't begrudge them their joy…but it stung because it only served to emphasize all that he had once had…and lost.

He shifted his gaze briefly to Tessa, who stood beside him, and caught a look of such raw wistfulness on her face that he very nearly put his own arm around her. He forced himself to look away before he did something that breached the boundaries of simple friendship. But the expression she wore tugged at him, stirring his curiosity.

Why had she seemed so vulnerable in that moment? It occurred to him that perhaps Tessa had secrets of her own, beyond what she'd already shared with him. He felt a driving urge to learn what they might be, but he held himself in check. If Tessa had secrets, they were hers. He had no business digging into her past, especially not as her coworker. If she chose to share her thoughts, he was certain it would only be as one friend to another. Until she took that step, it was really none of his business.

So why did he suddenly ache to know so much about her? The question rattled him.

Fortunately, Tessa's mother approached at that moment to offer him a glass of the wine he'd brought, distracting him. Connor moved off to check on the meal while Allan engaged him in questions about living in DC for so many years.

From the corner of his eye, he noticed Zoe grab Tessa's attention. She was a sweet little girl, a couple of years younger than Ginny had been when she'd been diagnosed. But whereas Ginny had had dark brown hair before it had fallen out due to the chemo, Zoe's was a honey blond, similar to Tessa's. She had a darker skin tone than Ginny, too, but perhaps that was only because his last memories of his daughter were of a pallid countenance, chalky with impending death.

He swallowed hard, nauseated at the memory, and tightened his fingers around his wineglass as Allan continued talking, oblivious to his distraction. But somehow, Tessa noticed. He felt her hand touch his back, a gentle brush of reassurance, and then it was gone. He turned his head and caught her eye, and she offered an encouraging smile. It was enough to help him regain his footing as he fell back into the conversation with her father.

Moments later, he was rescued by the announcement that dinner was ready. They filed into the dining room and prepared to take their seats as Zoe proclaimed, "I'm sitting in between Aunt Tessa and Noah."

Harper placed Grace in her rocker. "Noah is Aunt Tessa's guest, Zoe. Don't you think he should sit beside her?"

"He's my guest, too," she stubbornly declared. He was touched by the assertion, though it was likely Zoe had warmed to him only because she adored Tessa. Any friend of Tessa's was probably a friend of Zoe's, as well.

"I don't mind," he said, and that was all the encouragement the little girl needed to grab his hand and lead him to the table. She pointed for him to sit, but first he pulled out the seat next to him and gestured for her to climb onto it.

"Ladies first," he said.

Zoe seemed to like this, and obliged him by working her way onto the chair. "Now Aunt Tessa," she commanded.

Noah pulled out the next chair, gesturing for Tessa to sit. The look she gave him as she sat down nearly melted his heart. Clearly, by catering to Zoe, he'd done something right.

Once they were all settled, Connor started serving the dinner. Tessa had been correct. It was like eating a gourmet meal for free.

Tortellini with asparagus tossed in a lemon-mint dressing. Roast salmon with a citrus glaze. A salad of spring greens with Connor's house dressing. Toast points with brie and fresh strawberries. Noah couldn't remember the last time he'd eaten such a delicious meal.

Throughout dinner, the conversation flowed steadily around the table, with the discussion ranging from personal acquaintances, to work life, to the summer tourist season in town. He knew it was inevitable that one of them would ask about his job, but he was too busy enjoying the delicious flavors of the food to worry about it.

The asparagus turned slightly sour in his mouth, however, when Paige finally directed a question at him.

"So, Noah, you're a doctor?"

He reached for his water glass. "Yes, a pediatric oncologist."

"You must be a good influence on Tessa, then. She hasn't brought anyone around for dinner in ages."

"Noah and I are colleagues," Tessa pointedly reminded Paige as she lifted a bite of salmon to her mouth. He sensed the subtle warning there. She didn't want her older sister to make a big deal out of this. He felt both protective of her and at the same time, oddly disappointed. Not that he should have. Tessa was right. They were coworkers. Friends. That was all.

"Hmm, well, you've never brought *colleagues* around before. But then, I suppose you didn't have many interesting coworkers at the animal clinic."

Noah nearly winced.

"I'd have to disagree," Noah said. "We spent the morning there, and the people at the clinic were delightful. Did you know one of the staff members breeds prizewinning corgis? Apparently, she once bred for some of the royal family."

This observation earned him several seconds of silence before he heard Harper quietly utter, "Well played."

He slid a glance in Tessa's direction, hoping she wasn't embarrassed by his words.

But she was glaring in her eldest sister's direction.

"See? That's why I'm always telling you not to be such a snob, Paige."

"I'm hardly a snob," Paige tossed back. "But you have to admit, your skills were wasted at that clinic."

"Girls," their mother warned.

"Why don't I bring out dessert?" Connor suggested.

The announcement abruptly ended the exchange between Paige and Tessa. Noah was impressed. Obviously, this wasn't Connor's first family dinner.

"No, you finish eating. Let Noah and me do it," Tessa said.

He was doubly impressed. Tessa was a master at evading her sister, it seemed. Then again, she had likely had years of practice.

"Me, too," Zoe announced and began to climb down from her seat.

"No," Paige immediately chastised. "You sit in that chair, young lady, and finish your dinner."

"But I'm full!" Zoe protested.

"You can't be. You couldn't have eaten more than three bites."

"But I am," Zoe argued.

Paige sighed with exasperation. "Zoe, we have been through this. You know what the doctor said. You're losing weight, and you need to eat more. I swear, all you do is lie around and sleep. You complain that you don't feel well, but you won't eat anything to give you energy! Now, you sit down and finish your dinner."

Noah watched Zoe very carefully following her mother's admonition. She sighed with long-suffering patience and sat down in her chair, pushing at the food on her plate with a fork. Tessa was waiting for him, and as he stood there, he was vaguely aware that the rest of the family was staring.

"How long has Zoe felt ill?" he asked, trying to keep his tone casual.

Weston, who had been rather quiet throughout dinner, was the one who answered. "It seems like months. Since before Christmas."

Noah quickly calculated. At least six months, then. Maybe longer. "What are her symptoms?"

"It's just a lingering cold." Paige was the one who replied this time. She seemed unconcerned. "That's what her pediatrician says. We've taken her to the doctor on several occasions, and he said there's so much going around."

Noah couldn't blame Zoe's doctor, necessarily, for assuming the little girl just kept catching a bug. With the winter weather and then the change in seasons, it wasn't an unreasonable assumption. Still...

"You say she's been tired and has a loss of appetite?"

"Yes, that's correct," Weston said.

"Any bruising?"

"What?" Paige looked baffled.

"Does she have any bruises?"

Paige's response was wary and tinged with annoyance. "She's a kid. Don't they often get bruises?"

"Yes," Noah reluctantly agreed, "but does she get them after she's been playing or just from minor incidents?"

"Is there a difference?" Paige said.

Noah frowned. He felt Tessa's hand on his arm.

"Noah. What's wrong?"

He knew he shouldn't jump to conclusions. Not every child was Ginny. Not every kid was carrying a deadly disease inside of them. And the symptoms of leukemia were vague, often attributed to other conditions.

So a child had bruises. As Paige had said, children got bruises when they played. So she was tired. She was a kid, and kids were bundles of energy, but eventually they had to crash and rest up. Just because Zoe wasn't eating as much as her mother wanted didn't mean she had leukemia. Sometimes kids didn't eat at meals. They would get junk food or candy if they could, and it would ruin their appetite. He would embarrass Tessa if he pushed the issue.

But what if…

He shook his head. "My apologies. I…" He blew out a breath, uncertain what to say. He should have known better than to hope he could be a normal person for one night. Had he really thought his past would release him, even for a few hours? He carried it with him. Ginny's ghost rode on his shoulder, whispering in his ear wherever he went. He was well aware he couldn't save every child, but to start seeing the disease in perfectly normal, healthy children… "I suppose I have a hard time leaving work at work," he finished lamely.

The atmosphere grew awkward. Harper and Connor were sharing a look of concern, Paige's mouth was set in a straight line,

Weston's brow was furrowed and Tessa's parents were quiet. The girls, Molly and Zoe, were the only two who seemed unconcerned by his misstep.

"I should probably go."

Tessa's hand on his arm squeezed. "Noah, it's okay. You don't have to."

"Of course not." Allan Worth spoke up. "I have a hard time leaving work behind myself most days. We appreciate your concern over Zoe's well-being."

"But there is nothing wrong," Paige put in. "I'm her mother. I would know if there was."

"Yes, I'm sure you're right." Noah didn't want to argue further. He wasn't making a personal remark against Paige's parenting. The signs of leukemia were subtle. Most parents didn't realize what was happening until things got out of control. With all his training, he himself should have noticed Ginny's symptoms earlier. He should have been paying more attention. Why hadn't he paid more attention? He was a doctor; he knew better.

But he was being ridiculous, seeing the specter of cancer at a simple dinner party. He had embarrassed Tessa, tainting her hospitality. "I really should go. I have an early start at the hospital tomorrow."

He didn't, but it was a handy excuse. He could sense Tessa beside him, could feel her disappointment. He had let her down. He should have known that he would. He was good at letting people down. If they offered degrees in it, he would have earned a doctorate in that, as well.

"Thank you so much for dinner. It was incredible. Connor, you are truly a talented chef."

"Thanks, mate. Stop by Callahan's sometime soon. My treat."

It was a generous offer. More than he deserved for how he'd disrupted their family meal.

"I appreciate that." He had to get out now before he was too tempted to stay.

He finally turned to face Tessa. "I'll see myself out."

She was staring at him, her eyes filled with concern. "You don't have to go," she said again. He knew she would have said more, had her family not been watching.

"I do," he said. "But I'll see you at the hospital."

He hurried from the room before there could be further protests.

CHAPTER NINE

THE WEEK PROCEEDED awkwardly for Tessa. After all the ground she'd gained with Noah, she'd lost all of it during one family dinner. He'd been polite, even friendly, when they'd seen each other at work the next day, but she could feel he held something back. He had put up his walls again. The knowledge depressed her.

At first, she'd been devastated by his story about losing his family. But she hadn't invited him to the animal clinic or to the family dinner out of pity. Noah might be prickly at times, and he certainly made an effort to keep others at arm's length. He was wounded, and with good reason.

Yet he was sweet, too, in his own way. He insisted he didn't like animals, but he'd been kind and careful with the ones at the clinic. And in spite of his first reaction to Rufus, she had caught him scratching her bulldog behind the ears more than once when he'd been at her house the night of the storm. He'd been thoughtful enough to offer her a ride when he could have pretended not to notice her, or at most, offered to call her a cab. But instead he'd gone out of his way to see her home safely.

These were small things, she knew. But hadn't she been looking for tiny miracles? Wasn't that what had prompted her to leave the clinic and make a fresh start at the hospital? She wanted to make a difference in children's lives and to meet others who did, too. Though she might not have thought of him that way at first, she believed Noah truly wanted to help people. He might need to work on his bedside manner, but his heart was there, even when his words were not.

Noah Brennan was growing on her. And it hurt her heart to know he'd pulled back.

Her family hadn't said much following his abrupt departure from dinner. Paige mumbled something under her breath, but Tessa didn't catch the words, and Weston had shushed his wife before she could say anything more. Tessa had stayed through dessert, eyeing Zoe nervously. Could Noah's suspicions be correct? It seemed too impossible. Zoe didn't have leukemia. She was just going through a growth spurt.

But when Tessa had announced she was going home early, her niece had clung to her, begging her to stay. As a compromise, she and Paige had made plans to have Zoe spend the following weekend at Tessa's, a sleepover for just the two of them. This had pacified Zoe, and Tessa had been able to escape back home to analyze her thoughts.

And what had filled her thoughts had been Noah.

At work, they didn't talk about what had occurred. Several times throughout the week that followed, she opened her mouth to let him know it was okay, that he hadn't done anything wrong, but each time, something in his expression and posture stopped her. She didn't want to push him further away, and she sensed trying to draw him out would do just that. So she kept quiet, pretending nothing had happened, and so did he.

But the camaraderie they'd experienced for an all-too-brief moment was gone.

By the week's end, Tessa was exhausted. Not so much from her job—she'd gotten a lot of things in place for the gala in another couple months' time—but from having to take so much care around Noah. It was draining, her awareness of him and her subsequent caution about each word that left her mouth, trying not to make matters more strained between them.

She was looking forward to spending some time with Zoe on Friday night, but part of her wanted nothing more than to curl up by herself on the couch, watching Hallmark movies and eating ice cream. She put that attitude aside when Zoe walked in the door. She noticed the way Weston's eyes followed his daughter when he dropped her off. She wondered if Noah's questions had gotten to him, too. He seemed reluctant to leave.

"Was traffic bad?"

It took him a moment to respond. "No, no. It was fine. Thanks for watching Zoe this weekend. Paige is looking forward to a weekend off."

Her sister was driving to Findlay Roads an hour behind her husband, after wrapping up some last-minute details at her job. Weston had been able to get away sooner and had picked Zoe up from the nanny to bring her here. Weston and Paige were spending the night at the Delphine while Tessa and Zoe had their sleepover. Tessa noticed that

Weston didn't comment that he was also looking forward to the weekend. She suspected he wasn't very comfortable leaving Zoe.

"We'll be fine," Tessa brightly declared to allay his concerns. Weston had never minded leaving Zoe in her care, and she didn't think that was the problem now. But he was clearly uneasy.

Zoe was already distracted, however, with greeting Rufus. Her giggles as Rufus licked her chin made Tessa smile.

"Weston, is everything okay?" she finally asked.

He swallowed. "What? Oh, yeah. Yeah, everything's good."

But he was still watching his daughter. Tessa followed his gaze, trying not to absorb his worry as her own. Zoe was scratching Rufus behind the ears. She didn't look like a sick child.

"We'll be fine," Tessa said again. "You and Paige enjoy your weekend."

"Right. Okay." But still, he lingered.

"Would it make you feel better if I had Zoe call you later tonight, just to check in?" she offered.

Weston finally relaxed a little. "Would you mind?"

"If I can tear her away from Rufus, it'll be no problem."

He sighed. "Thank you, Tessa."

"Sure." She looked at Zoe again. "Zoe, you want to come say goodbye to your dad?"

The little girl got up off the floor, and Tessa watched her carefully. Was it her imagination or did Zoe move a little stiffly?

"Bye, Daddy!" Weston bent down, and she gave him a quick kiss on the cheek before she turned back to the dog.

"We'll call you later," Tessa reassured Weston as he opened the door.

He nodded, but his eyes were still on his daughter as she closed it.

HOURS LATER, Tessa had convinced herself there was nothing to worry about where Zoe was concerned. Her niece had been energetic during their evening together, all through a game of Candyland, making popcorn balls, a dinner of pizza—though Zoe didn't eat more than a few bites—and bathtime—she had laughed long and loud at Rufus's attempts to climb in the tub with her. They'd called Weston, as promised, and Tessa had been slightly irked when he didn't pick up. Of course, it was likely Paige had made plans for the two of them. Tessa placed her phone nearby, making sure the ringer was loud enough, in case Weston tried calling them back. She turned on a Disney movie, grabbed some blankets and curled up on the couch with her niece.

They were halfway through *Sleeping Beauty* when Zoe stirred beside her.

"Aunt Tessa?"

Tessa looked down and gasped. There was a trickle of blood from Zoe's nose that flowed down her chin and onto the blanket that covered her. Tessa moved quickly, thankful for her nursing training.

"Breathe through your mouth, baby," she instructed, shifting Zoe so she could lay her down on the couch with her head tilted back. "Pinch your fingers on your nose here." She tapped the bridge of the little girl's nose. "I'm going to get you a wet cloth, okay?"

Tessa hurried into the kitchen, yanked open the dish towel drawer and grabbed a rag from the top. Rufus, who had been curled up at her feet while they watched TV, didn't follow. It was as if he knew he had to stay by Zoe's side. She went to the faucet and turned on the water, dousing the fabric. She realized she was trembling, her hands shaking.

It's only a nosebleed, she attempted to reassure herself. *Kids get nosebleeds. It happens.*

But her mind refused to shut down her fear. She squeezed out the excess water from the towel as a memory hit her.

When the news crew had come to the hospital to film the segment about the animal therapy program, she'd sat in on the family interviews. Kyle Miller's mother had been asked how she first learned her son had leukemia. Her answer suddenly came back to Tessa with haunting clarity.

"I missed all the signs. They were so easy to explain. He had joint stiffness, and his appetite was poor. He had some bruising and nosebleeds. Nothing was alarming, not in and of itself."

Nosebleeds. Tessa felt as though she had been punched in the stomach. It was a coincidence. It had to be. Zoe did not have cancer. She hurried back into the living room as she began mentally ticking off a catalogue of symptoms.

Zoe had had a persistent runny nose for months. She'd complained of aches that they'd assumed were a growth spurt. Her lack of appetite was not something Tessa had noticed until it had been pointed out at dinner the other night.

She knelt beside her niece, who was preternaturally calm in light of the nosebleed. Tessa cleaned up the blood and told Zoe to keep her head tilted back. Zoe breathed through her mouth, and Tessa could see the gap where she'd lost a baby tooth, the adult one nudging its way in. She began inspecting the little girl's body. There were a few bruises, some a fresh bluish-purple and others a faded dark yellow. Tessa bit her lip. Rufus whined and put his paw on her leg.

How many bruises should an average child have? Zoe played like any kid, and in playtime, kids bruised. But how much was normal? Her heartbeat began to pick up speed. She checked Zoe's forehead. It was warm. But was that from being bundled together on the couch? Rufus huffed in annoyance, stepped a few feet away and lay down, though he kept his eyes on them.

She felt Zoe's lymph nodes. They were still swollen, as they had been the weekend before. She was battling something. Maybe it was a minor infection, a cold she'd picked up from playmates.

But what if it wasn't? What if Noah, after all his years observing this disease, had a sixth sense?

What if Zoe had cancer?

"You okay, kid?" Tessa asked her niece.

Zoe began to sit up. Tessa thought about stopping her but then decided to see if she became dizzy.

"I'm okay," Zoe reassured her. "It's just a nosebleed. I get them a lot."

Tessa's heart dropped into her stomach.

"Y-you do?"

Zoe shrugged. "Yeah. Mom says I take after Dad. He gets nosebleeds sometimes."

She sat down beside Zoe, wiping her face with the edge of the cloth. "How have you been feeling lately?"

Zoe made a face. "You sound like Dad."

Tessa's gaze flickered toward her phone. She reached across Zoe to tap the screen. She had no missed calls or texts. Weston hadn't tried calling them back.

Panic began creeping in. She had heard enough of the stories over the last few weeks at the hospital. There was not a second to be wasted when leukemia was diagnosed. Children were immediately rushed into treatment to eradicate the cancer cells before they had a chance to advance too aggressively.

She glanced at her phone again. She didn't want to worry Zoe unnecessarily, but what could it hurt to try calling Weston again?

"Speaking of your dad, let's see if he picks up this time, hmm? I know he wanted to talk to you before bed."

"But I'm not ready for bed yet," she protested, even as she yawned.

Tessa ignored her and dialed Weston's cell. She found herself counting the rings as she tapped her foot. She forced herself to be still.

"Hi, you've reached Weston, I'm unable to take your call right now…"

Tessa punched the screen to hang up and looked at Zoe. She seemed pale. There were dark circles beneath her eyes. Was that new or had Tessa just not noticed before? Tessa's anxiety was creeping upward, and she was beginning to feel desperate. What could she do? How could she figure out the truth about Zoe's condition?

Noah.

Of course. He would know what to do. He was the only person who could allay her fears.

"Zoe…how would you feel about Noah coming to see us?"

Zoe perked up visibly. "Noah? I like him."

"Me, too," Tessa agreed before she could consider just how much she liked him.

"What do you say we give him a call?"

Zoe nodded. Tessa's fingers were still shaking as she found Noah's number in her phone and tapped to dial. It rang several times, and she began to think he wasn't going to pick up. Was he screening her calls? What if he was holding his phone in his hands right now, looking at her name on the screen, and debating whether to send her call to voice mail? He kept his phone nearby at all times, in case of emergencies at the hospital. Of course, maybe he was working late and wasn't able to answer. She closed her eyes, silently praying.

And then his voice sounded in her ear, and it was so soft and sweet that she nearly sobbed with relief.

"Hello, Tessa."

The way he said her name…

"Noah, I…" She trailed off, uncertain how to continue. She suddenly felt foolish. What if she was being ridiculous? Paige would be furious at how she'd jumped to conclusions.

But Noah spoke again, and she suddenly didn't care.

"Tessa, what's wrong?" He knew. Even without her speaking a word, he knew she needed him.

She had seen too many children battling cancer in the last few weeks, had sat with them and listened to their stories. She'd heard Noah's own struggle. If she was paranoid, then so be it. Better to be safe than sorry.

"Can you come over?" she asked, her voice strained. "I need your help."

NOAH WAS OUT his front door before Tessa even finished explaining. He could tell she was being guarded in her choice of words. Zoe must have been beside her, listening in. Tessa was smart. She didn't want to alarm the little girl. But he was glad she had called. Ever since that dinner with Tessa's family, he'd had a growing uneasiness where little Zoe was concerned. He knew it was none of his business, and he was probably influenced too much by his own past. But he still couldn't shake the feeling that there was something wrong.

He made it to Tessa's house in less than ten minutes. He'd only arrived home a half hour before, and he was grateful he'd been so close when she called. She opened the door for him before he could even knock, ushering him inside with a breathless "Thank you for coming so fast."

Rufus was at her feet, and he jumped up, demanding a greeting. Noah bent down briefly to scratch the dog behind the ears and then straightened, looking to Tessa. She was dressed casually in loose-fitting pants and an oversize lightweight knit sweater. Her hair fell around her shoulders in golden waves, but her eyes were dark with worry. He had the sudden, overwhelming urge to pull her into his arms and reassure her, let her know everything would be all right. The thought brought him up short.

He'd done the same for Julia when Ginny had first been diagnosed. She hadn't thanked him for it, in the end. Her words still echoed in his head, the ones she'd thrown at him after Ginny's funeral.

You lied! You said she would be fine, that she'd go into remission! Liar!

He stiffened, holding himself back from comforting Tessa.

"Where is she?" he asked instead.

Tessa led him into the living room. Zoe

was spread out on the couch, watching a cartoon running on the television. She brightened when she saw him.

"Hi, Noah!" She offered a little wave.

"Hello there, Zoe," he said.

She scooted down on the couch and then pointed for him to sit. He did, but he also kept a cautious eye on her, mentally assessing her physical state. She was pale, and her eyes had a slight glassy sheen. Fever? It was a common symptom of undiagnosed leukemia.

"What movie are we watching?" he asked, trying to distract her from noticing his observation.

"Sleeping Beauty," she answered. "It's my favorite."

He swallowed. Ginny had always loved *Beauty and the Beast* best.

"I forget, what's the name of the princess in that one?"

"Aurora," Zoe promptly answered.

"Oh, that's right. She has brown hair, right?"

Zoe giggled. "No! Her hair is blond, like mine. And like Aunt Tessa's."

Noah looked over his shoulder at Tessa, who was standing there watching the exchange, nibbling on her thumbnail. Rufus had settled on the rug in between them.

"Yes, Aunt Tessa resembles Sleeping Beauty, doesn't she?"

Tessa appeared startled by this comment. He quickly turned his attention back to Zoe lest Tessa read something in his expression that he didn't want her to see. Zoe was studying her aunt with consideration, a light of awe dawning in her face.

"She does," Zoe breathed. "Aunt Tessa is really pretty."

"Aunt Tessa is very pretty," he agreed, keeping his back to the object of their discussion. "Zoe, would you mind if I did a quick examination? I know you haven't been feeling well lately, and I wanted to see if I could figure out why."

Zoe shrugged. "Okay."

"Could you sit up for me?"

She pulled herself up and sat on the edge of the couch. Rufus came over to watch the proceedings. Noah ran through a brief examination and asked a few questions as he did.

"Are you in any pain? Do you get fevers? How often? How often do you feel tired?"

Zoe answered them patiently, but it was difficult to get accurate answers from a six-year-old. He finished his examination and stood.

"You and Rufus hang out here for a few minutes while Aunt Tessa and I go in the kitchen to talk."

Having grown bored with the questions, Zoe was too absorbed in a scene with the dragon to make any protest. Tessa admonished Rufus to stay put and then led the way out of the room. When they reached the kitchen, she spun to face him.

"Please tell me we are both being paranoid."

He hesitated. "I'm not sure," he finally answered. Tessa's shoulders slumped. "At this point, I would certainly recommend more tests. The sooner the better. If this has been going on for months…" He trailed off but decided it was important to finish his thought. "Tessa, you know there's not a minute to lose here. Best-case scenario, she's fighting something viral. Worst-case—" He stopped. He didn't need to elaborate on the worst case.

They stood in silence for several minutes, the weight of their worry hanging between them.

"Tessa, I'd like to take her to the hospital. Run tests."

"Paige and Weston—"

"Could meet us there. If they're amenable."

She nibbled her lip, considering.

"Tessa…" He was trying to remain unbiased, to evaluate Zoe clinically and not emotionally. But there were too many variables in the equation. Too many what-ifs. He needed more information. "The only way to be certain is to run some tests."

Tessa released a pent-up sigh. "Let me try Weston again."

She pulled her phone out of her back pocket and dialed her brother-in-law's number. In the still silence of the kitchen, he could hear Weston's voice on the other end of the line when he finally answered.

"Tessa? Is everything okay?"

Tessa's eyes met Noah's, a dark question in them. "Y-yes. No." She drew a deep breath. "Do you think you and Paige could meet us at the hospital?"

CHAPTER TEN

TESSA HAD LOST track of the time. Somewhere between carrying Zoe to Noah's car and telling her they were going on an adventure and dozing in the waiting room at the hospital, she'd become disoriented. When she opened her eyes after falling asleep, she noticed the sun had risen, slanting in disjointed rays through the window blinds.

Weston was seated next to her, slumped in his chair. Not quite asleep but not awake, either. Paige was pacing, typing furiously into her phone. Who could she be texting at this hour? Maybe their parents, or Harper. She stirred enough to check her own phone. Her battery was hovering at ten percent. She'd let Zoe play games on it while they waited in between tests. There was a message, from Harper, saying she planned to stop by the hospital later that morning.

Tessa texted her to wait since they didn't know anything for sure yet. She stood to her feet, careful not to disturb Weston, and moved toward her sister.

"Paige?" she asked to get her attention.

Paige turned, a frown cutting across her features. "What?" she asked, her tone clipped.

Tessa didn't let it bother her. Paige could be abrasive even on a good day, much less one like this.

"You doing okay?" she ventured.

"If you must know, not really," Paige responded. "I don't see what everyone is so paranoid about. Zoe is *fine*. There is nothing wrong. I've always been a good mother. I feed her organic food. I use non-GMO. I do everything I possibly can—"

"Paige. This isn't about you," Tessa gently reminded her. "If Zoe really is sick, it's not a reflection on you as a mother."

Paige and Weston had always been very involved in their careers, and she wondered if that focus had added to her sister's guilt over this diagnosis.

Paige had never mentioned wanting kids, so Tessa had been surprised when her sister announced she was expecting. She sometimes wondered if her niece had really been a planned pregnancy, though Paige insisted she had been.

Tessa knew Paige loved Zoe. She just had a difficult time showing it. As the oldest, there had been more pressure on her to succeed, to live up to their father's high standards for success. As the baby of the family, her parents had had more relaxed expectations for Tessa. She had wondered, more than once, if that was why it bothered Paige so much that Tessa had bailed on her wedding and then her job to work minimum wage for nearly two years. Paige would never have done something so unassuming. She was driven to climb higher and higher, earn more money, gain more status.

But at what cost? Her sister was short-tempered much of the time, and now Tessa feared she was feeling guilty for circumstances beyond her control.

"Of course it's not," Paige responded to her reassurance. "It's just…I think I'd know if my daughter was sick."

Tessa was torn between wanting to calm her sister and yet not offering false hope. "The symptoms of leukemia—"

"Stop, Tessa. Just stop. You're not a mother. If you were, you'd understand. It's called mother's intuition for good reason. I would sense if my child was ill."

Her words could not have hurt any more if they had been delivered at the end of a sharp knife. Tessa folded her arms over her chest, trying to keep herself together.

Paige had no idea of Tessa's struggles with infertility. None of her family did. She wasn't a mother. She likely never would be, at least not biologically. The medical diagnosis she'd received almost two years ago had made that abundantly clear. She'd done the research, weighed the costs. The odds were against her ever holding her own, flesh-and-blood child in her arms.

This knowledge was at the core of every decision she had made over the last twenty-four months. She had left her fiancé, quit her job, isolated herself from her friends who had children.

Her heart hurt for what her sister was going through. But Paige could not know the cold, hard truth behind her words. Tessa's sister did not realize how she had wounded her. And Tessa was not about to tell her. But neither did she have the fortitude to continue their conversation. She wanted to take a break and head to her office downstairs, but she didn't want to leave the waiting room in case there was any news.

So she sat back down, choosing a seat several chairs away from Weston. She needed some distance, even if she didn't want to go far.

Another hour passed. Weston woke but he stared sightlessly ahead. Paige would sit for a few minutes then leap up to begin pacing once more. A throbbing pain began behind Tessa's eyes as she watched her sister's restless energy.

After yet another hour, Tessa felt, more than heard, the waiting room door open. Noah stepped inside, and Tessa's heart contracted. He looked exhausted. She remembered that she had torn him from a night's rest for this emergency. She needed to thank him. It was strange that she'd assumed he was cold when she first met him. The longer she knew him, the more she saw a steady kindness that warmed her. Just now, however, she was trying to read his expression, to determine Zoe's prognosis from his features.

Paige pounced on him before he could open his mouth. "This is ridiculous. You drag my husband and me out here, and we spend hours waiting for results. Where is my daughter?"

Tessa flinched. She should have warned Paige that the tests would take a while. But she didn't have the energy to reassure her sister at the moment. Paige's words from before had decimated her. All she cared about right now was finding out if Zoe was all right. She knew she'd never hear the end of it from Paige if her suspicions were wrong. But she would take a lifetime of that harassment over Zoe having cancer.

"Zoe is with the nurse. You'll be able to see her shortly." His tone was not unkind, but it was firm. Perhaps that was what she had missed during her last judgment of Noah's bedside manner. He probably handled all sorts of reactions from patients' families. Maybe, sometimes, a certain amount of grit was required. "Why don't we all go to my office, where we can speak freely?"

This suggestion seemed to throw Paige. She could empathize with her sister's struggle. Arguing in a hospital waiting room was one thing but sitting down in a doctor's office was another. It spoke of something serious, of news that had to be delivered in private. Even Tessa felt shaken by the suggestion. Although perhaps Noah simply wanted to take them somewhere where Paige could calm down.

Tessa sensed bad news coming and felt a tremble of fear. Noah caught her eyes, the expression in his own bleak. And she knew then, without him saying a word.

Zoe had cancer.

NOAH WAITED TO speak until they were in his office with the door firmly closed. Paige and Weston took the chairs in front of his desk. Paige had paled since he suggested going to his office. Despite her caustic reactions up to this point, he couldn't help feeling sympathy for her. Her world was about to change. Forever.

He knew the feeling.

He'd had to drag another chair into his office for Tessa. Now she sat, perched on its edge and off to the side, in between her sister on one side of the desk and him on the other.

He didn't waste time. He'd been where Paige and Weston were sitting, and he knew the most important thing they wanted to hear was "yes" or "no."

"Zoe's tests came back positive. I'm afraid she has ALL, which stands for acute lymphoblastic leukemia."

It never ceased to shake him how parents reacted after he delivered this devastating news. Most were in a state of shock, unable to wrap their minds around the enormity of the diagnosis. Some knew in an instant the battle that they were in for, and these would immediately burst into tears or break down crying. In one case, he'd even had a mother begin screaming hysterically. A few grew angry, threatening second opinions, too frightened to accept a fight they were unprepared for. He expected Paige to be in the latter group, but she surprised him by blindly reaching out her hand until she found her husband's and leaning in to him.

It gave Noah pause. He had assumed, during his limited observations of their relationship, that Paige was the strong one. Weston was, for the most part, quiet and unassuming. But the way Paige leaned on him now, he wondered if he'd had it all wrong. Maybe Paige was all wind and storm while Weston was the rock that would hold them steady through the upcoming battle.

"The good news is that ALL is the most common form of childhood cancers, and has one of the highest cure rates," he explained, beginning a speech he had offered many times before. "The bad news is that it's not an easy fight."

He steadied himself, trying not to think of Ginny. This was the hardest part of his job. More than fighting the cancer, he hated having to look parents in the eye and tell them their child was going to die if extreme measures weren't taken. And even with ALL's high cure rate, there were exceptions.

Ginny.

"We are getting Zoe ready for a blood and platelet transfusion right now. Next, we will need to place a port in her chest so we can deliver the chemotherapy."

Paige let out a tiny sob at the word *chemotherapy*, and Weston went white as a sheet. Noah shifted his gaze to Tessa, suddenly needing to look at her, to see how she was faring.

She was quiet but calm. She gave him a nod of understanding, and he experienced a new appreciation of her. She didn't shy away from battles, this woman. He admired that in her. He turned back to Weston and Paige to continue outlining the treatment plan.

"I know it's a lot to take in, but there is no time to waste. We want to get Zoe on the path to remission as soon as possible."

Weston tried to focus on him. "Then there's hope?"

He hesitated, remembering his words to Tessa. *Hope is a disease.*

"There is a very high remission rate for ALL," he said. "But you have to be prepared for the road ahead." He drew a breath and began offering information. It would be a challenge for them to remember it all, which was why the staff would supply literature and offer to answer questions throughout the course of treatment.

Over the next few weeks, Zoe would be spending the majority of her time at the hospital, receiving treatments while he and the other staff tracked her progress. He explained that Zoe would need intrathecal therapy in the first month in order to administer the chemo into her cerebrospinal fluid.

"Intra...thecal?" Weston's tongue struggled with the words. He looked from Noah to Tessa. "What's that?"

This part was particularly difficult for parents to hear. "Lumbar punctures," he said.

The reaction was immediate. Paige's grip on her husband's hand tightened. Weston gave a little gasp. From the corner of his eye, Noah saw Tessa's head lower, as if unable to witness her family's distress.

At some point, one of the nurses would go over the treatment in more detail, including the fact that intrathecal therapy occasionally caused seizures in some patients. But he didn't want to add that possibility to their burden right now. They would have their hands full dealing with Zoe as she experienced the standard side effects of treatment, including diarrhea, nausea, vomiting, fatigue. He was giving them the larger scope at the moment. Other details could be addressed later.

"There will be at least a couple intrathecal treatments in her first month, possibly more depending on how the cancer responds. We will continue with this course for a couple of months until we reach the intensification stage."

He knew Paige and Weston were overwhelmed, but he wanted to at least give them an overview of what their lives would look like for the next six months. He sensed Tessa paying close attention, cataloguing the details for when her sister and brother-in-law had recovered from their shock enough to ask questions.

After he felt he'd provided sufficient treatment descriptions, he asked if they had any questions. The couple appeared shell-shocked.

"Is our daughter going to die?"

It was the most common question he heard from parents, but voiced now, by Paige, it softened him toward her.

"I will do everything in my power to keep that from happening," he said, knowing he could make no guarantees. Julia's heartbreak prevented him from making promises he couldn't keep.

You said she would live! You lied!

"I don't get to decide what happens to these children, but I will fight for them with every breath I take." That was the vow he had made after Ginny's death. That was how he tried to make amends for his failure to her. It was his absolution, should he be worthy of it.

"I know this is a lot to absorb right now, and you'll likely have more questions later. Feel free to ask them at any time." He drew a deep breath. "I'm sure you want to see Zoe now."

This offer seeped through their shock and moved both of them to their feet. Typically, he would have led them to the patient himself, but he'd found the conversation had drained him more than usual. He needed a minute to regain his composure. Perhaps it was the personal connection he had to Zoe, even though he'd only just met her. Maybe she reminded him too much of Ginny. Or maybe just having Tessa in the room had infiltrated too many of his barriers.

"Tessa, would you mind taking Paige and Weston to Zoe's room?" He consulted the chart. "She's in 414."

He didn't quite meet Tessa's eyes, but he sensed her watching him carefully.

"Of course." There was hesitation there. She knew too much about him now. It was why he'd kept himself guarded from others. He didn't want her pity, didn't need her to worry if he was going to be all right. She had changed him too much already, her quiet kindness drawing him out little by little. He couldn't give her any more opportunities to get into his work…or his heart.

"Do you—"

"I just want to review Zoe's chart a bit more before we proceed."

His words were cold, a chilly difference from his tone when he'd spoken to Paige and

Weston. Tessa backed off. He felt it even though he didn't look at her.

"Okay," she said and moved to usher her family from the room.

Only when the door was closed behind them did he lower his forehead to his desk and squeeze his eyes shut to hold back the tears for all he had lost, and the struggle for Zoe still ahead.

THE NEXT FEW hours were overwhelming. Tessa took the job of communicating with the family. She placed calls to Weston's parents on the West Coast, updated Harper via text and then rang up her mom and dad. No one had told Allan and Vivienne Worth what was happening while they waited for answers. But now that they knew the worst, Tessa had to tell them their granddaughter had cancer.

They took it well. She was able to catch them at home, together, before her dad headed to the Delphine for the day. She was grateful they were in town at the moment and not at their penthouse in DC. Findlay Roads was closer to the hospital so they'd be able to get there sooner.

"How is Zoe?" her mom asked.

Tessa felt a little dart of pain to her chest. "I haven't gotten to see her yet. Paige and Weston are with her and the nurse right now."

"And how are they?" her dad questioned. She had asked her mom to place themselves on speakerphone so she could talk to them both at the same time.

"They're...in shock, I think. But obviously distraught."

"Zoe's a tough kid. She's going to get through this."

This was what Tessa loved most about her dad. He might have exacting expectations, and he could be an intimidating force. But when faced with a crisis, all those elements made him someone you could rely on. He would have done well as an army general, leading men into battle. And that was what it felt like they were doing right now. Heading into battle.

"I know," she answered, more because she had to act confident than because she really felt it.

"Find out if Paige and Weston want anything from their house. I can make the drive into the city to pick up some things for them," Allan offered.

"I'll get together some food," her mom said. "I'm guessing they haven't eaten much. Or you. I'll be there as soon as I can."

Tessa felt some of the burden ease from her shoulders. She loved how her family drew together during tough times. When her grandmother had been ill, she'd been the only one living in Findlay Roads, so the bulk of Nana's care had fallen to Tessa. But her family had helped out when and where they could—visiting, staying overnight to give Tessa a break, bringing food to store in the freezer and asking what she needed.

It was a nice reminder that she always had her family's support. It made her doubt her decision not to tell them the real reason she had left Burke standing at the altar almost two years ago. She swallowed at the memory. But she didn't want her family's pity. She couldn't bear the thought of her sisters, especially Paige, trying to offer their advice. She knew they'd mean well, but how could they understand? And right now, all the family's focus needed to be on Zoe.

"Thank you," she managed to force out. "I'm sure Weston and Paige will appreciate the help."

"You tell Zoe to hang in there," her dad said.

"Send our love, and we'll be there soon," Mom added.

"Okay. I will."

She wrapped up the call but remained standing in the empty waiting room. She should go check on Paige and Weston, see what they needed. And she hadn't had the chance to talk to Zoe. Her niece had still been with the nurses when they'd emerged from Noah's office.

Noah.

She was grateful to him. If it hadn't been for his keen observations, who knew how long Zoe would have gone undiagnosed? Tessa wasn't certain how early they'd caught the disease in her niece, but every day was an advantage. She was heartsick at what lay ahead for Zoe, but she was also glad more time hadn't passed before they'd caught the signs. Thanks to Noah.

"Tessa?"

She turned at the sound of her name. Elise, one of the nurses, was standing in the doorway to the waiting room. "Your niece is in her room. She's asking for you. Her parents are with Miranda, going over the treatment schedule."

"Of course, I'm coming. Thanks."

Elise, bless her, looked concerned. She understood what a tough blow this was for families.

"What's Zoe's room number again?"

"414."

"Okay, I'll be right there."

She offered a wavering smile, and Elise took the hint. She stepped out of the waiting room, leaving Tessa alone once more.

Tessa drew a deep breath, gathering her composure. There was a mirror in the waiting room, and she checked it, to make sure there was no evidence of tears or distress. She wanted to be strong for her niece's sake.

The face that stared back at her was open, pleasant. She tested out her smile. It appeared natural. But her eyes... There was sadness there...and uncertainty. She blinked, but it remained. Maybe that look had been there for a long time—ever since her doctor had sat down with her and explained the symptoms she didn't understand in the weeks leading up to her wedding.

Early-onset menopause.

She remembered her reaction clearly. The baffled uncertainty.

"But I'm not even thirty years old yet. How can I be going through menopause?"

"It's somewhat rare, but not entirely unusual," Dr. Natalie had explained.

"Okay, so what are my treatment options?"

Dr. Natalie fell silent after this question, and it was then that the enormity of her diagnosis began to sink in.

"We can manage the symptoms, but, Tessa…there is no way to reverse it."

Dr. Natalie explained that hormone therapy might relieve her symptoms, but it could not restore what was being taken.

Tessa had trained as a nurse, but she was still slow to reach the most heartrending conclusion of her diagnosis. It wasn't until the doctor started discussing premature ovarian failure that it hit her.

"Wait, does that mean… I mean, I can…I can still have kids, right?"

Dr. Natalie looked at her with pity. That was when Tessa felt the weight settle on her shoulders, a mantle of shock and embarrassment.

"There are options," Dr. Natalie began. "In vitro treatments, supplementation or egg donation."

Tessa felt her world coming apart at the seams.

"Egg donation?" she'd rasped, having to

force the words past her tightening throat. "You mean, not my own? The baby wouldn't be mine?"

Dr. Natalie was so unbelievably calm that Tessa wanted to slap or shake her. The violence of this kind of reaction only served to unsettle her even more.

"A family member might—"

"No." She was not about to go begging her sisters to use their eggs so she could conceive.

"You don't have to worry about any of that right now. Take some time to let all this sink in..."

And she had. With only two weeks before her wedding, she began researching her options. She didn't tell Burke. She didn't tell anyone. But she went online, visited message boards and forums, and her sadness grew into a full-blown depression. It was difficult enough to read other women's sorrow over their inability to conceive. They suffered through treatment, cycles of hope, disappointment and grief. But then she stumbled upon forums for men whose wives were unable to conceive.

The messages there twisted her up inside so that at one point, she had to run to the bathroom, gagging into the wastebasket. How could she tell Burke she would likely never bear his child, if there was any chance this would be his response?

My wife and I tried IVF over and over. It never worked. I started seeing another woman, and when she got pregnant, I left my wife...

No matter how much you love her, if you want a biological child, that love will eventually turn to hate. It's better off for both of you if you leave her and find someone else...

It's a tough choice, but you owe it to yourself to carry on your family line...

Just do what's best for you. Your wife will understand...

I love my wife, but the idea of adopting someone else's kid leaves me cold...

I can't look at her the same way...

And on the messages went, some more cruel than others. The hardest were the ones where the guy obviously loved his wife but didn't know how to deal with having his hopes of his own kids being taken away. The ones that didn't want to leave but couldn't reconcile how to stay.

Some men spoke up and defended their wives, reminding others that it was not their fault, and that the world was not the place it had once been. It was perfectly acceptable in this day and age to adopt or remain childless. No shame in it.

But Tessa had always dreamed about being a mom, longed for the day she'd have children of her own. It seemed grossly unjust that her body had betrayed her the way that it had. Everyone had always told her she'd be a great mother—she'd heard it nearly every day when she'd worked as a pediatric nurse, parents marveling at her care and skill with their children.

She burned with resentment at her own womb for failing her, stealing her future hopes and her lifelong dream. She ached with shame and sorrow and fear, and she couldn't bring herself to share it with anyone. She was embarrassed, feeling as though she was somehow letting others down by admitting they were wrong. So she carried that burden alone, for weeks, right up until the day of her wedding when she realized she could not possibly ask Burke to join his life to hers when the family they'd dreamed about could never happen. Or at least, not happen as they'd planned.

Burke was a good man. She knew he

would have married her regardless, supported her no matter what. But she had always had a sense of something between him and Erin, and she could not bear to think of him comparing her to someone else, especially in this regard. So she ran. No explanation. No excuse.

Her family had thought she was crazy. They had no context to her decision, nor the decisions that followed. She'd quit her job because she couldn't be around children and parents on a daily basis. She wasn't sure she'd ever tell them. Because she knew they'd try to convince her it was no big deal, that plenty of women had the same struggle, that there were options, she could still find fulfillment, and so on. But those words would ring hollow. She had already tried them out on herself, hundreds of times. It couldn't change the way she felt.

CHAPTER ELEVEN

ONE SIGHT OF her niece, and Tessa forgot about her own heartache. Zoe looked small and vulnerable in the hospital bed, the white sheets nearly matching the pale shade of her skin. Her eyes were wide with uncertainty, darting around the room to take in the machines, the sterile counters and cupboards, the fluorescent lighting.

For a hospital room, it was actually quite cozy. The walls were painted a cheerful turquoise blue, and the artwork depicted cartoon fish in a rainbow of colors. There were chairs with blond wood and cushions to match the walls. A flat-screen TV hung opposite Zoe's bed. One of the nurses had turned it on to the Disney channel. Despite these little touches, however, the room was still a clinical environment, and Zoe knew it. Tessa could tell by her expression, the anxiety plainly written on her face.

"Hey, kiddo," she greeted as she entered the room.

Zoe's eyes skittered to hers, and for a brief moment, relief registered there.

"Aunt Tessa!"

Tessa moved closer and leaned in for a hug. "I heard you've had a busy morning so far."

Zoe's lower lip trembled. "I got stuck with needles." She raised her arm, showcasing her IV as proof.

"I know, sweetheart, I'm sorry. Needles are no fun."

Zoe nodded her agreement. "Mom and Dad are here," she said.

"Yeah, I was with them earlier. Grandma and Grandpa are coming later, too."

She brushed the hair back from her niece's head, taking a moment to appreciate the soft, fine strands in her fingers. Within a few weeks, Zoe's hair would begin to fall out. She wondered if it would distress Zoe or if she'd see it as an odd adventure, marking her as special. This was how Tessa would try to present it to her, at least.

Zoe grew quiet for a couple of minutes, her gaze focused on her arm and the IV tube. Tessa forced herself to be patient, wanting

Zoe to work through her thoughts and emotions.

"Aunt Tessa—" she finally raised her eyes "—when can I go home?"

Tessa swallowed, pained by the simple question. "I'm not sure yet, but it's going to be some time. Did your mom and dad talk to you, tell you what's going on?"

Zoe gave a short nod. "They said I'm sick. Like really sick."

Tessa drew a deep breath. She wasn't sure just how much information Paige and Weston would have given their daughter. They probably hadn't had much time to help Zoe process what was going on.

"You are sick," Tessa affirmed, "but that's why we brought you here to the hospital. So Noah can make you better."

This perked her up a bit. "Noah is going to fix me?"

Tessa didn't want to make promises. "He's going to try."

Zoe watched her, as if looking for signs that she was telling the truth. Tessa wasn't sure how much her niece, at the tender age of six, understood about cancer.

"Is it going to hurt?" she asked, her voice a threadbare whisper.

Tessa's heart broke at the question, but she would not lie. "Yes, sweetheart, it's probably going to hurt sometimes."

Zoe's eyes filled with tears, and Tessa rushed to reassure her.

"But I'm here, and so are your mom and dad, and Aunt Harper and Uncle Connor, Grandma and Grandpa, and Molly and Grace…we're all going to be here for you, so you don't have to be afraid, okay?"

Zoe didn't respond. She blinked, and the tears overflowed her eyes and onto her face. Tessa grabbed a tissue from the counter and used it to dab at Zoe's cheeks.

"Aunt Tessa…am I going to die?"

Tessa swallowed. Zoe understood more than she'd given her credit for. She knew the seriousness of cancer. And while Tessa refused to lie, she also didn't want to reply in a way that would panic her niece even more.

"Zoe, have you seen all the kids around here?"

She shrugged. Tessa realized that she'd probably been tied up with nurses most of the night, so she may not have met the other patients in the ward.

"There are lots of kids here, and many more who come to the hospital every day to get treatments because they're getting better. They don't have to stay here all the time now, but they come back to get their medicine and stuff. There are so many children out there who get better."

She didn't know what else to say, how else to explain that most kids survived...but some did not. She thought of Noah and his daughter, Ginny. Leukemia was much more treatable than it once had been. But nothing in life was guaranteed.

How had Noah survived it, the loss of those he loved most in the world? Tessa didn't think she'd have the strength to go on. Just her own diagnosis of premature menopause...that alone had shattered her. That was the loss of a child she had never known or held close. How much worse must it be to have loved that child and have them torn from you?

"I'm sorry," Zoe said, drawing Tessa's focus back to her.

"What in the world are you sorry for, love?" she asked, smoothing Zoe's hair once more.

"It's my fault. Mom told me that I should be more careful because I kept getting the bruises and she said I needed to eat more, but I didn't." Zoe's tears came in force. "I'm sorry, Aunt Tessa! I'm really sorry!"

"Shh, shh, Zoe, it's okay." She moved to sit on the edge of the bed and drew her niece into her side, rocking her awkwardly as she tried to maintain her balance. "This is *not* your fault, Zoe. Nobody is to blame for this, do you understand?"

Zoe kept crying, but Tessa didn't let her go. She just held her and let her cry, trying her best not to weep along with her.

NOAH WATCHED FROM a distance as Tessa's family rallied to support Zoe. It seemed as if they each contributed, and they assembled with the efficiency of an army. Tessa's father was the head of the unit. He met with Noah for details on Zoe's treatment and asked surprisingly intelligent questions about the latest clinical trials and what Zoe's options were.

Given her background in pediatric medicine, Tessa was often present for these sessions and contributed explanations for her dad's benefit. Noah tried to keep most of his attention on Allan Worth as he spoke because if he didn't, he'd easily get lost in Tessa's eyes.

Having her call on him to help had only

deepened his conflicted feelings for her. He was rarely relied upon as a friend anymore. That was his own doing, of course. But having Tessa need him had awakened a dormant desire he didn't even know he still possessed. He could not, however, allow this to affect his work. He had many patients, and he distributed his care equitably among them. But he found himself welcoming Allan's questions. It kept his own mind buzzing with the best ways to treat not only Zoe but his other patients, as well.

It was also apparent to him that Tessa had inherited her caregiving skills from her mother. Vivienne was the one who made sure Paige and Weston were taking enough breaks, getting proper nourishment, and filled in the gaps for them when necessary.

Connor and Harper brought food, and usually enough to feed not only their family but others, as well. Noah supposed that made sense, given Connor's job as a chef and restaurateur, but he was impressed just the same. Sometimes Harper had their baby, Grace, with her, along with her adopted daughter, Molly. The nurses loved cooing over Grace, and Noah approved of how friendly Molly was with the other kids on the floor. She never stared or asked uncomfortable questions. She seemed to accept them at face value, perhaps because her cousin was going through the same situation. Molly kept Zoe company in between tests and treatments. Even though she was several years older, she whispered and giggled with Zoe like they were two teenage girls.

And then there was Tessa. He supposed, in some ways, it was opportune that Tessa worked at the hospital. She was able to be there for her niece even more than the rest of them. Ana had given her latitude to take as many breaks as necessary, so Tessa often spent part of the morning and afternoon in her office and then brought her laptop with her to sit in Zoe's room and work while her niece dozed or if Paige and Weston needed to step away. He marveled at how driven Tessa was. She kept up with the planning for the gala, along with her other fund-raising and PR projects, in between everything else going on.

He learned that Connor and Harper were caring for Rufus so Tessa could be at the hospital more. Noah had noticed that Zoe asked for Tessa more than her parents. The two obviously shared a close bond, which didn't seem to bother Paige much.

Then again, Tessa had that nurturing instinct; her very presence was calming. He'd found that to be true himself, gravitating to her when he was out of sorts or had a bad day because just being near her steadied him somehow.

Unfortunately, that frightened him, as well. He'd grown far too fond of Tessa, and had to continually remind himself to keep his heart in check where she was concerned.

He'd seen how good she was with Zoe and with other children on the floor. She often stopped to say hello to the kids and their families. She remembered them all. Every name. Every hobby. Their fears. Their hopes. Where they came from and the distance they had to drive. How many siblings they had, and she remembered them, too, so she could greet them when they were there. She asked after treatments, encouraged the weary and always left the kids with a smile on their face.

She was a wonder, and one that he found difficult to resist.

But when she was unaware he was watching, he saw her unfiltered fear. And the sight of it brought back a flood of memories, too forceful to repress. Julia, late at night, leaning over their daughter's hospital bed with her hands folded in prayer. Julia, holding on to Ginny's body as it grew cold and screaming at anyone who tried to take her dead child from her arms. Julia at Ginny's funeral, practically unresponsive but for the tears leaking from her eyes.

Tessa was not Julia. He was well aware of that fact. But he could not bear the thought of seeing a woman he loved going through such an experience again. His loss with Ginny and Julia had been too sharp, too great. He had barely survived it. At times, he wasn't even sure he had. He was marked now. Changed. Different. His scars were too rigid.

Life was full of sorrow. That was the lesson he had learned over the last few years. If it wasn't leukemia, it might be something else. He was a doctor. He saw it every day. If he risked his heart again, there would inevitably be more heartache, in one form or another. And he would drown in his grief and regret until he was a shell of a man, worthless. He'd been blinded by his pain the last time. Who was to say the same thing wouldn't happen again? Tessa deserved someone who could put her needs before their own. He had failed to do that for Julia; he could not risk doing it to Tessa, as well.

At least, by walling off his heart, he could still do some good in this world. He could give children the tools to fight their disease. It was the only absolution he had left. And if he fell in love, and he lost a second time, he would never deserve forgiveness.

So he kept his distance from Tessa. She might know his secrets, the darkest parts of his soul, but he trusted her with his past. He did not, however, trust himself. She had gotten too far under his skin, and he had to take several steps back to clear her from his mind and heart.

When he noticed her in Zoe's room late at night, keeping watch over her niece, he did not stop in to talk to her like he wanted. He didn't enter, lean down to drop a kiss against her hair, breathe in the sweet scent of her skin. He didn't touch her, didn't look her way, didn't breathe her name.

He walked right by the room, keeping his gaze averted.

TESSA WALKED INTO Ana's office and stopped abruptly at the sight of Don Hess, from the hospital board, seated across the desk from her boss. She was even more surprised to see Noah was also there, leaning against a wall with his arms crossed. She and Noah hadn't spoken much over the last week. At least, not outside of discussions about Zoe and her treatments.

Something had changed between them, but her days were too filled with Zoe and work to analyze it too deeply. Or maybe she didn't want to think about it. She had let herself get too close to Noah. Her heart did involuntary things when he was around. Like now. Her heart rate sped up as she took in the sight of him, his expression aloof but emotion broiling beneath the surface.

"Dr. Hess, how nice to see you."

She plastered an expression of pleasure on her face even though she was feeling anything but pleasant at the moment. She was tired, having spent the night in a restless and uncomfortable sleep on the chair in Zoe's room, and she had limited energy to address whatever the reason she'd been summoned.

"A pleasure, as always, Tessa." Dr. Hess was beaming at her, though she couldn't imagine what she'd done to earn such a greeting.

"Have a seat," Ana said, gesturing toward

the only other available chair in the room. She glanced at Noah, but he avoided her gaze, seemingly content to stand.

"First of all, let me express my sadness over your niece's diagnosis," Dr. Hess said. "It is a hard weight for a family to bear, and I hear you two are very close."

His words flustered her, and her curiosity grew as to why Dr. Hess had asked for this meeting. When Ana had called her to her office, Tessa had assumed it was merely to check in on her progress with the gala.

Tessa had been keeping up with her work, but she hadn't been home much in the last week. She'd taken to showering and dressing at the hospital so she could be nearby.

She felt a moment's panic. She thought she'd stayed on top of things, but maybe Ana had called Dr. Hess in to tell her she wasn't juggling her work as well as she believed.

"Um, thank you," she said in response to Dr. Hess's words. "It's been a challenge, but we're up to it. Our family has really pulled together."

Dr. Hess nodded. "Ana says you're doing a wonderful job with your role here at the hospital, even with everything going on. Thank you for your conscientiousness. I imagine it's not easy."

Tessa blinked. Okay, so he wasn't here to reprimand her. So what was going on? She looked at Noah, her eyes questioning. He met them briefly, shrugged, and then glanced away again. She didn't say anything.

"Tessa," Ana finally spoke, "the reason Dr. Hess and I called you and Noah here today is because we have a proposal."

Tessa frowned.

"Given the situation your family recently find themselves in," Dr. Hess picked up the conversation, "we realized we might have a rare opportunity on our hands."

She cocked her head but said nothing.

"We all know that our goal is to bring more awareness to the hospital and our pediatric oncology department. At our last meeting, you had an idea in your proposal about doing a web series."

Tessa had suggested leveraging the current interest in reality TV and social media to launch a behind-the-scenes look at families struggling with leukemia. She'd proposed a weekly video upload to the hospital website so viewers could follow patients' progress through diagnosis, treatment and hopefully remission. She'd argued it would be a good way for others to feel invested in what the hospital was doing, but it was a project she hadn't planned to tackle until the following year, well after the gala ended.

"I hadn't fully developed the details," she said, still uncertain why Dr. Hess was bringing this up now.

He waved away her words. "Of course, we recognize that. However, given your niece's illness, we thought Zoe's might be a good case to follow."

Tessa's head whipped in Ana's direction. "You want to use Zoe?"

Ana gave a short nod. "And you and your family. Of course, as you already noted in your proposal, Dr. Brennan would be an important part of the story, as well."

Tessa shook her head, trying to process this suggestion. It seemed inappropriate somehow to use Zoe in this way. Maybe the whole idea had been flawed.

"You've already made it evident that you have a talent for these things, Tessa. You did exceptional work with the news crew when they came to feature the animal therapy program. With your personal investment in the project, we believe it will be even better than you intended."

"I see."

She looked at Noah. He remained silent. Why wasn't he speaking up? He hated this sort of thing. Surely he wouldn't agree to it. At least not now.

"I'm not sure now is the best time. My focus is on the gala, getting everything in order. And Zoe's diagnosis is still so new to her."

"The gala isn't for another two months, and Ana tells me you've already made great strides in getting things in place for the event. Besides, this series could be part of the gala."

Tessa was uncertain. On the one hand, Dr. Hess made a good point. But from a personal perspective, she wasn't sure she was ready to take this on, especially when it was her own niece who would be involved.

"Noah, what do you think?" She looked at him, convinced that he would argue against the idea. He hated the spotlight, and she'd expected a battle about the web series from the first.

He pushed himself off the wall and unfolded his arms. "I think it's a great idea."

She blinked. He...what?

"But...Noah..." She floundered.

"Tessa's original proposal was right. Giving others a glimpse into what we do would raise their awareness and understanding of pediatric cancer, and hopefully prompt them to make donations to research and to the hospital. Zoe's a great kid, and Tessa will do a wonderful job leading her through the process."

"But y-you'd be involved, too," Tessa reminded him.

"Of course. I will do whatever I can to support the project."

Her eyebrows furrowed in confusion. What was going on? This wasn't at all the Noah she knew.

"Well, I suppose I'd have to ask my family if they'd be on board." Tessa wanted to make certain Zoe understood what it all meant.

"Understandable," Dr. Hess said. "Provided they're amenable, we'll have Legal go over all the necessary paperwork. Ana has already reached out to a local production team about filming."

Tessa was dazed. How much had she missed during her late nights at Zoe's bedside?

"Thanks for being a team player on this,

Tessa. You, too, Dr. Brennan," Dr. Hess added as an afterthought.

"I am always at the service of the hospital."

The sarcasm in his tone was lost on Dr. Hess, but it drew Tessa's attention. She arched an eyebrow in question, but he didn't acknowledge it. She looked toward Ana, but her boss was typing away on her keyboard, presumably putting things in motion.

"Great!" Dr. Hess enthused. "This is going to be a wonderful opportunity to raise more money for the kids."

Tessa could only manage to nod and smile. Noah slipped out of the room without saying anything.

CHAPTER TWELVE

NOAH HAD JUST finished reviewing a patient's chart with the nursing staff when Tessa found him. He knew he shouldn't have been happy to see her. There was no good reason for the way his heart increased speed as she approached. He'd been doing his best to remain nonchalant in her presence, but his heart couldn't lie. The more he tried to convince himself getting close to Tessa had been a bad idea, the more he longed to be near her.

"Are you seriously okay with this?" She began without preamble.

If he feigned ignorance she'd hang around longer.

"With what?" He grabbed a chart at random and opened it, pretending to review its contents.

"Come on, Noah. With this whole reality web series thing?"

He glanced at her and immediately realized that was a mistake. Her eyes were large and questioning, the brown in them golden and warm despite the dark smudges beneath her eyes that spoke of the long days and nights she'd been spending at the hospital. He experienced a tug of concern.

"You're not taking very good care of yourself," he observed, bypassing her question.

She sagged slightly. "There was a time you would have just told me that I look terrible." She made an attempt to smile, but it was weak, and her words stung.

"Am I really that awful?"

Her expression softened, and the sight of it melted his heart. "No. But you're like those chocolates with a hard outer layer and a chewy center."

"So I'm chewy?" he teased her, keeping his expression stoic.

"What? No. That's not..." She drew a breath. "Can we please get back on track here?"

He pretended to refocus on the chart, though he'd far rather keep staring into her eyes.

"We need more donations to help fund the research that saves these kids' lives. The web series will help with that," he said.

"I know that," she returned, "but I didn't expect you to get on board with it so quickly."

He shrugged. "What can I say? You've convinced me of the merits of these initiatives."

She fell silent, and he peered at her from the corner of his eyes. She was nibbling at her thumbnail, deep in thought. He closed the file and put it away. He wanted, more than anything in that moment, to pull her into his arms and reassure her. But then, what right did he have to do that? He'd done the same for Julia, countless times, and in the end, he'd only made a liar of himself.

He couldn't tell her the truth. He dreaded the idea of the web series. A film crew would be, at best, a distraction and, at worst, an impediment to doing his job. But his treacherous heart had agreed for one reason.

Because doing the series would bring him nearer to Tessa. He knew he should keep his distance. After how he'd so thoroughly failed his wife, how could he possibly think he wouldn't do the same thing should he fall in love again? He was damaged now, scarred in a way that made him blind to the needs of others. Tessa had called him out on it already, about the way he spoke to his patients and their parents.

But, if he was being entirely honest, the web series really was a great idea. And Tessa would be brilliant at it. Who was he to stand in the way of spotlighting the work the hospital and the kids did every day?

"Tessa."

When he said her name, she looked at him. He had never been so conflicted in his life. He wanted nothing more than to touch her. He was a fool. Letting Tessa in had been a mistake, one that could cost him too much in the long run. But that didn't mean they couldn't work together, did it? Especially if it benefited his patients and the hospital.

"You'll do fine," he said. "And if, at any point, I feel like this project is jeopardizing Zoe's treatment, I will put an end to it immediately. Agreed?"

His words seemed to ease some of her doubts. Her shoulders relaxed. "Thank you. I appreciate that."

He nodded. They stood there for another minute, and he wondered if she was as reluctant to part ways as he was.

"I guess I better go present this idea to Paige and Weston."

"Do you think they'll agree?" Somehow, he had a feeling convincing her family wasn't going to be a problem.

"They'll probably be okay with it."

Still, she lingered, making it more and more difficult for him not to reach out and touch her, to offer some sort of reassurance.

"Okay, well. I'll talk to you later."

"Later," he agreed.

She finally turned and walked away, and he watched her go, his heart filled with both longing and disappointment.

CONVINCING PAIGE TO do the web series was a greater challenge than Tessa had expected.

"You mean it would be posted right on the hospital's website? So everyone can get a glimpse into our lives?"

Paige had her arms crossed over her chest as she sat across from Tessa in the hospital commons. Tessa held a cup of tepid tea in her hands while Paige's fingers nervously fiddled with the lid of her disposable coffee cup.

"Think of it more as giving people a chance to see the struggles of a family battling cancer. The hospital is hoping the series will raise awareness for research funding and trials to help other kids like Zoe."

Paige took a sip of her coffee, made a face and put it back down.

"Can't you do something about this?"

Tessa frowned in confusion. "About what?"

Paige held up her cup. "This coffee. It's terrible."

Tessa didn't respond. Paige didn't cope well with things outside of her control—whether it was poor coffee or her child's cancer diagnosis. She continued to play with the lid of her cup until Tessa reached out and took it from her, putting it aside to wrap her hands around her sister's.

"Paige. Are you okay?"

Paige's stare might have withered someone who wasn't accustomed to her sister's moods. "My child has cancer, and I totally missed the signs. How do you think I'm doing?"

"Oh." Tessa let a minute or two tick by, waiting for Paige to say more. Her sister fidgeted, which was unusual for her, but finally started speaking.

"I know I'm not the best mother," she admitted in a low whisper, as if ashamed to speak the words out loud. "But I never… I wouldn't… If I'd suspected something was wrong…"

Paige's eyes filled with tears as she looked at Tessa. "I would have demanded tests immediately if I'd had any idea."

"I know. Just because you didn't understand the signs doesn't make you a bad mother, Paige."

Her sister pulled her hands away to wipe at her eyes but didn't meet Tessa's gaze. "You and Zoe have such a special bond. She reminds me a lot of you, when you were a kid."

"Really?" Paige was several years older, and sometimes, Tessa forgot that her sister had the advantage of watching her grow up.

"Definitely. You were always playing with those baby dolls of yours," Paige said. "You never went anywhere without them. You would hand them to me and Harper and tell us we had to feed them or rock them or whatever." Paige's lip twitched with amusement. "You'd get so worked up if you found them lying on the bedroom floor or forgotten somewhere. One time, I left a doll in the car, and when you got home from school and found it, you were so mad that you wrote me a ticket in crayon for being a bad mommy."

Tessa didn't speak, and Paige's eyes filled with tears once more. "I was never cut out for this. You were always so much better at this stuff than I could ever be."

Tessa flinched but ignored the sting Paige's words caused. Her sister needed her right now, and it wasn't Paige's fault that motherhood was such a sensitive subject for Tessa. Fortunately, her sister didn't notice her momentary reaction.

"Zoe's like you," Paige went on. "She'll try to hand me one of her dolls, and she'll say... she'll say, 'Take good care of her, Mama...'" Paige broke off, the tears overflowing her eyes. She looked at Tessa with something akin to desperation in her gaze. "It's like those dolls. I just didn't pay enough attention." She lowered her forehead into her hands so that Tessa couldn't see her face, though Tessa still heard her say, "Why didn't I pay more attention?"

Tessa was grateful the commons cafeteria was practically empty this time of day. She didn't mind other people's stares, but she wanted to spare her sister an audience while she grappled with her fear and grief. She knew Paige didn't have many chances to be vulnerable. She put on her typical brave

and blustering front when she was with Zoe
and even Weston. In a way, Tessa was honored that her sister had broken down in front
of her. It was a rare thing for Paige.

She moved around the table to lay her cheek
against Paige's back, holding her as she cried.
They remained in that position for some time
until Tessa felt the sobs ebb and then stop.
Only then did she straighten and take her seat
again.

Paige drew a deep, haggard breath. "I realize I haven't been the nicest sister to you over
the last couple of years. I just couldn't understand your choices. But that was unfair of me.
I guess you never really know what another
person is going through, do you?"

It would have been the perfect moment
to open up, to share with Paige everything
Tessa had struggled with since her diagnosis.
But she didn't say anything. She still wasn't
ready to explain her actions to her older sister. Not even now, when Paige was the most
open and vulnerable she'd ever seen her.

"I'm sorry that I was so hard on you."

"It's okay." After all, no one was harder
on Tessa than she was on herself. She knew
leaving her job had been a foolish move, but

she'd let her heartbreak lead her. She didn't regret not marrying Burke, now that he was happy. But she mourned the loss of her hopes and dreams, and she blamed herself for not being able to stand up against the grief.

"It's not okay," Paige responded, "but knowing you, I'm not surprised you'd say that."

They sat there in sisterly silence for a few more minutes before Paige spoke again.

"This web series... It will be good for you? For your job?"

"It will," Tessa admitted, "but that's not why you should do it. If you choose to go through with it, it should be because it will benefit other families like yours, other children like Zoe."

Paige considered this. "That's good, then. It would be a way to turn all of this into something positive."

Tessa nodded. "Exactly."

"And if it helps you, too, all the better. But it's not just about me or Weston. It's also about Zoe. We should talk to her and see what she thinks."

"You're absolutely right. Do you want to talk to her about it or should I?"

"Why don't we do it together?"

ZOE WAS ENTIRELY on board with the web series. Her first question was, "Will it be on YouTube?"

Tessa had overlooked the fact that kids Zoe's age loved streaming videos. Apparently, some other patients on the floor had showed Zoe a few online videos of children in similar situations, and she was excited at the idea of being one of them.

Tessa wanted to make sure her niece fully understood what she was committing to, however, so she forced herself to bring up an unpleasant topic. She and Paige sat on opposite sides of the hospital bed. Weston was taking a much-needed break and had headed home to rest and shower.

"I'm glad you're excited about this, Zoe, but I just wanted to make sure you're okay with it. Do you remember what we talked about, not long after you were admitted to the hospital, about the chemotherapy and your hair?"

Zoe frowned, remembering. "Yeah, that my hair will probably fall out, and I'll be bald. Like Grandpa Everett."

Grandpa Everett was Weston's father, who was bald as an egg.

"Yes. When we film these videos, your

hair will eventually start coming out, so you'll be bald in a lot of the videos."

This set Zoe back for a minute. She stared down at the bedspread and considered.

"But that happens to everyone when they get the cancer medicine, right?"

"A lot of the time," Tessa agreed.

Zoe came to a decision with relative ease. "Then it's okay. Dad said that's part of my superpower. It's how people will recognize that I'm a superhero."

Tessa looked at her sister and saw Paige was smiling with tears in her eyes. "Your dad's pretty smart," she remarked.

"I know," Zoe promptly replied. "He says that's how I got to be so smart, too."

Paige laughed. "Fair enough."

"So you're sure you're okay with this, Zoe?" Tessa pressed. She wanted her niece to be positive about the idea but not to feel pressured.

Zoe nodded. "We're gonna be famous!"

"I don't know about that, but we'll be doing something that might help other kids in the future."

A film crew showed up at the hospital the next day. Tessa was in charge of giving them a tour of the hospital, introducing the staff and her family, and coordinating with the producer so they could begin filming immediately.

They arranged for interviews with Paige, Weston and Zoe, and then with Noah, to introduce him as Zoe's doctor. When she told him about the interview, he showed the first hint of disapproval about the idea.

"What about my patients? I can't neglect my obligations to them."

"You won't be," Tessa pointed out. "Ana has already instructed the other doctors take some of your workload so you can devote the appropriate amount of attention to this project."

Noah frowned. "Yes, but…"

"I thought you were all gung ho on this."

"I'm not sure I'd say gung ho." He cleared his throat. "Will you be there? For this interview, that is?" The words were patently nonchalant. If she didn't know better, she'd almost think Noah was hoping she'd be there. That was a ridiculous thought, however. He'd been cool and distant over the last few days. He obviously regretted the way he'd opened up to her. Given the secret she'd held so tightly over the last two years, she couldn't blame him.

"I'll be there," she said. "It's my job. Ana wants me present for as many of the interviews as possible."

"Ah." He paused. "Well, I suppose I don't have much choice."

It wasn't a very enthusiastic response, but it would have to be enough.

CHAPTER THIRTEEN

DESPITE HIS CYNICISM, Noah was impressed with the film crew. They stayed out of everyone's way as much as possible, and even on the rare occurrence where they were asked to move some equipment or had to leave a room, they did so with polite speed.

The producer and crew were certainly respectful of his time and obligations. If he was called away to an emergency or because another doctor needed his opinion, they patiently waited until he was able to return.

It was, much more than he had expected it to be, a positive experience. But it was made all the more so by Tessa's presence. At least until he noticed how friendly one of the crew members was becoming with her.

He first noticed it in the middle of his second interview on camera. He was asked to explain leukemia in layman's terms. He'd begun by saying, "White blood cells are the good guys, the body's knights in shining armor. They fight off infection and disease. But with ALL, the white blood cells don't mature. They're like untrained soldiers in the body's system who haven't been trained to fight. So more and more of them start crowding out the mature white blood cells, the knights. When this happens, the body doesn't have enough of the good guys to battle infections, so eventually, something as simple as a cold can cause...death." He faltered on the last word, thinking of Ginny. Something simple. That was how she'd died. It wasn't the cancer that had killed her, in the end. It was a minor infection that her body had not been equipped to handle.

He blinked and realized he'd been asked another question. But when he tried to focus, he noticed Tyler, the lighting technician, leaning in close to Tessa, whispering something in her ear. She laughed, her nose crinkling in that adorable way it did when she was amused by something, and he felt the sting of jealousy. He wasn't good at making people laugh. He never had been, and after Ginny's death, he never would be. He wasn't witty or clever. He couldn't tell jokes to save his life—he was too dry and droll. And it had never bothered him. Not once.

Until that moment. What in the world had this guy said to make her smile like that? She whispered something back, and Tyler laughed quietly in return, his body vibrating with humor. Noah scowled in their direction.

"Dr. Brennan?"

His attention snapped back to the producer.

"I'm sorry?"

"I asked if you could talk about the warning signs of ALL and then discuss what symptoms Zoe had when she came to the hospital."

"Oh. Right. Of course." He did his best to speak coherently, listing the symptoms that were easily misdiagnosed due to their subtlety. He then tried to expound more on what blood tests could reveal. But he talked on autopilot, his attention fixed on Tessa as she and Tyler continued to speak some distance away.

Whatever the other man was saying, Tessa had to lean in to hear. Her face was frustratingly close to his. What were they talking about? Was it something to do with the series? Then why not have Noah or her sister present?

A little voice reminded him that it was

none of his business what Tessa spoke about, or to whom. His goal had been to keep a wall between them, wasn't it? Not that agreeing to do this series would help with that. He should be making an effort to see less of Tessa, not more. And he certainly shouldn't be irritated that some other guy was talking to her. It wasn't as if she was dating him.

His heart tripped over itself at the thought. What would it be like to date Tessa Worth? He'd never dated much before marrying Julia. He'd had a couple of high school girlfriends, but he'd met Julia in college, and there'd been no one else after that. The reminder of Julia brought a familiar pang of regret. He still missed her, but those emotions—the love and affection he'd felt for her—had been tempered over time by the grief they'd shared. Their relationship at the end had been a mire of despair. He'd lost Julia long before she took her own life. He'd spent too many long hours and late nights at the hospital, and when he was home, his mind was on Ginny.

He had failed his wife over and over, and the memories of his love for her were far in the past. But still, they had shared a child, and he had needed her after that loss. And she'd needed him. He wished she'd reached out to him. He would have moved heaven and earth to help her deal with her grief and avoid the decision she'd made to take her own life.

"Why don't we take a break?"

It took him several seconds to refocus his attention on the cameraman and producer before him. He realized he'd trailed off some minutes before. He wondered how long they'd been trying to get his attention before making this announcement.

"Oh. I'm sorry—"

"It's fine, Doc. Don't worry about it. You've got a lot going on. We get that." The producer for this project, Nia, was a short young woman, one half of her head shaved while the other fell in a long, dark curtain down the side of her face. She was intelligent and respectful. He liked her.

"It's okay. We've got some good footage here. We can follow up with you later." She turned to her crew. "Let's take lunch, guys."

The group relaxed, putting down their equipment and walking away. His eyes wandered involuntarily back to Tessa and Tyler. They were still in conversation, and he felt that annoying sting of jealousy again. He chafed at his own reaction. He didn't want a relationship with anyone. It was too great a risk and too much of a distraction. So why did he want to go over there right now and insert himself between Tessa and this guy?

He decided to check in on Zoe. She was doing well with this initial phase of treatment, but he also wanted to ensure the film crew wasn't taxing her. She was in her room, a tray of lunch in front of her while Weston sat beside her, encouraging her to eat.

"Hey," Noah greeted as he entered the room.

Weston looked happy to see him. "Hi, Dr. Brennan."

"Weston, you can call me Noah. I've told you, I prefer it."

The man was unfailingly polite. Noah couldn't always say the same for his wife, but Paige was obviously trying. Her interactions with him had improved dramatically over the last couple of days.

"Paige is in the commons, getting something to eat," Weston said.

Noah frowned. "We can always have food brought to the room for you. You don't have to go all the way to the cafeteria."

Weston shrugged. "I think she wanted a break."

Noah understood. Sometimes, parents just needed to take a step away, to breathe, to not have to keep a mask on in front of the patient. It took a toll, being strong for a child. Noah knew. He'd lived it.

"Why don't you go join her?" he suggested. "Zoe and I can hang out here for a bit. Right, Zoe?"

The little girl brightened at this. "Just you and me?"

"Sure. If you don't mind my company."

She beamed, her pleasure radiating past her pale skin and bruised arms. "Yes, please."

"Are you sure, sweetheart?" Weston asked. "Mom and I will just be downstairs. We'll be back soon."

"I'm okay, Daddy," she assured him. "Dr. Noah's here."

Her confidence re-centered him. It was so easy for children to maintain hope. At what point had he lost that? Although, the death of his hope had probably been a gradual thing, defeated by each blow of loss and failure he'd endured.

Weston left the room, and Noah took his seat by Zoe's bedside. He studied the uneaten items on her lunch tray.

"I take it we are not a fan of pudding?" He pointed to the untouched dish.

She wrinkled her nose. It wasn't uncommon for leukemia patients to experience a diminished appetite as the results of the chemo, the various medications and even their environment. The hospital made every effort, especially on the children's floors, to create a warm and hospitable atmosphere. Even so, it was unfamiliar terrain. The change in routine sometimes affected their eating habits just as much as their treatments. Still, it was important for them to eat.

"How about we share these pretzels?" he suggested, reaching for the bowl.

He'd found that kids were more responsive to the idea of a shared meal. He grabbed a pretzel and waited until Zoe picked one up, too. She nibbled at it, watching him. He crunched into his, and she imitated him, taking a bigger bite. His eyes wandered briefly to the door, wondering if Tessa was still with Tyler. Maybe he'd invited her to lunch. The thought turned the pretzel tasteless in his mouth.

Zoe struggled through the pretzel and then placed her hand back in her lap.

"How are you feeling?" he questioned.

She shrugged and stared at the remains of her lunch. Noah popped the other half of the pretzel into his mouth and reached for a second. Zoe mimicked his movements but didn't take a bite. Noah turned the pretzel in his fingers, suddenly feeling awkward. He dealt with children on a daily basis, but Zoe was different. She was Tessa's niece, and he was acutely aware of that connection.

"Are you excited about being on the hospital website?" he asked.

This question perked her up. She nodded and even took a small bite of her pretzel.

"I heard you did a really good job on your first interview."

She straightened even more, her smile widening. He popped the whole pretzel in his mouth, just as Zoe asked, "Are you going to marry Aunt Tessa?"

The surprise of her question caused him to start and the pretzel lodged in his throat. He sputtered for several seconds, working to dislodge the obstruction and regain his composure. He had to grab one of the paper cups from the counter and fill it with water from the tap, gulping desperately until he was finally able to get the pretzel down.

When he turned around, Zoe was staring at him, her eyes wide and innocent.

"Your face is red," she observed.

"It's because of the pretzel," he rasped out, unwilling to consider that her question about Tessa had caused the color.

"Well? Are you?"

His eyes flicked to the door, hoping no one was listening in to their conversation. He had a limited view of the hall, but it was empty. He returned to his seat by the bed.

"Your aunt and I are just colleagues."

Zoe's face twisted into an expression of confusion. "Collies?"

"Colleagues. Coworkers. We work together," he scrambled to explain. "That's all."

"But you came to dinner at Aunt Harper's house," she pointed out.

"Yes. Well, that was… We were… I…" He fumbled for an explanation that Zoe would understand. He certainly couldn't tell her about his past, or the fact that he wasn't willing to risk his heart again. "We're just… friends," he offered.

Zoe narrowed her eyes, clearly not buying this excuse.

"Why are you so sad all the time?"

He had forgotten how blunt children could

be. It had been too long since he'd held a conversation with a child that didn't involve reassurances about treatments and protocols.

"What makes you think I'm sad?" he asked.

Zoe was quiet for a moment, considering the question. "You don't smile," she finally answered. "And your eyes, they're like Rufus's."

The observation startled him. "Like Rufus's?"

"Yeah. Tessa took me to the animal place, when she worked there, and Rufus had just come to stay. When she showed him to me, his tail wagged, but his eyes were really sad. Aunt Tessa said he'd had a hard life and needed someone to love him."

Noah sat there, stunned by the little girl's keen observation. He touched the watch on his wrist, thinking of Ginny and how much she had known that he hadn't given her credit for. She'd known she was dying. He remembered her hand in his, tiny and pale in the larger span of his palm. She'd been so weak, but it seemed to comfort her when he held her hand like that. She'd looked at him out of eyes that were a faded gray, so similar to his own but with the light slowly ebbing from them.

"Smile for me, Daddy," she'd whispered.

It had taken the last of his diminished emotional strength to offer her a weak and watery grin. And it had taken every ounce of hers to reach up and touch her finger to the tears that had been rolling down his face, smile notwithstanding.

She'd slipped into a coma soon after that, and within twenty-four hours, she'd been gone. That was his last moment with his little girl: her request for his smile. He remembered thinking at the funeral that she had taken it with her when she left. He hadn't believed he'd ever find it again.

But then Tessa had come along with her gentle strength and quiet understanding. And for the first time since Ginny had slipped away, he'd found himself smiling again. At least for a little while.

"Are you in love with Aunt Tessa?"

Zoe's question drew him from his memories. Her voice was tired.

"You should rest, Zoe," he murmured, reaching out to smooth a hand over her hair. Several strands came free in his fingers.

Her eyelids were heavy, but she obviously

wasn't done yet. "She loves you," she said, the words weighted with growing exhaustion. Despite how softly she spoke them, for Noah, they were as loud as a shout.

"How do you know?" he asked, embarrassed to be asking such a question of a six-year-old but desperate to hear the answer.

"Because Aunt Tessa doesn't smile that much anymore, either. But she does when she's with you."

Noah reached out and grasped Zoe's hand in his own. He looked at their joined fingers.

He would give anything to hold Ginny's hand once more. But his little girl was gone. Maybe it was time to learn to smile again. Because wherever she was right now, surely she would see it. Surely she would know that his love for her would never fade.

"Rest, Zoe. Everything will be all right."

Zoe's lips twitched into a smile as her breathing deepened. Noah held her hand for a very long time, anchoring himself to a life he hadn't felt he deserved as he finally let go of the daughter he'd lost.

CHAPTER FOURTEEN

THE HOUSE SMELLED of paint and bleach—the scent of something new, the world scrubbed clean.

"Let's open some windows and air this place out," Tessa said.

Her dad frowned. "What's wrong with it? I think it smells fine."

"That's because you've gotten used to the smell of the hospital, so antiseptic smells normal to you. But when Zoe gets here, it should smell like a home."

"Tessa's right," Harper said as she waved a rattle in front of Grace. "Let's light a candle or something. Make it smell inviting."

"I'll ask your mother," Allan said and wandered off in search of his wife.

Harper and Tessa shared a smile. It all felt blessedly normal. Zoe was finally coming home. After almost six weeks of in-hospital treatment, Noah had announced the leukemia was in remission, and Zoe could now switch to a maintenance schedule.

It would still mean a lot of time at the hospital, but at least she could resume some semblance of a regular life. That included moving into the new house Paige and Weston had purchased. Since the next couple of years would mean frequent hospital visits, they'd rearranged their lives to make things as easy as possible for Zoe. Paige would work from home as much as she could and commute to DC when necessary. Weston would have a longer commute each day, but his boss had agreed to a shortened workweek so he could also work from home part of the time. And this way, they'd be closer to the rest of the family.

Tessa was glad to see Paige and Weston adjusting their lives, placing Zoe at the center. Her niece would thrive as a result, and her journey to health would be a much more positive experience.

"Is Noah coming?" Harper asked, her tone tellingly casual as she pretended to focus on Grace.

"I think so," Tessa replied, her voice equally nonchalant. "Paige invited him."

Her emotions were conflicted on the subject of Noah. Something had changed in him over the last several weeks. He seemed…at peace. He smiled more. He asked her opinion. The brittle edges that had often surrounded him had softened. When he said her name, there was a warmth in it that left her tingling.

And frightened her. As long as Noah had been emotionally wounded, had kept a wall in place, she'd been able to guard her heart. But now, it was almost as if he was deliberately wooing her. His little kindnesses were adding up, especially after the weeks she'd spent at Zoe's bedside.

She'd run herself ragged between juggling the duties of her job, planning for the fall gala, and making sure Paige and Weston had all the support they needed. It seemed Noah had noticed her exhaustion because he'd gone out of his way to offer silent support. She'd come in to her office on several occasions to find a mug of hot tea waiting— her favorite, lemon mint from the Lighthouse Café.

The first time it had happened, she'd been baffled until she noticed the name the barista had scribbled on the cup for the order. She'd been touched by his thoughtfulness. And several times since she'd come in to find a cup of tea. She was never quite sure how he managed to know exactly when to have it there for her. She'd thanked him after each incident, but when she asked how he'd managed it, he just grinned and raised a finger to his lips to convey he wasn't sharing his secret.

There were other things, too. If he got lunch for himself, he always doubled the order and gave her half, a welcome gesture on several occasions after she realized that she'd neglected to grab a bite to eat for herself.

He seemed to have mentally catalogued all her favorite things. He knew she didn't like pickles on a sub. He always ordered her wheat bread, not white. He made sure there was an extra side of dressing for salad. How had he noticed these little quirks of hers? How long had he been paying that much attention? It wasn't anything important, but somehow, it moved her to know that he took the time to address these little details for her.

Twice she had fallen asleep in Zoe's room and woken to find herself covered with a spare blanket from the hospital's linen stores.

She felt fairly certain it had been Noah who had placed it over her both times.

He checked in on her in her office occasionally, too. Once, he had brought her chocolate from the vending machine and perched on the edge of her desk, asking where she was at in her planning for the gala, as they finished the treat together.

These tiny things had begun to add up, and she found herself looking for them now, her heart in a grip of anticipation whenever Noah was nearby. Whatever demons he'd been wrestling, they seemed to have left him, and in their place, Noah had become someone new. He was the same brilliant doctor, the same caring physician, and a thoughtful friend, but he was something else, too. She was afraid she was falling in love with him, and that would never, ever do. Not after Burke, and certainly not after her experiences of the last couple of years.

She was broken inside, and she had yet to find a way to overcome her body's betrayal. She knew all the thin condolences Noah would say if she shared her secret— that she could adopt, that there were other ways to feel fulfilled without being a biological mother…but that wasn't good enough for her. Not now and maybe not ever. Until she could find her way to forgive her body and love herself, how could she possibly think about loving someone else?

So she swallowed back her feelings and told herself, for the hundredth time, that Noah's gestures meant nothing. He was only being a considerate coworker. She shouldn't assume he meant anything more, and therefore, she had nothing to worry about.

But despite this, she couldn't stop the way her stomach flip-flopped when he approached, or the leap of her heart in her chest when he said her name. She could not turn off her growing feelings for Noah. And that scared her, perhaps as much as finding out Zoe had cancer.

The thought of her niece brought her around again. "Do you think Zoe will like the house?"

Harper looked up from placing a pacifier into Grace's mouth. "Definitely," Harper replied. "For one thing, she'll be living much closer to all of us but especially you. The cottage is only a short walk from here. She'll love being so close to everyone." Harper smiled a little wistfully. "It will be great, won't it? Molly will finally have Zoe close by, and Grace will have her cousin near her as she grows up."

Tessa swallowed and looked away. It was true that it would be wonderful for the cousins to be so close to each other. She only wished one day she'd have a daughter of her own to be part of their group.

"Harper," their dad called from the kitchen area, "your mother said you unpacked the box with the candles. Where did you put them?"

"Oh, she's right. I totally forgot." She bounced Grace in her arms as she spoke. "That's what happens, baby, when you keep Mommy up for three hours every night. I begin to forget things."

She moved toward Tessa and passed Grace into her arms without asking. "Let me find those candles, and we'll have this place smelling like home in no time."

Tessa accepted Grace without protest, the feel of her niece heavy and solid in her arms. She cradled her close and breathed in the scent of baby powder. Grace stared up at her with owlish eyes, blinking sleepily.

"Hello, little one." She took a few steps, rocking Grace ever so gently in her arms. She ran a finger down the baby's cheek, marveling at the softness of her skin. "You are a gift, you know that?" she whispered, battling the tears that threatened. Grace yawned but managed to raise a tiny fist in the air, a gesture of agreement. "Don't let anyone ever take you for granted." She sighed, feeling an empty ache that would never be filled. "I know I never would."

THE PARTY WAS SMALL, but Noah was still impressed. Paige and Weston's new house wasn't fully furnished just yet, but there were plenty of folding chairs and tables for guests to congregate at, and the place was welcoming with the smell of apple pie and sugar cookies. Harper had told him the scent was more from the candles she'd lit than any baking that had been done.

Still, as he'd found was typical with Tessa's family, there was plenty of food. Connor had done the cooking, but he'd admitted he'd had help from a friend—Erin Daniels, who was an impressive pastry chef in her own right. She'd provided fruit tartlets and a chocolate cake.

Noah wanted to try a little bit of everything, but for now, he also wanted to keep an eye on his patient. It seemed he wasn't very needed, however. Zoe was doing great. She was the star of the show, both literally and figuratively. The web series had been a tremendous success, garnering attention and accolades from multiple high-profile associations. There was even talk of several awards in the future.

The film crew had been invited to this party, not only to document Zoe's discharge but also to celebrate with the family.

Noah waved to Tyler, the lighting technician. He no longer harbored any jealousy toward the man. It turned out Tyler was already in a committed relationship and had recently gotten engaged to his girlfriend. He and Tessa had simply found common ground over a shared passion for bulldogs. In fact, the members of the film crew had become friends with many of the staff and families on the pediatric oncology floor. Over the last several weeks, the crew had become a part of the team, rooting for Zoe and the other kids as much as their families did.

The crew were gathered around Zoe now, asking her questions and recording her answers. Her bald head was covered by a knit cap that Vivienne had made for her. Her grandmother had used her time at the hospital to refresh her knitting skills. Noah had his own scarf to show for her efforts.

"How does it feel to be home?" Nia asked Zoe.

The little girl looked around. This house wasn't her home, really. Not yet. Noah hoped it would start to seem that way very soon for her, though. He knew that Tessa and the others had done as much as they could to make her bedroom feel like her old room. They'd brought her toys and furniture, her bedspread and photographs, and replicated Zoe's old room as much as possible. He had faith that Zoe would embrace living in Findlay Roads with all the resilience he knew children possessed. If cancer couldn't beat her, then moving to a new town would be no big deal at all. Especially with all her family nearby to support her.

Noah felt a nudge of jealousy, and he nearly laughed aloud. He was jealous of a six-year-old patient. But even while he knew it was ridiculous, a part of him recognized that Zoe had something precious that he did not—family to surround her, to support her, to love her. He had so isolated himself in recent years that he had none of those things.

Involuntarily, his gaze moved to Tessa.

She stood across the room with Grace in her arms, talking to Ana, who had also been invited to the homecoming. Tessa had yet to greet him, and it was taking all his willpower not to immediately move toward her and take her in his arms. Over the last few weeks, his feelings for her had deepened.

Ever since his talk with Zoe, he'd experienced a fragile sort of peace. The feeling was entirely new to him, and he sometimes feared it wouldn't last. But so far, it had held steady. It was as if he had been able to truly say goodbye to his daughter, without grief and guilt preventing him from letting her go. He was still working through Julia's death, though, weighing out how much of it was his responsibility. He'd begun to see a grief counselor again to find his way past the loss. It had helped.

But it wasn't the only thing that had motivated him to move forward. Tessa had played a large part, as well. Her friendship had been the catalyst, the thing that he treasured enough to want to find a way out of the dark. She had been his beacon, the light guiding him back, whether she knew it or not. She challenged him but supported him at the same time. She was sweet and kind, but he recognized a steady strength in her. She had held Paige and Weston up, had been the rock they leaned on throughout the weeks of Zoe's treatment. It was her determination that had gotten Zoe tested for leukemia in the first place.

He loved her for that. And for so many other things. The way she stopped to talk to patients, to allay their fears and brighten their day. No matter what task had brought her to the fourth floor, she was never too busy to encourage the children or their parents, to offer a greeting to the staff. She was the kindest, sweetest person he had ever known. And somewhere along the way, between darkness and light, he had fallen in love with her.

He wasn't sure if she felt the same about him. Or whether he deserved it even if she did. But he was just hopeful enough these days that he was willing to try to be worthy of her. It was why he had started a personal campaign to woo her after Zoe had told him Tessa loved him. Because even though he knew he had a long road of healing ahead of him, he wanted to try to be the man she needed, someone she could turn to.

"She's a wonder, isn't she?"

Noah jerked out of his reverie, belatedly realizing that Allan had come to stand beside him. He cleared his throat, feeling awkward for staring at Allan's youngest daughter.

"Y-you mean Tessa?" Noah fumbled, uncertain how to respond. He liked Allan, and he thought Allan liked him. But mutual respect didn't necessarily condone watching a man stare openly at your daughter.

Allan nodded in response to Noah's question. "Tessa is the youngest of my daughters, but sometimes, I think she's wiser than either of her sisters."

Noah frowned, thrown by this observation. "She's certainly a remarkable young woman," he offered with some hesitation. Not because he doubted his own words—Tessa was definitely something special, in his opinion. But he wasn't entirely sure where this conversation was headed.

"Don't get me wrong," Allan continued. "All of my girls are special, in their own way. Paige is brilliant. She's driven and sharp. Sometimes, too much so. She's always been so focused on climbing the proverbial ladder, and I can't fault her. For most of my life, I was the same way. And maybe I'm the one who put that pressure on her, to succeed at all costs. It's only been recently, spending more time in this town, among these people, that I realize the rat race isn't all it's cracked up to be." He took a sip of the punch he held. "I think Harper is the one who first started helping me to see that. She chose to restart her life here several year ago, and while I was baffled by her decision at first, I see how happy it's made her. She's a wife and a mother, and she loves working with Connor at Callahan's. It's partly what inspired me to build up the Delphine in town, not only to take advantage of the tourist boom here but to see what it was about this place that rooted two of my daughters here." He sighed. "But Tessa. She's the one I worry about."

Noah frowned. "Why do you worry about her?"

Allan didn't respond at first. Noah followed his gaze to where Tessa stood, still in conversation with Ana. He watched as she rocked Grace back and forth with ease, keeping up a steady dialogue with her boss at the same time. She was a natural caregiver. He wondered what it would be like when Tessa had children of her own.

"There's something..." Allan began, drawing Noah's focus back to him. "I don't know.

Perhaps because she's my youngest. I worry about her more than the others. She's always been tenderhearted, the peacemaker in our family. And believe me, that is no easy job with sisters like the ones she has."

Noah had to chuckle softly in agreement. "I can believe that."

"Sometimes I think Tessa gets so caught up in taking care of other people that she forgets to take care of herself."

This, too, was something Noah had witnessed. It was partly why he'd begun doing a few little things for her, such as bringing her tea and ordering lunch. If Tessa thought someone else was in want, she'd forgo her own needs to make sure the other person was taken care of. It was just who she was. And Noah had to admit that he loved it about her, even while he worried about it.

"Well." Allan took another swig of punch. "I think you're much the same. You don't take care of yourself as well as you should, perhaps."

Noah wasn't going to argue on that score. He just said, "It goes with the territory, being a doctor. And particularly one that deals with children. I want to be available as much as possible to them."

"A noble outlook," Allan replied. "As long as you don't sacrifice your own needs and wants to do it." He paused. "You and my daughter have grown pretty close since she started working at the hospital."

This pointed remark flustered Noah. He cleared his throat awkwardly. "Um, I guess you could say that."

Allan slid him a knowing glance. "Did she tell you she left her fiancé at the altar a little over two years ago?"

Noah didn't rise to the bait. He sensed Allan was testing him.

"She mentioned it, yes."

"She wouldn't explain why. She refused to talk about her decision, just kept saying that marrying Burke wasn't right." Allan shrugged. "I can't pretend it was a great loss. I never thought Burke was worthy of her, and my suspicions were confirmed when he fell for his former sister-in-law. Conned a business deal right out from under me, too. Cost me a bundle of money, although I learned my lesson, and it all turned out well enough in the end. A small price to pay if it meant Tessa didn't end up with someone she wasn't meant to marry."

Noah had a hard time following Allan's

logic. But he supposed Allan was trying to illustrate that he was protective of his youngest daughter and he wanted to encourage Noah's interest in her.

But Noah was already in love with Tessa. What her father said or did about it made no difference. All that mattered was whether Tessa felt the same way about him as he did about her.

"You said yourself that Tessa is wise. I'm sure whatever choices she's made, she knew what she was doing."

"Hmm."

This noncommittal response left Noah clueless as to whether Allan agreed or disagreed with him. Noah liked Tessa's father, but the man was used to taking charge, to directing the future the way he wanted it. Only, when it came to matters of the heart, you couldn't force things. Life was too uncertain for that. That was what he had learned from losing Julia. He had loved her. Perhaps that love had been strained to the point of breaking, but he had loved her up until the end. It was just that, in his grief, he had forgotten to pay attention to hers. Until it was too late.

He swallowed the reminder of his failings and turned to Allan instead.

"You know what I think?"

Allan looked at him with a questioning gaze.

"I think you are a very lucky man to have been blessed with the family that you have," Noah continued, "and I hope you never, ever take that for granted."

And with a nod of his head, he left Allan and went to join Tessa on the other side of the room.

CHAPTER FIFTEEN

TESSA HAD KNOWN where Noah was from the moment he entered the room. Hard as she might try to ignore his presence, she found her attention wandering from Ana, her gaze flicking briefly to make sure he was still in her peripheral vision. She only lost track of him once, when Ana excused herself to go greet a few of the web series' crew members. When Tessa's eyes moved to check if Noah was still across the room with her dad, she was startled to see her father standing alone, looking rather contemplative.

Grace had fallen asleep in her arms and was growing rather heavy. Tessa shifted the baby a bit, and when she glanced up again, Noah was standing in front of her.

"Hey," he greeted.

Her stomach performed a somersault that was becoming an all-too-familiar reaction when Noah was present.

"Hi," she whispered, not so much because

of Grace but because her voice failed her when Noah looked at her the way he was right now. His gaze didn't waver, his eyes so intent on her that she had to look away or melt beneath the warmth of his stare.

"You made it," she commented and then bit her lip at the obviousness of this statement.

"I made it," he repeated.

She forced herself to meet his eyes, trying to appear casual. "I just thought, with your schedule, and everything…" She trailed off.

"If there's an emergency, the hospital will call." He finally pulled his gaze away from hers to scan the party. "Besides, I couldn't miss Zoe's big moment."

Zoe looked their way just then, as if she'd heard her name. She beamed beneath her knit cap and waved. Her adult tooth had filled in the gap in her smile in recent weeks, so she no longer presented a childish grin. Noah waved back and smiled. Now it was Tessa's turn to stare.

"You've changed," she murmured, unable to keep the observation to herself. She'd recognized it weeks ago now but seeing how easily he smiled at Zoe made her stop and marvel. Noah didn't look at her.

"Have I?" he asked, but she sensed he wasn't really asking. He already knew the answer.

Grace sighed in her sleep, and Tessa rocked her gently. "You've found a way to smile again."

He turned his face toward hers. "Maybe I found a new reason to smile."

His eyes held hers for so long that she feared others would begin to notice. She cleared her throat and dropped her gaze. "I better lay Grace down."

He didn't follow as she threaded her way through the crowd, needing to catch her breath but also longing to stay in his presence. She found Vivienne and placed Grace in her grandmother's arms. With her hands free, she moved to check the refreshments and make sure none of the snacks or drinks needed refilling.

Paige found her just as she'd finished pouring more pretzels into the plastic bowl.

"I was just coming to do that," her sister said.

"Don't worry, you should be out there celebrating."

"So should you," Paige replied. Tessa fished a pretzel out of the bowl and crunched on one end. Paige did likewise. "Seriously, Tessa, you are very much a part of this celebration." And then, much to her surprise, her sister pulled her into her arms and hugged her long and hard. The minutes stretched by until Tessa found her grip tightening until they clung to each other, survivors of the storm.

Paige's voice was thick with gratitude and tears as she said, "I could never have gotten through this without you. And if you hadn't called Noah that night...who knows how long Zoe would have gone undiagnosed?"

She finally pulled back and looked at Tessa, placing one palm on either side of her face. "This celebration is for Zoe, but I hope you know that you are the hero of this story. If it wasn't for you..."

Tessa marveled as Paige wiped at her tears. She had witnessed Paige cry before, though not often. But these tears were something different. They were tears of humility and hope, and Tessa had never seen the like of them in her sister's eyes.

"Hey." Tessa grabbed her sister's hand. "Zoe's going to be okay. You know that, right?"

Paige let out a soft little laugh. "Don't you

see? That's why I can't stop crying. Because I *do* know it. I feel like…like I've been given a gift. A second chance. I don't plan on wasting it. So that's why I have to tell you that you are the best kid sister a girl could ask for. Harper, too, but don't let on that I said so."

Apparently, not everything changed. But Tessa was relieved, in an odd way, that Paige's rivalry with Harper would continue.

"Did I hear my name?" Harper appeared behind Paige. "And did you just say that I'm the best sister a girl could ask for?"

"Tessa. I meant Tessa."

"Yeah, but you threw me in there, too. No take-backs."

Paige and Harper continued to playfully argue, and Tessa felt a familiar ache as she watched them. One day, she would have liked to have daughters. To grow old and see them mature into women. She blinked back tears over what was never meant to be. Would she ever be able to forgive her body for its betrayal? Would there ever come a day when she didn't experience a stab of grief at unexpected times? At least, for now, she told herself she was blessed to have her sisters.

Paige and Harper were still bantering as she threw her arms around them both. The gesture stunned them into silence, and after a moment, their arms circled around her.

"I think I'm going to like living so much closer to you guys," Paige said.

"Haven't I been telling you to move here for years?" Harper replied. "I mean, not to say I told you so or anything…"

"What do you mean, 'I told you so'? I'm the one—"

"Paige?" Harper's interruption silenced her sister. "Let's just enjoy this moment, okay?"

And for once, Paige took Harper's advice, drew her sisters close and didn't say another word.

NOAH STAYED UNTIL the party wrapped up. He lingered long after the other guests had left, answering Paige and Weston's questions and attempting to alleviate their concerns about caring for Zoe now that she was home. They'd taken classes on how to clean her chemo treatment port, the proper nutrition she should be getting, warning signs to watch out for, follow-up visits and a myriad of other details they needed to know now that they'd be caring for Zoe outside of the hospital.

While he spoke with Paige and Weston, the rest of the family cleaned up from the party. Zoe and Molly sat with Grace on the couch, taking turns waving toys in front of her and then falling into giggles as she cooed and grabbed for them. He was satisfied to see Zoe looking well, if a little tired. He reminded Paige and Weston to encourage her to rest.

Harper and Connor were the first of the family to leave, showering Zoe with kisses and the promise to let Molly come visit soon, and then bidding farewell to the rest of the group. Having imparted as much information and reassurance as he could, Noah knew he should head for home, but still, he waited. Allan gave him the in he'd been looking for when he asked Noah if he'd mind helping Tessa carry a few things out to the car.

Tessa was quiet as they loaded a box and several bags into Allan and Vivienne's SUV. He didn't break the silence, content to simply be in Tessa's presence. But as they were heading back inside, he said, "It's a beautiful night out. Do you mind if I walk you home?"

Tessa lived near enough to Paige and Weston's new house that it was an easy walk. It was the perfect opportunity to spend a little extra time, just the two of them. His offer appeared to startle her, however. She blinked up at him, her hair burnished gold in the dying light.

"Um, what about your pickup?"

He shrugged. "I'll come back for it. It's not far. Besides, a walk will do me good. I don't get enough fresh air. It probably makes me cranky."

His teasing tone elicited a smile from her, and his heartbeat sped up at the sight, but Tessa still seemed uncertain. "I don't want to inconvenience you."

He made a face. "You, an inconvenience? After all the effort you put into drawing me out of my shell?"

Her laughter only made him fall even harder for her.

"Well...okay," she finally agreed when her humor settled. "Let me just say goodbye to Zoe and grab my house key."

Noah waited outside. He'd already spoken to Zoe earlier, sharing his joy that she'd been released from the hospital and cautioning her that the battle still wasn't over. He'd emphasized the victory in her release, however, and encouraged her to keep fighting. He also made sure she knew that he was in the fight with her, that just because she was no longer in the hospital didn't mean he wouldn't be there for her.

He touched his bare wrist, thinking of Ginny.

He'd surrendered his watch to Zoe, earlier in the evening. He'd waited until she had a break from all her well-wishers and while Molly was off getting them some snacks. Then he'd sat down next to her and removed the timepiece from his wrist, holding it in his palms as he spoke.

"I've told you about my daughter, Ginny," he said, surprised, as he always was these days, that he was able to say her name so easily, "and how she gave me this watch. I've worn it every single day since her death, as a reminder. Of time. Of how little there sometimes is. And it's never enough." He drew a deep breath. "I didn't get enough time with her."

He swallowed. Zoe was quiet, but her eyes were knowing. He had seen such a look before, in many of the children he treated. Forced to grow old before they should have to, in order to fight a battle that didn't discriminate by age. Children like Zoe knew more than they should…but it made them stronger than most people could ever hope to be.

"But while Ginny's time here was short, I treasured every single second of it." He held the watch out. "I believe, Zoe, that you are going to have plenty of time, a long life to fulfill your dreams. You still have a long road ahead of you, and I'm sure there will be a few rocky days ahead. But you hold on to this watch and remember that you'll come out on the other side, whole and well with an entire world of possibility awaiting you. And when that day comes, I want you to pass this watch on to the next person who needs a reminder…or just a little hope."

Zoe didn't speak, but she held out her wrist, so he could place the straps around it, tightening the bands as small as they would go. It was still loose around her wrist, but she pushed it up her arm to hold it in place. And then she threw her arms around him, and her hug was enough to speak all the words that neither of them could say.

Now, as he waited outside for Tessa to reappear, he stared up into the night sky, drinking in the sight of so many stars. He'd made the right choice, moving here, to this town. He hadn't imagined the miracle that had occurred—this slow healing of the wounds he'd carried for so long. But he was grateful for the chance to begin again, to cherish his memories more than he mourned them. It was a gift.

Like Tessa. She was a gift, too. If only he could find the words to tell her so.

His heart tripped over itself as he heard the front door open, and Tessa stepped out onto the porch. She held her keys in one hand and her phone in the other, and her face was flushed, whether from her goodbyes or the anticipation of the walk ahead, he wasn't sure.

"Ready?" she asked, her voice a little breathless.

He smiled. "Ready," he replied and held out his hand to ease her down the steps.

TESSA'S HEART WAS beating double time even though Noah kept a leisurely pace on the walk from Paige and Weston's to her house. His request to walk her home had been unexpected, though not unwelcome. Still, she found herself flustered by her awareness of him beside her and was irritated by her own reaction.

They didn't speak right away, strolling

quietly together as they passed beneath the trees lining the street. Noah's arm occasionally brushed against hers, and with every touch, she jumped a little. If he noticed, he didn't remark on it, for which she was grateful. After a few minutes, she grew restless with the silence. She had the feeling that Noah wouldn't speak until she did, allowing her to find the pace of conversation.

"Thank you for coming tonight. It meant a lot to Zoe, seeing you there."

"I was honored to be invited."

"You're the hero of the hour, so of course you'd be invited."

He shook his head. "Zoe is the hero. Not me. I give her the weapons, but she's the one who fights the battle."

Tessa stopped walking and turned to face him. "Why do you sell yourself short that way? You do everything you can for those kids. You fight right alongside them. If that doesn't earn you some sort of accolades, I don't know what does."

Her own passion startled her. It was just that Noah tried so hard. He sacrificed his time and his tears for the children. It was more than a job for Noah. It was a crusade.

"You lost your daughter to this disease,"

she softly noted, "but that doesn't make you any less worthy to be the hero."

Rather than arguing or brushing her off, Noah took a step closer to her and looked down at her with such intensity that it stole her breath away.

Her brain fired a warning that she should step back, gain some distance before she found herself falling even harder. But her heart refused to cooperate, stubbornly keeping her rooted to the spot as Noah raised his arm and cupped her cheek with his palm. His skin was warm and soft against hers, both soothing and electrifying where his fingers stroked the gentle curve behind her ear. She shivered at the touch, and he misunderstood, asking, "Are you cold?"

"No," she answered breathlessly. "No, I'm not cold."

He didn't move, just kept looking down at her, his fingertips lightly caressing as he moved his palm down from her jaw to cup her chin.

"Do you need a hero, Tessa?" he asked. His voice came out low and gravelly, as if the weight of his emotion had turned the tone inside out.

Did she need a hero? She wasn't sure there

was any way to save her. She had come to think of herself as damaged in some way, defective so that no one could possibly want her. She was too scared and embarrassed to share her struggles with anyone. She didn't know how to fix the things within her that were broken, and it didn't seem right to put that burden on someone else. Especially someone like Noah, who had already shouldered so much grief in his life. A hero. How could she ask that of him?

"Noah, I...I'm not sure how to answer that."

"Then don't," he replied and leaned down to meet her lips with his. His kiss was gentle and sweet, without pushing her for anything more than this moment. She supposed if anyone understood the importance of living in the moment, it was Noah.

He drew her into him, pulling her body against his in a sheltering gesture. She gave in, molding herself against him and only finding the will to keep standing because of his strength. She had been kissed before, many times. She'd been engaged to be married, after all, so she was no stranger to closeness.

But never had she been held like this. Not

even by Burke, her former fiancé. Noah wrapped his arms around her as though she was infinitely precious, as if he didn't want to hold her too tightly for fear of breaking her.

And she was afraid that this was exactly what was happening. She was shattering, from the inside out, her heart splitting with longing and uncertainty. Tentatively, she wrapped her arms around his waist to hold herself steady. He felt it and deepened the kiss, his mouth warm and gentle against hers, still not pushing for more than she was willing to give.

When he finally pulled his lips away, it was only to whisper her name, murmuring it against the edges of her mouth and then planting delicate little kisses along the bridge of her nose and up to her eyelids. Noah made her feel prized and precious, but if she didn't pull away soon, she risked never regaining her emotional footing…and her heart.

"Noah." She murmured his name as both a plea and a prayer.

He stilled, though he didn't pull back right away. She treasured that moment, the way he held himself in check but didn't immediately let go. She wanted nothing more than to stay in the circle of Noah's arms. But Noah couldn't help her. He couldn't restore what her body had taken away, and she couldn't reconcile herself to the loss.

He rested his forehead against hers, and she let him, struggling to find the courage to step out of his arms.

"Tessa," he murmured her name once more, "I love you."

She jerked in disbelief, breaking their embrace. She took a step back, staring at him. He loved her? The thought left her both giddy and alarmed. He couldn't love her. He didn't know the full story, had no idea what he was giving up if he chose her.

Noah was a good man, but even good men placed a certain value in a woman's ability to conceive...didn't they? She didn't want him to think less of her, to look at her differently, but she knew that was inevitable. She just hadn't expected him to say that he loved her.

"Do you mean that?" she asked, her voice a rough whisper.

He was gazing at her carefully, as if trying to read her thoughts.

"I do," he replied, full of conviction. "You've changed me. You've changed everything for me. After Ginny and Julia died, my world became gray. But since you've come into my life, I see color…everywhere."

She swallowed, the sincerity behind these words moving her deeply. But it changed nothing. It meant little that Noah loved her if she couldn't love herself, if she couldn't accept what her body could not give her. She would live her life in a cocoon of shame and uncertainty, constantly grieving the child she would never have. She refused to ask someone to bind their life to hers when she couldn't even share the secret that haunted her.

She didn't want to lead him on. It wasn't fair. But when she opened her mouth to explain it, her heart quailed. She couldn't tell him. No matter how much she needed to, she could not. An insistent pounding began at her temples, her blood pressure rising. Unable to find the words, Noah filled the silence.

"I still have some grieving to do, and I'm not the man I was once. But do you think… that there's any chance…you could eventually feel the same way about me as I do for you?"

The nervousness in his words made her want to reassure him, to tell him that if she didn't already feel the same way, she was almost there. But to admit this would complicate matters in the extreme. She couldn't lead Noah along and pretend that there was a future for them when she didn't know the answer to that question.

"I..." Her voice trembled, and then she felt his fingers brush against hers in the small space that separated them. Their fingertips touched and then intersected, and the solid warmth of his hand in hers buoyed her up. "It's possible," she breathed, inwardly cursing the words the instant they left her mouth.

It's possible...if you can accept me for who I am and what I cannot give you.

She knew she should speak this thought aloud, now while the opportunity was before her. But again, her will failed, and she remained silent. Noah's reaction to her words caused a physical ache in her chest. His face lit up with hope, his mouth widening into a heart-stopping smile.

He pulled her back into his arms before she could stop him and pressed his lips to hers once more. She resisted the embrace for a moment, afraid to encourage something she couldn't guarantee. But his lips were so insistent, and her heart craved this feeling so much. For too long, she'd held back, anchored by the fear of how others would see her if they learned her secret, that for just one moment, she wanted to remember what it was to feel cherished.

So she let herself sink into Noah's arms, her lips moving hungrily beneath his. He held her tighter, and as she stood there, in the moonlight, she didn't allow herself to think of how Noah's affections might change once he knew the truth.

CHAPTER SIXTEEN

NOAH ASKED HER if she'd like to have dinner
with him the next day. Despite how her head
cautioned her to say no, her heart prompted
her to say yes. He picked her up at six the
following evening, staring at her for a full
minute as Rufus whined desperately for a
greeting of his own. She brushed her dress
self-consciously, wondering if the plaid vin-
tage dress was too much for a casual evening
out. Maybe this wasn't a date, but just a night
out as friends?

He quickly relieved her of that notion as he
stopped staring and moved forward to brush
a kiss against her cheek delicately. Her skin
prickled, goose bumps rising, just from his
nearness.

"You look beautiful," he said, though the
words weren't necessary. His reaction had
been enough. Still, it was nice to hear. He
paused long enough to crouch down and give

Rufus a decent scratch behind the ears before he asked if she was ready to go.

They drove to the waterfront as he explained that he'd reserved them a table at Callahan's. She felt a ping of uneasiness. She loved eating at her brother-in-law and sister's restaurant, but she didn't know how she felt about them seeing her on a date with Noah. Not because she was embarrassed to be out with him but rather because of the questions it might raise.

Her family had pried in subtle and not-so-subtle ways to learn what had gone wrong between her and Burke when she left him standing at the altar. She had never told Burke the truth, much less her family.

She'd only dated one guy since Burke, and that had been a disaster. She wasn't heartbroken over Miles Daly. In a way, he'd been little more than a test. She'd told him about her infertility one night, after they'd gone on their fifth date, and his reaction only solidified her internal struggles. The breakup with Miles hadn't been a great loss, but the blame she'd heaped on herself afterward was reinforcement that she hadn't forgiven her body for its betrayal.

It was tricky enough that she and Noah

worked together. If she opened up and told him everything, and then he rejected her as Miles had, she'd still have to see him every single day. She wasn't sure she could bear that kind of reminder.

But she'd agreed to this date, which meant she was considering a relationship. And if her family knew that, it would be much harder to explain why things hadn't worked out than it had been with Miles, whom her family had never met.

Her head began to pound as Noah pulled into the parking lot of Callahan's. She feared she might begin hyperventilating on the spot.

"Hey."

She tried to mask her turmoil, but she realized she'd failed when she glanced in his direction.

"If you'd rather not—" he hesitated, as though searching for words "—have dinner with me, I'd understand. I can take you back home. I know we're colleagues, and even though the hospital has no rules about co-workers dating—"

"No," she said, her heart again speaking despite her head's protest. "I mean, I do want to have dinner with you."

He didn't appear convinced, and he definitely looked concerned. Her stomach twisted so that she had to lay a hand over top of it to steady herself.

"And I'm starving," she said by way of excuse. "In fact, I've been craving Connor's crab bisque, so this is perfect." Her voice was too high-pitched, and she tried to level it out. "I'm looking forward to it. I mean, our date, not just the crab bisque."

Her cheeks began to flame as soon as she said the word *date*. She was making a mess of this, and Noah appeared bemused.

"Um, should we go inside?"

She scrambled to get out of the car before her mouth could run ahead of her brain once more. Noah came around the side of the vehicle just in time to help her out, and they walked side by side, not touching, toward the restaurant.

Of course, all the staff recognized her, and she tried to act casual as they greeted her the minute she stepped inside the door. She introduced Noah to a few people, and when they expressed their concern for Zoe, she made sure to point out Noah's role as Zoe's oncologist. He waved away the credit she attributed to him, but it felt strange and tense until they were finally led to a table with a view of the bay but still slightly secluded in the corner of the room.

Once they were seated, she relaxed a little. She didn't see Harper or Connor anywhere, though it was likely at least one of them was somewhere in the restaurant. She and Noah perused the menu in silence, but she already knew what she wanted so she took the opportunity to re-center her emotions. By the time Stephen, their waiter, appeared to take their order, she was feeling a little bit better about the evening.

They each ordered an entrée, and Noah chose an appetizer to share. Then it was just the two of them once more, without the distraction of the menus between them, and they sat in uneasy silence for a minute before Noah spoke.

"What's your favorite color?"

She had just taken a sip from her water glass, and the question took her off guard. She swallowed too quickly and then coughed, placing the glass back on the table as she cleared her throat.

"Sorry, um…what?"

"Your favorite color," he prompted. "I feel like we've become close, and yet there are so many little things that I don't know about you."

She was conflicted, touched that he was interested but also wary that he felt they'd become close. Once he learned her secret, would he be as interested?

"Oh. It's violet."

"Purple?"

She shook her head. "Violet is softer than purple, more subtle. It's not as bright."

"Hmm. I never thought about it, but you're right."

"How about you?" she asked.

"Blue," he replied.

"Turquoise, teal, periwinkle?"

He chuckled, and the sound was somehow soothing to her torn emotions. "I had no idea this question would be so complicated."

"Hey, you asked," she teased back.

Their conversation fell into an easy rhythm after that, and they shared little details about themselves right up until their entrées arrived, at which point the conversation shifted first to food, then family, childhoods and careers. The night flew by as they finished their meal and ordered dessert, and talk turned to the hospital, the gala in another two weeks and the success of the web series.

Tessa marveled at how comfortable she was with Noah. When she was able to stop worrying over what he'd think if he knew her secret, she relaxed and couldn't remember the last time she'd enjoyed herself so much.

They finished dinner, and Noah paid the bill while asking if she'd like to stroll along the waterfront and check out some of the shops. She eagerly agreed, nowhere near ready for the evening to end. They were just making their way back to the front of the restaurant when she saw them.

She involuntarily came to a halt. Noah, who had been holding her hand, felt her reaction and came to a stop, as well. She would have regathered her composure enough to keep walking, but it was too late.

As if sensing her gaze, Burke looked up and caught her eye, smiling when he recognized her. Her gaze moved slightly, and she realized he was with Erin, his wife. She schooled herself to relax. This wasn't the first time she'd seen Burke and Erin together, but it had certainly been a while, and she'd never encountered him while on a date of her own before.

There were no hard feelings between them after their breakup, but the ghost of her own mysterious defection on their wedding day made things awkward.

Noah looked back and forth between her and Burke. She could sense the question on his face even though she could only see it peripherally.

Burke stood and gestured them over to his table. Unable to think of a reason to refuse, she walked to their table with Noah still holding her hand.

"Hello," she greeted Burke and then Erin with a forced smile.

If there had even been any jealousy on Erin's part for her husband's former fiancée, Tessa had never witnessed it. Erin seemed secure in her husband's love, and Tessa supposed that was because the two of them had known each other since they were teenagers. Erin had been married to Burke's brother, Gavin, before Gavin died. Burke had had a very tumultuous childhood, and she didn't begrudge him the happiness he'd found with his former sister-in-law.

Burke and Erin were staring at her expectantly, and she realized, just a beat too late, that they hadn't met Noah.

"Oh! Burke, Erin, this is Noah. Noah, this is Burke and Erin." She stopped short of attempting to explain the complicated relationships between them all, but Noah must have remembered the name of her former fiancé because his hand tightened, almost imperceptibly, in hers. He used his free hand to shake Burke's, and then Erin spoke up.

"Oh, you're Zoe's doctor," Erin realized, her smile broadening. "Harper told me about you. She said you're amazing."

"Hardly that," Noah said self-deprecatingly, "but I'll have to thank her for saying so."

They asked after Zoe, and Noah said more than she did. Tessa began to relax, feeling the reassurance of Noah's hand in hers. She may have been uncertain about her and Noah's future, but she had nothing to fear here. She was happy for Burke, glad that he had found love with Erin. Any jealousy she might have experienced had evaporated in the time that had passed.

Burke and Erin were talking about Kitt, Erin's son whom Burke had now adopted, explaining that he was home with Aunt Lenora, Burke's great-aunt who lived with them.

"We're actually celebrating," Erin noted, her tone uncharacteristically shy.

Burke looked at her then, his face suddenly beaming.

"Oh?" Noah asked. "Are there some sort of congratulations in order?"

"There are," Burke said, "since we just found out that Erin is expecting."

The smile remained pasted on Tessa's face, though the announcement struck to her very core, wounding her more than any knife could have. Noah reacted accordingly with congratulations while Burke and Erin gazed at each other with the expressions of two people who were totally in love. Tessa felt sick. She was still smiling, but she couldn't open her mouth, couldn't voice the congratulations she didn't feel.

Erin was going to have a baby. Tessa had broken up with Burke for this very reason. Because she knew she'd never see this expression on his face if he'd married her. They'd never have a child of their own. She didn't regret her decision not to marry him. But to be confronted now with the fact that Erin would bear him a child when Tessa had known she never could… It hurt.

She nearly doubled over with the pain of it, the sharp reminder that her womb was an empty and barren thing.

"Are you okay?" She looked into Noah's eyes and saw his concern for her. "You're very pale."

"Am I?" She touched her cheeks. "Maybe it was something I ate." She didn't want to blame the restaurant when the meal had been absolute perfection, but she needed an excuse, some reason for her discomfort.

Burke and Erin were still focused on each other, though, so it appeared her reaction hadn't even been noticed. Erin looked so... content. Fulfilled. She was already a mother, and now she would be again. Tessa knew she shouldn't resent her. It wasn't Erin's fault that Tessa's own body had betrayed her. But everyone around her took their ability to conceive for granted while she wrestled on a daily basis with the fact that she would likely never carry a child in her womb.

"We should leave you two to your celebration," she announced, drawing Burke and Erin's attention back to her. "Please enjoy your dinner."

She pulled her hand from Noah's and started for the door, desperate to get there before the tears managed to find a way to fall.

CHAPTER SEVENTEEN

NOAH MUMBLED A farewell and hurried after Tessa as she fled the restaurant. She was walking ahead of him, heading for his pickup.

"Tessa!" he called. She had to have heard him—they were only a short distance apart—but she continued with dogged determination. She never wavered, never turned her head to check if he was following her. When she reached the vehicle, she stopped and moved her head from side to side, as if she were lost and wasn't sure which direction to take. He caught up with her seconds later and placed a hand on her shoulder. She whirled around to look at him, and he saw that her eyes were wide with unshed tears.

"Tessa." He whispered her name as uneasiness coiled in his stomach. "What's wrong?"

"Take me home," she choked out, her voice ragged. "Please just take me home."

He opened his mouth to ask more questions, to try and find out what had changed in the last few minutes to bring her to a state of tears and want to end their night so unexpectedly. They'd been having a good time... hadn't they? Until...

Burke.

She'd told him she no longer had feelings for her former fiancé. Had she lied? The idea left him hurt and bewildered, the food they'd enjoyed suddenly sitting heavy in his stomach. How could he have overlooked something so obvious?

He thought he'd been paying more attention to Tessa than he had with Julia. He was desperate not to make the same mistakes again. Was he really so clueless when it came to others' emotions?

"Please, Noah," she pleaded as one tear and then another fell.

"Okay," he relented. "Okay."

He opened the truck door and held it for her as she climbed inside. He waited until she was seated before he gently closed it and moved to the driver's side. The ride back to Tessa's cottage was painfully quiet. Tessa took a ragged breath once and then exhaled sharply. He turned his head to look at her, and her face, in profile, was red with tears streaming down her cheeks.

"Tessa," he murmured, "are you okay?"

She wiped at her tears, as though embarrassed, and just nodded. His uneasiness grew, smothering the happiness he'd been experiencing less than a half hour before. What did her tears mean? He had no context to the situation other than to assume the worst: that despite what she'd told him, she was still in love with Burke Daniels, and his announcement that his wife was expecting had thrown her into heartbreak. Once again, he had failed the woman he loved. He hadn't seen her pain...and to know that the cause was someone she'd once loved only added to his anguish.

He should have realized. How had he dared to hope again, to believe that love was worth risking his heart? True, it hadn't been death that had stolen Tessa away. It was only her past, the lure of the love she'd given up. But that was just it. Hadn't she said that *she* was the one to break things off with Burke? How could he have missed this? Maybe he was simply incapable of giving her what she needed. In which case...did it mean they shouldn't be together?

These thoughts tormented him throughout the drive, and when he pulled into her driveway, he turned to face her before she could try and escape.

"Tessa, talk to me." He tried to form the words, to ask if she still loved Burke, but he couldn't quite bring himself to say it. He'd opened his heart again. He'd given it to Tessa, and when she told him it was possible for her to love him, too, hope had settled into the dark and empty caverns of his loss. It was devastating to consider he'd lost her before they'd even begun.

She was quiet for a very long time, the tears still flowing and her breath catching in her throat several times, as though she were holding back sobs. She stared down into her lap, twisting her fingers in agitation until she finally found whatever courage she'd been seeking. Turning her head, she looked him in the eyes.

"This was a mistake. I'm so sorry. I can't… We shouldn't… Let's just go back to the way things were, okay?"

He didn't know his heart could break so thoroughly yet again. Hadn't it been scarred and hardened enough? It was stupid of him to think he'd found love once more. He didn't deserve it. Perhaps Tessa had realized that, too.

"I'm sorry," Tessa said again, and he felt a twinge of guilt. It wasn't her fault. He couldn't blame her for not loving him. She was sweet and kind, a light in the very dark center of his soul. He wasn't worthy of someone like her. Maybe he wasn't worthy of anyone. He might have come to peace with Ginny's death, but Julia's still haunted him. Perhaps curing his daughter had been beyond his control but recognizing his wife's pain shouldn't have eluded him. He should have been a better man. He *wanted* to be better, for Tessa. But maybe he wasn't capable of that. Perhaps it was time to let her go?

"It's all right," he said, his voice so low with sadness that he had to clear his throat and try again. "It's okay. I understand."

She took another breath, the sob catching before she could release it.

"It was probably a bad idea anyway. With us being coworkers and all," he said. He was just making excuses now, trying to smooth over the sting and sorrow. Maybe they could maintain the friendship they'd developed. But he knew that was a lie. He couldn't go back to seeing Tessa only as a friend. He'd allowed himself to wish for too much. But for her sake, he would make every effort to behave as though his heart wasn't broken, to act as though it wasn't a great loss. He loved her, though, and he wasn't sure he could pretend otherwise.

"I'm so sorry," she said yet again.

"Tessa, you don't have to apologize," he said. "It's not your fault."

They sat there a moment more, and Noah couldn't help wondering if she recognized what he did: that after she left him, things would never be the same again. If he could have stopped time in that moment, he would have, just to pretend for a little bit longer that there was hope for the future.

When Tessa finally placed her hand on the door handle and pulled, the sound was loud and final in the stillness.

He thought about getting out and going to hold the door for her, but he wasn't sure he could will himself to do it. Not when he knew that everything between them was so final. Tessa hesitated with her hand on the door anyway, and he prayed, for one wild moment, that something might have changed, that she'd tell him she was just kidding, and really, he was the one she wanted more than anything.

Just like he wanted her.

But after several more heartbeats, she pushed the pickup door the rest of the way open and climbed out.

"Thank you for dinner," he heard her say as the door slammed closed.

THE WEEK THAT followed was a contradiction for Tessa. While she was thrilled to have Zoe living nearby and witness firsthand how well her niece was doing on her outpatient regime, life at the hospital had become painfully difficult. She still saw Noah every day, but they had fallen into a routine of avoidance once again.

It hurt more than she could have imagined.

Noah was never rude. If they ran into each other, he was unfailingly polite but also distant. It reminded her of their first days working together at the hospital and how he'd been cold and unsociable. She didn't sense that same aloofness in him, but sometimes, she almost wished he'd behave that way again. At least his condescending demeanor had allowed her to dislike him. This formal politeness was difficult to bear. It was as if they really were no more than friendly colleagues. She hated it.

Gone were the moments where his face lit up when she entered a room. She hadn't even quite realized how much those little reactions meant to her until he began schooling his face to remote politeness when she appeared. She knew he was trying his best to make this easier on the both of them, but she couldn't escape the burden of guilt she experienced. If only she was *normal*, if only her condition didn't hang over her to the point where she couldn't discuss it with anyone.

She knew there was still a very remote possibility she could one day have children of her own. But with her background in medicine, she understood the odds were against her, as well as the costs associated with it. Infertility treatments weren't cheap, and there was no guarantee that they would work. On top of that was the emotional seesaw of hope, waiting and disappointment, a cycle that might be repeated over and over without success.

Of course, adoption was a possibility, but she wasn't sure she should consider that option. Not until she could find a way past her feelings of betrayal. Her body had failed her, utterly and thoroughly. Until she learned to accept that, it wasn't fair to even consider adopting a child.

Nor was it right to enter into a relationship. Not even with Noah, who had changed so much and shared his heart with her. He deserved someone who could help him over the walls of his grief, but she could barely get a handhold on her own. It was better this way, for the two of them to part as friends. After all, even if she told him the truth, he was kind enough that he'd tell her it didn't matter. But it did. It mattered to *her*.

She avoided saying anything to her family about Noah, at least right away. There was nothing to report anyway—none of them knew about the kiss after Zoe's party, nor about the date that followed.

But they suspected something, she was sure of it. Her uncharacteristic actions over the last couple of years had made them sensitive to her moods and decisions. She'd tried to downplay things, but that never worked, especially where her sisters were concerned. They saw right through her excuses.

They all liked Noah, not only for how he'd taken care of Zoe, but also for how kind he'd been to *her*. To all of them.

The memory of it made her heart ache anew, but she held fast in her decision not to share her heartbreak with anyone.

She did, however, finally have to admit to her family a little of what was going on.

Harper called to invite her to dinner that Saturday night at her and Connor's house. Paige and Weston, along with Zoe, were coming, too, but their parents were spending the weekend in DC, so they wouldn't be joining them.

Tessa hesitated, not really in the mood to be social, even with her family. But she hadn't seen Zoe all week, and part of her longed to hold Grace in her arms and ask Molly if she was excited about the upcoming school year.

"I'm not sure if I can make it or not," Tessa hedged as she held her cell phone in one hand and moved her computer mouse with the other, navigating through her emails as she finalized details of the gala taking place the following weekend.

Harper laughed, a flutter of amusement on the other end of the line. "Just invite him along, Tessa."

She swallowed hard, her hand stilling on the mouse.

"W-what?"

"Noah. We know you're hanging out with him, so just bring him along to the dinner. He's more than welcome."

Tessa pulled her hand away from her computer and placed it in her lap, picking nervously at the fabric of her tweed skirt.

"I can't, we…" She bit her lip, eyes closing. There was no point making up some ridiculous excuse. Better off to just tell her sister the truth and get things out of the way. "Noah and I are coworkers, that's all."

"C'mon, Tessa, you don't need to be shy. We all really like him. He's good for you."

Harper's words only made the situation worse. She closed her eyes and willed herself not to cry.

"I'm not being shy. I'm serious. Noah and I are coworkers. That's it."

Harper was silent for a full five seconds. "Tess…what happened?"

"Nothing happened. Noah and I have always just been colleagues."

She knew it sounded lame. All evidence pointed to the contrary. She and Noah had grown close, expanding beyond the bounds of employee camaraderie. Her family had witnessed it, both inside the hospital and out.

Harper was quiet again on her end. Tessa

prayed she didn't ask any more questions. Her throat was already thick with suppressed tears.

"Okay." Harper's tone was heavier than it had been moments ago. "But you'll still come to dinner, right?"

She knew her sister was worried and probably wanted her there as much to assess her emotional state as for company.

"Sure. I'll come." She didn't want to, but to refuse would only cause Harper to do something drastic like bring the entire family to her place.

"Good. That's good."

She felt bad for worrying her sister.

"Harper, I'm fine, okay? Don't stress about me."

"Well, you're my baby sister so that's kind of my job."

The words caused a flood of affection. "I know, but we're not kids anymore. I can handle stuff on my own."

"I never said you couldn't. The point is that you don't *have* to. You know I'm here for you, right? Paige, too. And Mom. All of us."

"Yes, and I love you all for it. But seriously, there's nothing going on. I'm fine." It was a lie she'd told so often by now that she was able to speak it without any sort of hesitation anymore. If only it would become true if she said it enough times.

Harper sighed but didn't push. "We'll see you at six on Friday night, then?"

"I'll be there," Tessa promised.

She quickly ended the call before Harper could change her mind and ask any more questions that Tessa did not want to answer.

CHAPTER EIGHTEEN

THE WEATHER ON Friday night was perfect for a cookout—mild and pleasant with a light breeze. Thankfully, other than Zoe asking about Noah, none of her family questioned her about him when she showed up alone—with the exception of Rufus—at Connor and Harper's for dinner.

They ate out on the back patio, and the conversation flowed around her with no references to the hospital. She wondered if Harper had warned them ahead of time to steer clear from any mention of Noah. If so, she was both annoyed and grateful. She didn't like being handled with kid gloves, but on the other hand, she hadn't given her family much choice. They sensed something was wrong, had sensed it for a very long time, but they also knew she stubbornly refused to talk about it. She couldn't expect any less for her behavior.

The steak Connor had grilled was delicious, done with his typical culinary skill. Tessa's jaw nearly dropped open when she caught Paige slipping Rufus a bite from her plate. The bulldog licked his chops and offered a little bark of thanks as Paige patted him on the head. Her sister had truly changed if she was willing to not only feed Rufus but pet him.

She was glad her dog had gotten the chance to enjoy the steak because she barely tasted it. Her mind kept straying, wondering if Noah had stayed late at the hospital or if he was home now. Was he alone? Did he miss her as much as she missed him? Several times during dinner, she cut these thoughts off and made an effort to join the dinner conversation, only to find her mind drifting again after a couple of minutes.

At one point, she heard giggling and looked up to see Molly and Zoe, heads bent together with Molly's hair brushing against Zoe's bald scalp, as they shared some girlish secret. It was only then that she realized Zoe hadn't asked to sit beside her, as she usually did. Zoe was in between her mom and her cousin, seemingly content at Paige's side.

The sight struck a chord of jealousy, which Tessa knew was ridiculous. She wanted

Paige and Zoe to have a good relationship.
And as she watched, Paige's arm automatically reached out to rub her daughter's back,
as though reassuring herself that Zoe was
still there and not some figment of imagination. Zoe turned to her mom and offered a
bright smile. Something about the sight…the
shared expression of love, of that bond between mother and child, of everything they
had conquered and all the days yet to come…
it struck Tessa hard, bringing together all
the frustration, grief and uncertainty of the
last two years.

She pushed back her chair abruptly.

"Excuse me."

The table fell silent at her sudden departure. She could feel the wall of quiet at her
back as she fled inside the house and into
Harper and Connor's kitchen. She thought
about leaving, but that would only make matters worse. She just needed a minute to compose herself and then she'd go outside again.

There was a stack of dishes in the sink,
and she zeroed in on them, grabbing a scrub
brush and attacking the bowl Connor had
used to whip the mashed potatoes. She
scrubbed with a singular determination,
trying to focus on the dried potato crust

clinging to the bowl and not her own shattered heart. She didn't know how long she stood there, but there was a stack of immaculate dishes piled beside her when she heard Harper say her name.

"Tessa."

She turned to see Paige and Harper standing in the kitchen, watching her with concern in their eyes.

"I'm fine," she said. She couldn't bear pity or whispers or the walking on eggshells when conversation about babies or children came up. She didn't want people to be afraid to talk about their families with her. This was her burden, and she didn't want to share it.

"Tessa," Paige said, "something is obviously wrong. Why can't you tell us what it is?"

Tessa felt the frayed edge of her nerves beginning to unravel further.

"I don't know how many times I have to say it… *Nothing is wrong.*"

"Tess," Harper tried to intervene, "we're just worried. We care about you."

Tessa reached for a nearby dish towel to wipe her hands. "I appreciate that, but you guys don't need to worry. I'm not a child."

"But you're our kid sister," Paige said. "We can't help it. Maybe it's a mom thing. You'll understand when you have kids of your own."

These words, from Paige's lips of all people's, finally caused Tessa to crack.

"You don't own the market on motherhood, Paige," she snapped, "and that's just the problem—I'll *never* have kids of my own, so I guess I can't possibly know what it's like to be you."

Her little outburst stunned them into silence. She'd never shouted at her sisters before. Not even as children, when they'd get into fights. In fact, she'd never fought with them. She'd always been the peacemaker, the one that pulled them all together. She was the good one. She remembered her dad once telling someone that Tessa was an angel. She didn't feel very angelic right now.

"Tessa." Paige's tone was scolding. "Don't be dramatic. Just because you and Noah are having some sort of spat—"

"Paige," Harper warned. Paige had never been the most emotionally astute of the three of them, but Harper could obviously see how close Tessa was to the edge.

"Well, it's true. She's finally getting her

life back on track, and it's obvious to everyone she and Noah are crazy about one another. Just because they've had some sort of tiff doesn't mean she has to act like an angst-ridden teenager."

Tessa threw the hand towel at Paige. It flopped against her face and then fell to the floor. If Tessa hadn't been so angry, it might have been comical, exacerbated by Paige's shocked expression.

"Noah and I are not together," she cried, "and we never will be! That's what I'm trying to tell you—I cannot have children! That's why I left on the day of my wedding. It's why I quit my job at the doctor's office—because I couldn't bear to work with kids every single day, knowing I'd never be able to conceive one of my own!"

The tears came then, tears she had wept in private and tears she'd swallowed in public, tears that had been pooling inside of her for months upon months. Tears to represent lost dreams. Tears to wash away her hopes. Tears of worry that she hadn't allowed when Zoe had been diagnosed. Tears to drown herself in sorrow. She found herself sinking to Harper's kitchen floor and weeping out every emotion she'd kept to herself for so long.

It was only moments before she felt her sisters beside her, one on either side, their arms coming around her in silent support.

For the first time since she'd been diagnosed with early-onset menopause and learned about her infertility, she let herself cry without inhibition, without fear of others finding out her secret or asking her questions. She just let herself weep, emptying out an endless stream of sadness and mourning. She choked out her story, her symptoms, the visit to the doctor, the diagnosis and all the months that followed.

"Why didn't you tell us?" Harper asked after her tears finally began to ease.

She sniffed, her nose clogged from her crying spell. "Because I didn't want you feeling sorry for me or trying to make it better and somehow making it even worse."

"And you didn't want us to look at you differently, to think less of you. Or like you were a failure."

Tessa frowned at Paige's assessment. "Yeah. Exactly."

Paige shifted slightly, leaning back against the cabinets, her arm brushing against Tessa.

"It took four attempts with in vitro for me to get pregnant with Zoe."

Tessa blinked. Harper must have been equally as shocked, based on the way she spluttered, "What? Really?"

Paige nodded. "My eggs weren't viable, and I just couldn't get pregnant. So we saw a specialist."

"You never mentioned any of that," Tessa said.

"This family and their secrets," Harper muttered.

"For all the reasons you just mentioned," Paige said. "I felt like a failure."

"I didn't even know you wanted to be a mom that much," Tessa murmured. "I thought with Zoe, that it just happened, so you and Weston went with it."

Paige shook her head. "We both wanted it. I mean, maybe it started out with Weston wanting it more, but the more difficult it became, the more obsessed I got with becoming pregnant. So then…" She swallowed. "When Noah first started asking questions about Zoe, that's why I got so defensive. Because I thought I had failed as a mother…again. That I had barely been able to conceive Zoe and then I was going to lose her because I hadn't been a good enough mom. When she was diagnosed, I figured I was being punished for not appreciating her more, after how hard it was to get pregnant with her."

"Paige."

"I know—" she cut Harper off "—I know. But it's one thing to understand the facts in your head and another to accept it in your heart."

The words struck Tessa. There were so many things she knew in her head but convincing her heart was another matter entirely.

"I finally decided, though, that it wasn't a punishment but rather a second chance. A reminder that my daughter is precious, and I should never take that for granted again. It's why Weston and I chose to move here. In fact, I've been talking to Dad... I think I'm going to resign my position at his firm in DC and take over as a general manager of the Delphine. It will mean a significant pay cut, but it'll be worth it to be able to have more time with my daughter."

"That's a great idea," Tessa said.

"I agree," Harper added.

"Well, I have to admit that this town has grown on me. It's a good place to raise a family."

Tessa felt Paige cringe as soon as she said the words. "I didn't mean…"

"See? That's why I didn't want to tell you. I don't want you guys to be afraid to say that sort of thing around me."

"You know you can always adopt," Harper suggested. "I love Molly just as much as if I had given birth to her myself."

"Yes, but it still means I will never carry a child in my womb."

"But maybe with infertility treatments, like Paige, you could."

Harper meant well, but she didn't understand.

"I've discussed those options with several doctors. Yes, it's a possibility. But the odds aren't good. It's really expensive, and I could have a dozen treatments, and it might never work."

"And each time," Paige added, "you get your hopes up, thinking this will be it. But when it isn't, it feels like you lost a child in some ways. Because you did. You lost the child that you're afraid you will never have."

Tessa stared at Paige, stunned that her oldest sister understood so well.

"So that's why you and Noah broke up?"

"We didn't break up," Tessa quickly pointed out. "We were never together."

Harper ignored this. "And Burke, too? What is *wrong* with these guys? Just because you can't have a biological child of your own—"

"I never told them."

These words silenced both of her sisters for a minute.

"You never explained to Burke why you stood him up at the altar?" Paige asked, an echo of disbelief in her tone. "You just let him think you didn't want to marry him?"

Tessa looked down and tugged at the hem of her shirt. "It was more than that. I mean, yes, I knew how much he wanted a family of his own one day. And after the childhood he had, he deserved one. Plus, I just… I had a feeling it wasn't right. I loved him. But it was as if the universe was telling me something when I found out I wouldn't be able to give him the family he wanted. And I learned about it only a couple of weeks before we were supposed to get married. At first, I didn't think I could call it off. But then, on the day of the wedding, I couldn't do it. I couldn't marry him without telling him the truth, and I just wasn't prepared to do that. So I ran instead."

"And you never gave him an explanation?"

Harper repeated. "He still thinks you just walkcd away?"

Tessa sniffed, feeling defensive. "It worked out the way it was supposed to. He married Erin instead. And…and I s-saw him the other night. He got what he wanted. Erin's p-pregnant." She had to force the words out before she choked on them.

"Oh, Tessa." Paige moved to wrap an arm around her, drawing her close.

"It's not about Burke," she managed to say, battling off another round of tears. "I'm happy for him. But it's just something I wouldn't have been able to give him. It's the thing I can't even give myself."

Harper got up long enough to grab another clean dish towel and handed it to her so she could wipe her face.

"And what about Noah?" Harper asked in a gentle tone.

Tessa shook her head. She didn't want to talk about Noah.

"If it wasn't related to your condition, then why did you guys break up?"

Tessa signed in exasperation. "Harper, we were never together so how could we break up?"

Her sisters shared a glance over her head

but Tessa didn't have the energy to remark on it.

"I think you should tell him," Harper said. "You're basing everything on the assumption you'll be rejected. How do you know unless you try?"

"I *did* try," she argued. "You remember that guy I dated for a few weeks this past winter? Miles?"

"Oh, yeah. The mystery man," Paige said.

"We called him that because we never got to meet him," Harper spoke apologetically.

Tessa ignored these comments. "We went on a handful of dates before I mentioned my condition. It's not like we were getting really serious, but I just... I needed to see his reaction." She wiped at her nose with the dish towel. "I wish now that I hadn't. He finished out the date, but then he called me the next day to say we really weren't right for each other, that we had different priorities. As if I *chose* this problem."

Harper uttered a few choice names for Miles beneath her breath.

"But you can't give up. Noah's different."

Tessa knew what Paige was trying to say, but she was still scared. Her sisters were right; she hadn't dated Miles that long. But that was sort of the point. If it hurt that much when Miles rejected her, how much more devastating would it be when Noah did?

"I know that. But it's not just about Noah and how he might react. It's about…me. Learning to forgive myself, to accept that my body failed me. If I can't do that, then I don't deserve to be in a relationship with someone. It's not fair to them, especially not Noah. He's already been through so much."

"Maybe that's exactly why you two are meant to be together," Paige suggested. "Because if anyone is strong enough to stand with you, it's Noah."

Paige had a point about Noah's strength. To have come through the loss he had suffered and still be willing to love again… It left her in awe. But that was exactly why Tessa felt Noah deserved better. He'd had enough challenges in his past relationships. She didn't want to add to that burden.

"You should at least talk to Burke," Harper said. "You owe him an explanation."

"I did explain," Tessa defended. "Sort of. I just didn't give him all my reasons."

Paige and Harper's silence chastised her.

"Burke has moved on! He and Erin are sickeningly in love, and they're going to have a baby together. The last thing he wants is me telling him the real reason I didn't marry him. It's better just to leave things as they are."

"Better for who?" Harper pushed. "Burke is happy now, but he still deserves to hear the real reason. You were going to spend the rest of your lives together, and he has no real understanding of why you didn't show up that day. Plus, laying everything on the table might make you feel a lot better."

Tessa considered Harper's words. Was there a possibility her sister could be right? Would telling Burke lift some of the guilt and shame she felt so acutely? If it helped, even in some small measure, to come to terms with her situation, then maybe it was worth a shot.

"Paige, what do you think?"

Though she normally preferred Harper's advice to Paige's, her oldest sister had some understanding of what she was going through.

"Talk to him," Paige agreed. "I don't know if you owe it to him or not. But you certainly owe it to yourself."

She wasn't sure she was ready for that conversation. But she had to admit that telling her sisters hadn't been as terrible as she'd imagined it would be. They weren't treating her like they pitied her, and the weight of this secret she'd been carrying for so long didn't feel quite so heavy at the moment.

"I'll consider it," she said.

"Okay. And remember, we're here for whatever you need," Paige said.

Harper took her hand and squeezed it. "Even if it's just a reminder that while you may not be a mother, you are still the greatest sister, aunt and daughter that this family could ask for."

These words offered a small balm of reassurance. She may not have a child of her own and maybe she never would. But she had her family, and that was a very precious gift indeed.

CHAPTER NINETEEN

THE AFTERNOON WAS CHILLY, and even though they were sitting in the warmth of the sunshine, Noah still made sure John was covered well with a blanket. He suspected that his father-in-law was enjoying being outdoors. Though John didn't speak, he had turned his face upward as if drinking in the sun's rays. Noah hadn't talked much during this visit. His mind was full of Tessa, of her rejection, of how awkward things had become between them.

Because she found his attention unwanted, he'd stopped the little signs of affections he'd shown her. But he'd become so accustomed to her being part of his daily life that a couple of times, he'd begun to order tea for her before he remembered he shouldn't, and once, he distractedly doubled his lunch order for them to share. When it arrived, he found he'd lost his own appetite, and both sandwiches went uneaten.

They still saw each other at the hospital, but they made every effort to keep their interactions professional and focused on business. He missed her. He missed being able to text her or talk about his day, and he missed the little stories she shared about her family or something one of the patients had said to her. He even missed Rufus, something he never thought would happen. But at some point, he'd developed a real affection for that dog.

Just like its owner. He sighed, and John lowered his face from the sky, almost as if he was preparing to listen to whatever Noah might have to say. He wasn't sure how much John understood of their conversations, but the words he'd come to speak today were not easy ones.

"John, I have something I need to ask you." He cleared his throat. His father-in-law stared straight ahead, and Noah had no idea whether his announcement had penetrated or not.

"I loved your daughter." He put the words out there and then leaned forward, placing his elbows on his knees and resting his forehead against his clasped hands. "From the moment I met her, I knew she was the one for me. It was in the cafeteria at college, and she was trying to decide between the fish sticks or a hamburger. It wasn't a very appetizing choice." He laughed softly at the memory of Julia's scrunched-up nose as she looked back and forth between her options. "Do you remember how she used to wrinkle her nose when she wasn't sure what to do?"

He glanced at John briefly. He wasn't quite sure, but it almost seemed as if a corner of the older man's mouth twitched.

"I offered to buy her lunch at the pizza place across campus. It meant I'd be late for my next class, but there was just something about her... I couldn't let her get away." He held the memory close for a moment, turning it over in his mind, before he released it.

"Well, you already know the story of how Julia and I met and married." He felt the tears rise. "The thing is, John...I need you to know that I loved her. Right up until the end. I may have failed her, but I did love her."

He remembered Julia's face, on their wedding day, on the day Ginny was born, and on the morning they placed their daughter's body in the ground.

"But that man, the one who loved your daughter... He doesn't exist anymore. I am not the boy who bought her pizza or even the one who saw her buried next to Ginny." He swallowed hard against the emotion clogging his throat. It took him a moment to find the courage to speak again.

"I have to bury that man, too, now. I have to lay him to rest next to his daughter and wife or else the man that remains, the person I am… There will be nothing left of him but to end up beside them anyway."

He breathed deeply and then exhaled. John still stared sightlessly ahead. "I would give anything to bring them back, you know," he whispered roughly. "If giving my life would restore theirs, I would do it without hesitation. But I was never given that option. And I'm left here, to make whatever life I can, in the aftermath."

He closed his eyes and lifted his face to the sun, as John had been doing before he started speaking. It was warm and soothing on his face, and for a strange and crazy moment, he imagined he could feel Julia's fingertips tracing his jaw, as she had the first time they'd kissed. And then that memory shifted to Tessa, the feel of her in his arms and the taste of her on his lips.

"I fell in love again, John," he admitted,

his voice still a whisper. "She's very different from Julia. And she doesn't love me back." The admission hurt, but he was determined. Tessa may not love him, but she'd taught him how to love again. For that, he would forever be in her debt.

He opened his eyes and looked at his father-in-law. "I have to let go of the past. I have to move on. I think Ginny would want that. And while I know Julia blamed me at the end, I believe the two of them are together again now, and that she'd feel the same way." He licked his lips. "I'll never be able to atone for my failures. I realize that. But I'm not sure I can even keep trying if I stay stuck in this bubble of grief and isolation. As difficult as it is, I want to find a way to live, to breathe again. Tessa made me realize that. There's a whole life ahead of me, and it would be an insult to Ginny's and Julia's memories if I didn't try and live it."

He sniffed. "So what I'm asking from you, John…is your blessing. I get that you can't grant absolution, and you told me, before all this happened, that you didn't blame me. But I need something else. I need to know you want this for me, as much as I want it for myself." He reached out and gripped the older man's hands in his own.

"We are all that is left of the battle we waged," he said, his voice low. "And you will always be family to me. So grant me this one thing. Give me your benediction to move on."

Noah wasn't sure what he expected. John hadn't spoken in so very long that he wasn't really anticipating that he'd talk. Noah wasn't sure if there was any way his father-in-law *could* communicate, and he wasn't even sure if he understood all that Noah had said. But his face turned, and John's eyes focused on him. Tears filled the older man's eyes, slipping from the rheumy blue and over his wrinkled cheeks. And Noah knew that he had heard every single word.

Noah tightened his grip on his father-in-law's hands and felt tears falling from his own eyes.

"I'm sorry," he whispered. "I am so sorry. For everything."

And then, John blinked. Once but slowly. His eyelids closing as though acknowledging the debt and forgiving it.

The last of Noah's grief and guilt lifted then. His burden eased. Ginny and Julia settled into a hollow of his heart where he knew they would never be forgotten…but at peace.

"Thank you," Noah breathed, grateful. He leaned forward to rest his forehead against the other man's. "Thank you."

They sat like that together, saying the last of their goodbyes to the ones they had lost, and feeling the sun warm them with the promise of the future.

IT TOOK HER a couple of days to work up the courage to speak to Burke, and even now, as Tessa waited for her former fiancé to show up at the lighthouse, she had to steel herself to keep from running away. She didn't think Burke would much appreciate being stood up twice, however, even if this was just a casual get-together. He'd seemed curious when she called and asked if they could meet, but he didn't press her for details, which she was grateful for. Still, she was uneasy as she paced in front of the lighthouse, glancing around every so often to see if Burke was approaching.

She'd chosen the lighthouse because, even if there were others nearby, it was unlikely their conversation would be overheard. She'd thought about the nearby Lighthouse Café, but it was too easy for others to eavesdrop. And even while Findlay Roads had grown in recent years, it was still a small enough town that gossip would easily spread when she was spotted with her ex-fiancé. Not that she was overly worried about that. Anyone who knew Burke and Erin recognized how in love they were. And once the news of Erin's pregnancy spread, it would be even more evident.

Still, she didn't want to answer questions from acquaintances on why she was meeting Burke. The lighthouse was a less conspicuous venue, and it was a lovely day to be outdoors. The air was cool, but the sun was warm and bright. The leaves were just revealing the tint of fall in their veins, with a handful of gold- and red-tipped sprigs sprinkled throughout the branches. The breeze from the bay was tinged with the scent of foam and sand, and she closed her eyes, breathing in all the memories she had of this town she called home.

"Hey, Tessa."

She jerked at the sound of Burke's voice, annoyed that she'd allowed him to sneak up on her. It threw her off, and she'd already been feeling unbalanced.

"Oh, um…hey."

He offered a friendly smile, and she managed to relax a little. She and Burke had always been comfortable around each other. It was one of the things that had made their relationship so easy and obvious. It seemed natural that two people who got along so well should end up married. But she realized now, as she was sure Burke did, too, that there was more to marriage than just being able to get along. However, she hoped there was still an element of friendship between them. Burke had always been a good friend, even if he wasn't the man she was meant to marry. Knowing that, her nerves eased.

"It's a nice day. You want to walk?" he offered, gesturing toward the promenade. He must have sensed her uneasiness. The movement would give her something to focus on other than her anxiety.

"Sure."

They moved toward the promenade that wound through the park, circling the Chesapeake Bay. Burke didn't press her for the reasons she'd called him here, and she used the easy silence to gather her wits before she began speaking.

When they came to one of the wrought iron benches that lined the boardwalk, she asked if he'd like to sit. They moved together toward the bench and took a seat. Tessa kept about two feet of space between them, needing the buffer for what she was about to do.

She twisted her fingers in her lap, not certain where to begin. Part of her wished she had never asked Burke here, but another part knew that her sisters were right. This was something she had to do if she wanted to heal.

"Tessa, whatever this is about, just tell me—are you okay?"

It was sweet of him to be concerned, especially since they were no longer in the kind of relationship that required it.

"I'm...fine." The word came out forced. She wasn't, and she knew that, but she was working on it.

He eyed her doubtfully and she finally found the courage to speak up.

"I owe you—or rather, I owe us *both* an explanation on why I left you standing at the altar."

Burke frowned. "Tess, it's okay. I mean, as long as *you're* okay. You gave me your reasons when you came back, when I was living at the Moontide."

"Yes, but…I need to tell you the *real* reason."

This silenced him. She hadn't been sure whether Burke had bought her weak explanation when she'd gone to talk to him after their failed wedding. She'd given excuses, none quite satisfying and none exactly the truth.

He didn't protest, so she continued.

"Shortly before we were supposed to get married, I was experiencing certain… symptoms." She blushed, unable to share the more intimate details with him. "My doctor ran some tests, and the results came back that I…I was experiencing…" It was embarrassing for her to talk about, no matter how close she and Burke had once been.

"Tessa. It's me. You can tell me."

She nodded, swallowed and took a deep breath. "I was going through early menopause."

He frowned, and she could see him working through the implications of this, trying to pinpoint what it had to do with their former relationship.

"Okay," he finally said. "Why didn't you say anything?"

"Because…because you and I had talked

a lot about raising a family together, and this diagnosis meant that…" She trailed off, biting her lip to regain the balance on her emotions. She had known it would be difficult to say the words, but she forced her way through them. If she didn't speak them now, she might never find the nerve again.

"It means that I probably won't be able to ever conceive children on my own. So, all those dreams we had to create a family… I couldn't give that to you. At least, not in the way that we planned."

She didn't look at him but focused her attention on the bay instead, watching the way the sun angled across the waves in sharp, gilded planes. "You know how much I've always wanted to be a mother, and from the moment I met you I was sure you'd make a great dad. I mean, you've already proved that with Kitt and now…now you'll have the chance to raise a child from infanthood on up."

He didn't say anything, but after a moment, she felt his hand reach out and grab hers. The simple gesture nearly undid her. She looked at him, tears in her eyes, and was stunned to see his own were shiny with emotion.

"This isn't the first time Erin's been pregnant. The Christmas before last, after we were married, she told me she was expecting. I was overjoyed." He glanced away, shaking his head. "She lost the baby two weeks into the new year. It was hard. Really hard. For both of us. We're both thrilled and scared that she's pregnant again."

"Burke, I'm sorry. I had no idea." Tessa couldn't believe her own selfishness, her narrow assumptions. Even for Erin and Burke, the road hadn't been easy. The two of them sat in silence for a moment more before Burke spoke again.

"Why didn't you just talk to me?" he asked. "You never should have had to face that alone. I would have supported you however I was able to."

She smiled sadly, her view of Burke blurring through her tears. "Of course you would have. You're a good man. And that's why I couldn't tell you. Because you would have married me anyway, out of a sense of obligation. And I always would have wondered if you still would have chosen me, in spite of the fact that we might never have been able to have kids together."

Burke continued to hold her hand as she

blinked away her tears. His gaze remained steady on hers. She felt a well of regret and grief open up inside her until the tears overflowed.

"Oh, Tessa."

Her eyes slid closed. "Please, don't feel sorry for me."

"How can I not?" he replied. "You made a lot of assumptions, and to be honest, I'm a little hurt by them."

Her eyes flew open. She had never wanted to hurt Burke. When she'd left him standing at the altar, she was aware it would wound him, but better that than a lifetime of resentment and the tedious parade of fertility treatments and disappointments.

"I never wanted that," she said. "That's exactly what I was trying to protect you from. You'd been hurt enough in life. You didn't need any more."

He shook his head. "I'd like to think you trusted me enough to make that decision for myself. We were engaged, about to share a life together. You should have told me rather than deciding it was something I couldn't handle."

The words threw her. "I never considered it that way. I thought I was doing the right thing, by not telling you. It made it easier for you to walk away."

He let go of her hand and reached out to draw her into a hug instead. It was unexpected but welcome, the touch more brotherly than romantic.

"Tess," he breathed into her hair. "Nothing about love is ever easy. Whether it's good or it's bad or somewhere in between, it comes with tears and triumphs, just the same." He hugged her hard and then released her.

"So." He hesitated. "I take it nothing's changed? I mean, you're not…cured or anything like that?"

She shook her head. "No. There's no cure. There's only hope and grief and hope again."

He nodded, accepting these words. "Then I'm sorry. Because you're meant to be a mom. I don't want to be all insensitive and say you should adopt because I'm sure that's not exactly a solution when I know how much you wanted to experience actually being pregnant."

She was touched that he'd remembered. They used to joke about how pregnancy would suit her, being all fat and glowing. Chances were, she'd never know what that was like now. But for the first time since she'd learned about her diagnosis, she was willing to consider that there were other options, other things to anticipate beyond carrying her own child.

"Is that why you left Callahan's like you did the other night? After you found out Erin's pregnant?"

"Yeah. I'm sorry about that. I should have congratulated you both, but it just…hit too close to home, I guess."

In truth, she thought Burke and Erin hadn't noticed her abrupt departure. They'd been so captivated by each other and their good news. She didn't think anyone had really seen how she was hurting.

Except Noah. He had seen. She hadn't treated him very well for it, either.

"That guy you were with. The doctor."

"Noah," she offered, his name soft on her lips.

"Yeah. He seemed nice. Like he'd be good for you."

"He is," she admitted, realizing the truth behind those words. She'd begun to find healing with Noah, and he seemed to have found the same with her. But she'd sabotaged it to minimize the risk of being hurt again.

She was only just realizing that she had hurt herself more than Noah ever could.

"Have you said anything to him? About the infertility thing?"

She shook her head. "No, he and I aren't... anymore."

She could feel Burke staring at her and finally met his eyes.

"You should tell him."

"I can't. That wouldn't be fair."

Burke made a face. "You still don't get it, do you, Tess? It isn't fair to make the decision for him. If you like this guy, and if he likes you...you need to tell him. If he decides it's a deal breaker between you, then that's on him, not you. And you'll know you deserve better. Someone willing to love you despite all the rest. And if he's smart, he'll realize you're worth fighting for."

Maybe Burke had a point. Certainly, he'd given her a new perspective to consider.

"Tessa, love and relationships are about so much more than having kids or raising a family. You know that."

She did. But it was hard to feel like she was the failure in the equation.

"I can't tell you what to do. And while you and I weren't really meant to be, if we had it to do all over again, I still wish you'd explained to me what was going on. We could have postponed the wedding, taken some time to figure it out if necessary. But the point is, we'd have made those decisions together."

Burke's assessment soothed her. *Together.* The thought was encouraging. From the beginning, she had assumed she was in this alone. But that was her own fault, wasn't it? She had never told anyone, other than some guy she barely knew. It was no wonder she'd gotten the reaction from him that she had. She'd set herself up, reaffirming her mistaken belief that no one could want her if they knew her secret.

She trusted Burke, and what he said made sense. She realized she'd sabotaged herself again by breaking things off with Noah without giving him the real reasons beyond her decision. Maybe Noah would feel the same way Miles had. Maybe he wouldn't want anything to do with her if he found out. But she had to give him the choice. Her own fear of rejection would have to take a back seat to her hope. She wouldn't allow herself any less.

"I really am happy for you and Erin, you

know," she told Burke. "After what you both have been through, you deserve it. I'm sure this baby will be the best of both of you. And if he or she grows up half as wise and kind as their dad, they'll be pretty special indeed."

He beamed at these words, the promise of impending fatherhood evident in his smile. A small part of it pained her, just a little, and she suspected maybe she'd always experience that ache when she saw others' happiness where their children were concerned. But it didn't mean she couldn't find happiness of her own.

"If you're available for babysitting, I can't think of anyone I'd trust more with my son or daughter."

The offer moved her, more than she could ever tell him.

"Thank you. I'd really like that."

Burke leaned back and gazed out over the bay. She did the same, enjoying the peaceful moment between them and holding close the hope that there would be many more peaceful, happy afternoons ahead for her.

CHAPTER TWENTY

NOAH STEPPED INTO the ballroom of the Delphine resort and paused on the threshold, awestruck by the grand scope of the room. Allan Worth was not one to do things by halves, but still, the ballroom of his Findlay Roads luxury resort was impressive. No wonder Tessa had suggested holding the gala here.

The ceilings were edged with decorative crown molding with a motif that represented crashing waves, the detail evident from the light of the dozen chandeliers spread across the room. The walls were papered in gold threaded with pale blue accents. The carpet was an interlocking design of swirls in colors of gold and a seafoam that perfectly picked up on the blue in the wallpaper.

A hundred tables must have been scattered throughout the room, each draped by a crisp white tablecloth and holding a vase with blue stones, a branch and a calla lily. The effect was rustic but elegant. No less than he would have expected for Tessa being in charge.

There were two very large flat-screen televisions mounted in separate corners of the room. Each was streaming muted episodes of the web series. He saw his own face flash briefly on the screen before he looked away. He noted several large placards around the room featuring the faces of his patients along with facts and statistics about childhood cancers. The attendees mingled around these displays, a glittering exhibition of some of the wealthiest and most successful people affiliated with the hospital.

Noah stepped farther into the room and continued to scan its occupants. He told himself he was looking for any familiar face, but the truth, he knew, was that he was looking for Tessa. They'd been so formal and professional with each other in the last two weeks that he didn't expect things to be any different tonight. But being out of the hospital setting and in such a charming atmosphere, he couldn't help hoping… Well, he wasn't sure exactly what he hoped for. He was only sure that Tessa was at the center of it.

"She did an amazing job, didn't she?"

He turned at the sound of Ana's voice at

his elbow. She was sipping from a fluted glass, presumably champagne, and admiring the decor of the ballroom, as he had been doing a moment before. She handed him the second glass she held, which he accepted, though he didn't drink.

"I have to admit, when you first hired her, I never would have expected..." He trailed off. There were so many things he hadn't expected. Not just Tessa's skill at her job but the way she had come into his life, a breath of fresh air and sunshine, to chase away the funereal gloom.

She might not love him. Her heart might still long for her former fiancé, though he didn't understand why she had left him at the altar if that were the case. But maybe, one day, her feelings would change. He hoped he'd be there and have the chance to win her if that happened. For now, it would have to be enough that they were colleagues. And his next step was to try and reestablish the friendship that he'd unintentionally fractured. He planned to take the first steps toward that tonight, if possible.

"I confess, I had a few doubts myself. Tessa is more than capable, but when I first met her, I worried that she was too...soft for the job. But she has proven, especially through the situation with her niece, to have both an iron strength and a notable kindness."

Noah liked that. It summed Tessa up very well.

"It's a wonder she's still a single woman," Ana remarked, and Noah tried not to flinch.

"Well, Tessa may have a wealth of skills, but we have just established that subtlety is not one of *yours*, Ana."

She laughed at the jab but, thankfully, didn't pursue the subject further. He was left to scan the ballroom once more, not caring if he was obvious about it, as he wondered where Tessa was hiding. Perhaps she was still attending to details for the event. That would make sense. He longed to see her, however, even if it was only for a moment.

He was distracted as several people recognized him, whether from the web series or the advertisements noting him as a keynote speaker at the event, he couldn't be sure. Ana helped answer questions about the hospital and his role, and the crowd grew as he shared his passion for his work and the need for continued funding for patients. As the questions continued, he realized with some surprise that he was actually enjoying himself. He didn't mind being the center of attention in this instance, sharing stories about his patients and his work at Chesapeake View. He credited his ease to Tessa. She'd changed the way he looked at these events, shifting his viewpoint so he could see the good in them. He continued the conversation until his audience was distracted by something Ana pointed out on the television screens, allowing him a reprieve.

Finally able to pull away, he turned and immediately locked eyes with Tessa, who had apparently been watching as he fielded questions from the gala's attendees. He moved toward her without hesitation, before someone else could interrupt.

As he drew nearer, he was able to take a good look at her, admiring the cut of her navy blue gown and the tousled upsweep that held her blond hair in place. His heart began to hammer madly with each step he took closer to her until they finally stood face-to-face.

"Hello, Tessa," he greeted, his fingers flexing at his sides with the desire to touch her. "You look…beautiful."

He watched her eyes shine as he spoke the

last word, gratified that every bit of feeling he possessed must have been conveyed in how he said it.

"Thank you," she murmured and then, "Can we talk? In private?" she added.

His interest stirred. There was no way he would deny such a request.

"Of course."

She took his hand, and the touch of her skin on his only increased his curiosity and longing. He allowed her to lead him around the perimeter of the ballroom and toward the French doors that opened onto the outdoor balcony. He feared they might be intercepted along the way, but they managed to escape the gala without anyone stopping them to chat. Once they were outside, Noah breathed in the crisp evening air and felt himself relax. Tessa had done an amazing job with the gala, but the crowd and the stuffy atmosphere left him uncomfortable. He much preferred it out here...with Tessa.

He felt a twinge of sadness as she released his hand, leaving it cold and empty. She took several steps away from him, then turned to face him, her eyes luminous in the light of the moon, as she said, "There's something I want to tell you."

Inadvertently, he found himself bracing for whatever was about to come next. Perhaps it was because he'd delivered bad news to people so many times in his life that he could read in Tessa's tone and posture that this wasn't good. He couldn't, for the life of him, guess what she might be about to say. That she was leaving the hospital? That was the worst scenario he could think of at the moment. She may have rejected him, but as long as she worked at the hospital, he still got to see her on a daily basis.

"I owe you an apology for the other week, when we had dinner, and I said that—" she drew a breath, her eyes wide and full of regret "—that it was a mistake."

He wanted to step closer to her, to bridge the distance between them, but he didn't trust himself. He didn't think he'd be able to keep from touching her, especially after the feel of her hand in his as they'd made their way out onto the balcony.

"You don't need to apologize," he said. "I understand. I appreciate that you were honest enough to not want to pursue a relationship with me while you still have feelings for Burke."

She blinked, and then her eyes widened

even farther. He could see the moon reflected in the warm brown of her eyes.

"Is that what you thought?" she breathed in disbelief. "That I was still in love with Burke?"

He frowned. "We were having a good time...until you saw Burke and Erin."

Her eyes slid closed, and she drew a deep breath. He was baffled, hopeful and wary.

"So it wasn't because of Burke?"

She opened her eyes. "No. I'm not in love with Burke. I hope he and I can be friends, but I don't love him. Not like I..." She swallowed, and he tensed, his body straining toward her. "...I love you," she finished.

A rush of happiness washed over him, and he smiled, moving toward her. When she took a step back, though, he stopped.

"Wait. There's something you need to know."

He did as she asked, waiting, though every nerve and cell in his body cried out for him to take her in his arms.

"About two years ago, not long before Burke and I were supposed to be married, I received a diagnosis from my doctor."

Noah noted that Tessa's entire body was taut, as if poised to flee. Whatever she was about to share, it was obviously something that caused her a great deal of anxiety. He frowned, still waiting.

"I was experiencing early menopause. My entire reproductive system was aging before its time." She licked her lips, tears filling her eyes. His mind was skipping through the possibilities of this diagnosis, trying to get to the heart of her devastation.

"It means the odds of me ever conceiving a child were—are very slim." She drew a ragged breath. "Burke and I used to talk all the time about starting a family together. We didn't plan to wait, after we were married. I wanted to get pregnant right away, and he was ready to be a father. So when I found out I couldn't bear children, I took the coward's way out and stood him up at the altar."

She paused, perhaps weighing the consequences of this decision. "I couldn't bear it if he didn't want to marry me, so I took that decision away from him to protect myself and my heart." Her eyes slid closed again, as if she was too ashamed to look at Noah. "I know now that was wrong and unfair. However Burke felt about my infertility, I should have let him make his own choice. But I don't regret it, in some ways, because

Burke found happiness with Erin. That's who he was meant to be with all along. And I... Well, I think that for a long time, I believed no one could love me with this condition. But more than that, I couldn't love *myself*. I assumed how other people would look at me based on what I saw as my own failings." She opened her eyes. "But now I realize that's a very narrow view. Or at least, that's what I'm trying to tell myself these days. For me, children were always supposed to be a part of my future. I once refused a date with a guy in college because I knew he never wanted to have kids." She laughed, somewhat ruefully. "I guess I must have always had a very black-and-white view of the world."

She stopped speaking, and Noah ached to fill the silence, but his mind was still processing everything she had just told him.

She cleared her throat. "Anyway. That's why I pulled away from you. Because even though I know you lost a child, Noah, you have to realize that I'm sure you were and would still be an amazing father. I didn't want to take that away from you. And if you and I..." She trailed off, and he could see her working to hold her tears in check. "You'd have to appreciate that even if there was a future between us, it's likely we would experience quite a bit of disappointment and hope and consideration where children are concerned. I haven't fully accepted my limitations just yet," she added, "but I'm trying. Because I don't want this to be what defines me. At least, it shouldn't be."

He weighed through these words, recognizing what she was saying. There were all sorts of options for a situation like Tessa's, but he knew she might not want each one.

As for him, he'd never really considered whether he'd want to be a father again. With Tessa, surely he'd have wanted children. But he couldn't just say it didn't matter until he knew, in his heart, how much it did. And given all that she'd just shared with him, he worried that he'd somehow let her down. He hadn't seen her pain. Just like he hadn't seen Julia's.

"Maybe all this is a bit premature," she went on when he didn't say anything, "but I love you. And I believe you when you said you loved me. So if this is going to affect any chance of a future together, I think it's better we part ways now, no hard feelings." She lowered her head. "But I wanted you to know. Not just because of our potential future. But also because you're my friend." She raised her head and looked at him. "You've become my very best friend."

He opened his mouth to speak, but she raised a hand to stop him. "You don't have to say anything right now. In fact, I think I'd prefer it if you didn't. Because when you do, Noah...you have to be sure about what you want. Because if it's *me* that you want, it has to be with all the heartache and possibilities."

His heart strained to speak, but he honored her wishes and nodded. She gave a little nod in return, and her shoulders squared. He couldn't imagine the weight she had carried all this time, and the courage it had taken to share it with him. He wanted to honor her request and not make any instant decisions.

She didn't linger. She brushed by him without another word, the edge of her skirt brushing against his tuxedo. It took every ounce of willpower he possessed not to reach out for her as she passed by. But he waited, knowing that he couldn't ask for her heart until he had the answers she needed.

Noah didn't immediately follow Tessa back inside. He took a moment to compose himself, to come to grips with the news she'd just delivered. He was standing, staring out into the night, when he heard the doors behind him open, and someone else come onto the balcony.

He turned, hoping it was Tessa, but found her father, Allan, standing there instead. He held a glass of champagne in his hand. He raised it.

"A perk of donating the venue," he said. "I get to attend the party."

He took a sip, and Noah turned back without saying anything. His mind was still full of Tessa and what she'd shared. He was only barely aware of Allan stepping forward to stand beside him, not saying anything more as a minute, then two, passed by.

"My father was a cold man."

This unexpected statement caused Noah to glance at the other man.

Allan continued, "He came from nothing, and he pulled himself to the top, one ladder rung at a time. My mother told me he wasn't always cold, but by the time I was old enough to really have a sense of him, of his *presence*, he was someone to be admired and respected, not one to shower his loved ones with affection or share his emotions."

Noah wasn't sure where Allan was going with this, and he was momentarily irritated. He liked Tessa's father well enough, but he wanted time alone, to work through his feelings where Tessa was concerned. But the other man seemed oblivious to these emotions as he went on.

"Growing up, I was in awe of him and all he'd accomplished, how far he'd come. He was the strongest man I knew."

Allan paused to take a sip of his champagne.

"And then my mother died. Her illness was brief, not allowing us enough time to accept the loss before it actually occurred. I remember the graveside service, watching this man who'd never shed a single tear in his life, break down. He was on his knees, sobbing as if his heart had been torn in two, and the pain was more than he could bear."

Noah knew that feeling. He knew it all too well.

"I watched my father…break. For a young man who had never seen him as anything but a titan, it shook the foundation of my world. He had taken everything life threw at him and stood strong in spite of it. But losing the love of his life was more than he could bear. He kept working, but his spirit was no longer in it."

Allan looked down into his glass.

"This was before I met Vivienne," the older man explained. "So I had a hard time imagining what it was like to care for someone so much that losing them was akin to losing the better part of yourself."

He turned his gaze on Noah then.

"He lived on for a good many years after her, and he retained the success he'd gained… but he never reached for more after that. I think he was just going through the motions after she was gone. It rattled me in a way I can't really express. But then I met Vivienne, and I knew I was falling in love with her. And that scared me even more. I didn't want to lose her, but I didn't want to end up like my father one day."

Allan glanced away again, but Noah kept his eyes trained on the other man, captivated by his story.

"That year, on the anniversary of my mother's death, he and I went to her graveside together, just like we had every year since her passing. We would stand in silence because while her loss had changed him, it hadn't made him any softer. He still wasn't a man to talk about his feelings." Allan paused, and Noah sensed he was taking a moment to gather his emotions.

When he spoke again, his voice had a faint rasp that spoke of grief. "After we stood there for some time, I couldn't bear it anymore. My heart was full of Vivienne, but my head was warning me to turn back before I got in too deep." He swallowed. "So, I asked my father…'If you could do it all over again, would you still fall in love, knowing what it costs? Was it worth it?'"

Allan swirled the liquid in his glass. "What struck me was that he didn't hesitate. Not even for a heartbeat. He looked up at me, and his eyes were bloodshot with tears. He still missed her. He would always miss her. But he said to me, 'I would give anything to do it all over again.'"

Noah realized he was gripping the railing in front of him, so intent was he on what Allan would say next.

"That wasn't good enough for me, though," Allan said. "I pushed him on the subject and said, 'Even if this is how the story ends, every time? With you standing over her grave?'" Allan drew a deep breath. "And my dad stared back at the flowers we had laid on the grass, rested his palm on her headstone, and answered, 'I would take this grief every single day for a lifetime if it meant I could have just one more moment with her at my side.'"

Allan fell silent then, and Noah's grasp on the railing eventually eased. He understood this story. Perhaps better even than Allan, given the grief he had already experienced in his life. He wasn't afraid to love Tessa anymore. He was only worried that he couldn't be what she needed, especially after what she'd just revealed. He had failed one woman in his life with disastrous consequences. He couldn't bear to fail Tessa, too.

"My father lived to see me marry Vivienne, and he was there for Paige's first birthday. And then he was gone."

Allan drained the last of his champagne and cleared his throat. "I didn't know much about my parents' marriage, not really. I was their child, but I was an outsider to their relationship. But I can tell you what they taught me."

He focused on Noah once more. "No life remains untouched by sorrow. There is no relationship that doesn't experience difficulty. But I've seen you fight for those kids, and

I know that's what you are, Noah. You're a warrior when it comes to people you care about. And my little girl, well… She's definitely worth the fight."

The words struck a powerful chord because he felt the same way. He would have battled dragons for Tessa, real or imagined. If she needed him to fight with her, to fight *for* her, against infertility or anything else, he was all in. He had made mistakes in the past. But he could use those mistakes to build a better future.

With her.

"Well, I better get back to the party. I know I'm biased, but I have to say, I think my little girl did a good job with this gala."

Noah nodded, speaking out loud for the first time since Allan had joined him. "She's pretty amazing."

Allan smiled, as if knowing his work was done. He raised his empty champagne glass in salute and headed for the doors, leaving Noah alone once more.

Once he was gone, Noah released a breath, feeling the last weight of doubt lift from his shoulders. He marveled at Tessa's courage, at what it must have cost her to share her secret. It renewed his hope. They both had burdens, but in sharing them, the load would be much lighter. As long as they kept doing that, they could weather any storm. He released the balcony rail and straightened.

Tessa had wanted him to be sure, before he asked for her heart. And he was.

He'd never been more certain of anything in his life.

CHAPTER TWENTY-ONE

TESSA HAD WANTED a moment alone after talking to Noah on the balcony, but she was scarcely back inside the ballroom before she was approached by Dr. Hess.

"Tessa, darling." He reached out to lay a hand on either side of her arms and drew her in for a brief kiss to her cheek.

She was tense, wanting to turn around and see if Noah had come back inside but knowing she had to give him space.

"Hello, Dr. Hess," she greeted.

"You've done an outstanding job here, my dear. Everything is just perfect. People are raving about it."

"Thank you," she said. "I hope it does a lot of good for the hospital."

He clasped her hand in his. "I have no doubt on that score. How could they not be compelled to give after seeing all these moving stories about the children? I'm eager to hear Dr. Brennan's speech. If there are any doubts as to the worthiness of this cause, I'm sure he will eliminate them."

At the mention of Noah, her heart stuck in her throat. It had been selfish of her to choose tonight, of all nights, to unburden herself. She hoped her confession didn't affect his ability to give his speech. She should have been more sensitive to that. But she couldn't wait any longer. She'd made strides in the last few days by talking to her sisters, and then Burke, and then having a long, healing talk with her parents about all of it. They had been encouraging and supportive, and that helped. But telling Noah… That was the hardest conversation by far, and she'd feared if she didn't do it while she had the nerve, then she would retreat and leave the truth unspoken.

"The hospital is lucky to have you," Dr. Hess was saying, and Tessa was touched by such high praise from someone of Dr. Hess's stature. "And dare I say, I think you'll be with us for a very long time."

She recognized what he was saying. When her year was up, the job was hers. It should have brought her joy. But right now, her mind was on Noah. She thanked Dr. Hess for his kind words and gracefully disentangled herself from the conversation to attend to other details of the gala.

The event moved along seamlessly, from Ana's welcoming speech to dinner and dessert. They showed excerpts from the web series, and announced the awards it was nominated for. Nia, as the series' producer, had been invited to say a few words. Tessa flitted from here to there, never stopping, and never allowing herself to search the room for Noah no matter how much her heart demanded it. She didn't glimpse him, even once, throughout the evening. She wasn't sure if he was hiding or she just kept missing him during her rounds, but she did not give herself the luxury of trying to find him in the crowd.

It wasn't until it was finally his turn to ascend the podium, as the keynote speaker for the gala, that she let herself search the room for him. It was part of her job to make sure he was in place for his portion of the event. She needn't have worried. He was already by the stage, waiting to be introduced as Ana stepped up to the podium.

"Many of you are familiar with Dr. Noah Brennan's work in our pediatric oncology department." Ana ran through Noah's education and accolades, but Tessa barely heard.

Her attention was riveted on the man standing off to the side, head lowered as he waited to be called forward.

She found herself studying him with an increasing longing in her heart, the set of his shoulders, the cut of his jaw, the lines of his hands as he clasped them together in front of him. She felt it then, with both relief and regret. The way she loved Noah was deeper than any emotion she'd experienced before. Burke had been a friend, someone she certainly admired and felt affection for, but her emotions for him were a pale thing compared to the depth of longing she experienced for Noah.

She was glad she'd told him her secret. Because whether he chose her or not, she needed him to know, as her friend if nothing more.

She loved him, and suddenly, that was all that mattered. Maybe her grief over her diagnosis had been because she hadn't loved Burke enough. She hadn't been prepared to view marriage as a partnership, for better or worse. She had only seen the thing she wanted, and when it was taken away, she felt as though she had nothing left. But that wasn't true. With Noah, she had so much.

His friendship. His support. His kindness. His love.

She took a small step toward him just as Ana finished her introduction and he raised his head. She stopped, coming up short, as he moved toward the podium. Her breath caught in her throat as he kept his eyes lowered for what seemed an agonizing length of time. The room sat in rapt attention, and she couldn't help feeling a flutter of pride. He'd certainly captured their attention.

But when he raised his head, it wasn't the audience he looked at. It was her. Somehow, he instinctively knew where she was, his stare cutting across the crowd to find her. He held her in the warmth of his gaze for several long seconds before shifting his concentration to address the gala attendees.

"I came tonight armed with statistics, details on clinical trials, and information on how to better the programs and treatment at Chesapeake View Children's Hospital." He drew a deep breath. "But I can bore you with all of that for hours, and none of it might make a difference. So instead, I want to tell you a story."

He paused, and Tessa forced herself to stay

rooted to the spot instead of closing the distance between them.

"My daughter, Ginny, was diagnosed with acute lymphoblastic leukemia at eight years of age."

And so he began his story, leaving nothing out. He shared every detail—not focusing so much on the treatments but rather on the emotions, what it felt like to be a parent whose child was diagnosed with cancer. And he told them about Julia, her decimating grief. His feelings of helplessness. His determination and doubt. And when he finally had to admit that Ginny had become one of the children who did not defeat leukemia, his voice was sad…but not so thick with loss that he couldn't find his way through.

The ballroom was so silent that Tessa could hear the soft breaths of those around her. Even the servers had stopped, everyone listening to what Noah would say next.

"For a long time, I've resisted being a voice on behalf of both patients and parents, but recently, someone changed my mind, reminding me that maybe I can speak about this better than anyone."

He glanced in Tessa's direction, and she smiled her encouragement.

"So the message I want to give you tonight is about hope. How it turned me inside out, how I felt it had betrayed me until I realized it was the thing pulling me along in the wake of my loss. Hope held me up when I couldn't stand myself. Hope is what we give to these families every day, and that is something that has no price tag."

His eyes swept the room for a long moment before they finally found her again. He kept his attention focused on her as he continued.

"What you have to know," he began again, his voice so low that without a microphone, it never would have carried, "is that I am no stranger to grief. I know how hard life can be. I know what it is to have your dreams stolen."

He was talking to her. In this crowd full of people, these words were for her alone.

"You give me hope. Not that life will be easy. Not that I will never grieve again. But that I don't have to do it alone, not as long as you're standing with me, and I'm with you, and we're fighting together. That's what hope is. Believing that neither of us is on our own, and as long as that's true, we will weather whatever comes."

Her throat closed, and her heart hammered. The words were as much a pledge as any wedding vows he might have made.

"There are no guarantees. There never are. But I will make you one. As long as you're willing to try, then so am I."

He seemed to have forgotten his audience, and while some of them were still hanging on to his words, believing them to be about the hospital, others were shifting their gazes, noticing that his attention was focused on only one person. Her.

The silence dragged out until he stepped away from the podium. She sensed more and more people looking at her, but it didn't matter. She wasn't paying attention to them anymore. She only had eyes for him.

"I love you, Tessa Worth." Even without the microphone, in the utter silence, the words carried to her across the distance that separated them. "And it's you that I want. Just you. Anything else, we will figure out and face together."

Tears slipped from her eyes. She felt them on her cheeks, but she didn't make a move to brush them away.

"All you have to do…" he said, the words soft but strong, "is say yes."

She smiled through her tears, her heart swelling with joy.

"Yes," she whispered, but the word came out so quietly she thought he might not have heard.

But he did. The second it left her lips, he stepped away from the stage, threading his way through the ballroom's tables to try and reach her.

"Yes," she said again, louder, to encourage him.

He was hurrying, but it wasn't fast enough. She began moving, too, holding up the skirt of her gown as she tried to close the distance.

"Yes!" she called. "Yes, yes, yes!"

Until he was in front of her, pulling her into his arms, and drawing her against him. His kisses covered her tears, reassuring her that he loved her.

"If you want children one day, we'll figure it out together. We'll do treatments, or adopt, or anything that you want. I'll support you however I can. But it's you that I want. You, more than anything."

She molded into his arms, tucking herself into the shelter of his embrace and knowing that, no matter what, she had him, for better, for worse, forever.

"You're what I want, too," she said into his chest.

He eased her out of his arms so that he could look into her upturned face.

"What did you say?"

She reached up to rest her palm against his face, overwhelmed by the love she felt.

"You're the one I want, too."

The words drew a smile, perhaps the biggest one she had ever seen yet on Noah's face. As he lowered his lips to hers, she was vaguely aware of applause echoing around the ballroom, but she didn't pay it much mind.

She had Noah, and he had her.

That was more than enough.

EPILOGUE

"I'M SO GLAD the weather is warm enough that we could celebrate on the patio," Tessa remarked as she bounced Grace on one knee. The little girl was growing quickly and Tessa couldn't believe she was now a year old.

Beside them, Harper admired the view of the bay from where they each sat in one of the outdoor chairs at Callahan's. "I love that our restaurant sits along the waterfront. Thank goodness that Connor's dad owned the property long before the tourist boom came to town. It's prime real estate now."

"Did I hear you mention Dad?" Rory Landry asked as she took a seat next to Tessa. "Hand that niece over, Tessa," she said, without waiting for Harper to reply. "You get to see her more than I do, with me living in Nashville."

Tessa surrendered Grace into the other woman's arms without objection. She couldn't imagine how Connor's sister did it, living so far away from family. But then, Rory and Sawyer were often on the road, traveling the world due to his crazy concert schedule as an award-winning country musician and their constant charity events to raise awareness for Alzheimer's foundations.

So far, Sawyer had exhibited no symptoms of the early-onset version of the disease, but Tessa knew the couple lived each day as if it were precious, never sure how long they had together. They had made a point to clear their schedule for this weekend, though, so they could attend little Gavin Daniels's christening. Sawyer had been best friends with the baby's namesake. Burke's brother and Sawyer had gone through high school together and then Army basic training. And Rory and Erin had always been close. They had been determined to be here for little Gavin's big day.

Tessa's gaze shifted now to where Burke and Erin stood, greeting their guests while their oldest son, Kitt, looked on, watching over his newborn brother as Erin held the infant in her arms. Tessa felt that familiar pang at the sight, but it didn't linger. Every day, she was learning to let go of her grief and jealousy. It helped that she and Noah had begun discussing their options, including adoption. The idea was growing on her, though she wasn't ready to make any decisions yet. After all, Noah had only just officially proposed last month. They had a wedding to plan, which would keep them both busy enough in addition to their duties at the hospital. Dr. Hess had made true on his promise. Tessa's job as the hospital's marketing and PR coordinator was secure.

Plus, she had another role to consider.

"I think I better help Erin out by offering to hold my godson for a bit."

Harper reached out to touch her hand briefly before she stood. She returned the gesture by brushing her fingers along Harper's shoulders as she moved away. It felt good to have her sister's love and support.

"Take your time," Rory called after her, though her attention was focused squarely on Grace. "You're not getting this little one back for a while!"

Tessa tossed a smile over her shoulder. She didn't mind sharing Grace with Rory. She only hoped her niece understood one day just how blessed she was to have a family who loved her so much.

As she walked by, she caught sight of Zoe and Molly, giggling together as they hovered near a tray of cupcakes. They met her eye, and she gave them a warning glance. They grinned impishly and hurried away from the table, across the restaurant patio and over to where Connor and Sawyer were deep in conversation. It was good to see Zoe with so much color in her cheeks. There was a crown of hair on her scalp now that she had achieved full remission from her leukemia. It was just another reminder to Tessa that this was a day of blessings.

Erin saw her coming and let out a breath of relief, passing Gavin into her arms without Tessa having to ask.

"Thank you," she said, turning toward Tessa for a moment. "He was starting to get a little heavy."

Tessa tucked Gavin's baby blanket more tightly around him. It was a warm spring day, but she didn't want the breeze from the bay giving him a chill. "Of course," Tessa said to Erin, "after all, that's what godmothers are for."

Erin reached out to squeeze her arm.

"Thank you, for you and Noah agreeing to share the honor with Sawyer and Rory."

"We were happy to." She looked into Gavin's face. The newborn's eyes were scrunched up in sleep, seemingly uninterested that he was the honoree of this christening luncheon. "After all, a baby can't have too many aunts and uncles."

"You're right about that," Erin murmured. "And godmothers are important."

Something in Erin's tone caused Tessa to raise her eyes. The two women shared a meaningful glance.

"Don't leave godfathers out of that." Tessa grinned at the sound of Noah's voice, tingling with pleasure as he wrapped his arms around her from behind and looked over her shoulder into Gavin's face. The baby yawned widely and tugged one arm free from his blanket to wave a first in the air. Noah reached out a finger to trace the tiny knuckles. Gavin opened his hand and latched on to Noah's knuckle.

"I'm telling you now, this kid is going to be a champion arm wrestler," Noah announced.

Burke, who had been in midconversation

with his good friend Neal Weaver, shifted his attention to Noah. "Of course he is. He's a Daniels. His namesake was undefeated when it came to arm wrestling."

Erin laughed softly. "Yes, he was."

There was a moment of silence for Gavin, Burke's brother and Erin's first husband, who had died a few years ago.

Tessa was grateful for how gently Noah broke the quiet by saying, "He's a fortunate little guy, then. I was cursed with these delicate doctor's hands, and I've never won an arm wrestling match in my life."

This remark earned a round of laughter, and Tessa's heart warmed. With her free hand, she reached for his and gave it a squeeze.

Erin and Burke's attention was quickly diverted by more guests. Tessa took the opportunity to move away, bouncing Gavin gently in her arms as Noah directed her toward the railing that overlooked the lighthouse in the distance.

He wrapped his arms around her once more, drawing her back against his chest. Gavin sighed with contentment, and Tessa's heart did the same. The sun glinted off the waves of the bay, scattering sunbeams like diamonds across the water. The air was fresh with the scent of spring…and hope.

Tessa shifted her gaze to look into the baby's face. His eyes fluttered open, blinking against the light.

"What do you think the future holds for him?" Tessa asked, daydreaming aloud. "I hope he never knows sorrow or pain, and that all his days are bright."

Noah pressed a kiss to her jaw, and she shivered with happiness at the gentle touch of his lips.

"That is a lovely thought, Tessa, though he'll likely face his own share of joy and sadness."

"Hmm. You're probably right," Tessa reluctantly agreed. "But then I pray he also knows love. The kind that stands strong, like that lighthouse—" she turned her attention to the structure in the distance "—and holds firm no matter how hard the waves crash against it."

"That sounds like the perfect benediction for a christening day," he remarked, his voice low as he nuzzled her neck.

"I hope so," she replied, turning her head slightly so Noah could move from her neck and up her jaw, making his way toward her lips. "Because I know how that kind of love feels. And I wouldn't trade it for anything."

And then Noah's mouth found hers, and he demonstrated his agreement without words as the waves of the bay lapped gently against the Findlay Roads shore.

* * * * *

Get 4 FREE REWARDS!

We'll send you 2 FREE Books plus 2 FREE Mystery Gifts.

Their Family Legacy
Lorraine Beatty

The Rancher's Answered Prayer
Arlene James

Love Inspired® books feature contemporary inspirational romances with Christian characters facing the challenges of life and love.

FREE
Value Over
$20

YES! Please send me 2 FREE Love Inspired® Romance novels and my 2 FREE mystery gifts (gifts are worth about $10 retail). After receiving them, if I don't wish to receive any more books, I can return the shipping statement marked "cancel." If I don't cancel, I will receive 6 brand-new novels every month and be billed just $5.24 for the regular-print edition or $5.74 each for the larger print edition in the U.S., or $5.74 each for the regular-print edition or $6.24 each for the larger print edition in Canada. That's a savings of at least 13% off the cover price. It's quite a bargain! Shipping and handling is just 50¢ per book in the U.S. and 75¢ per book in Canada.* I understand that accepting the 2 free books and gifts places me under no obligation to buy anything. I can always return a shipment and cancel at any time. The free books and gifts are mine to keep no matter what I decide.

Choose one: ☐ **Love Inspired® Romance**
Regular-Print
(105/305 IDN GMY4)

☐ **Love Inspired® Romance**
Larger-Print
(122/322 IDN GMY4)

Name (please print)

Address   Apt. #

City   State/Province   Zip/Postal Code

Mail to the Reader Service:
IN U.S.A.: P.O. Box 1341, Buffalo, NY 14240-8531
IN CANADA: P.O. Box 603, Fort Erie, Ontario L2A 5X3

Want to try 2 free books from another series! Call 1-800-873-8635 or visit www.ReaderService.com.

---

*Terms and prices subject to change without notice. Prices do not include sales taxes, which will be charged (if applicable) based on your state or country of residence. Canadian residents will be charged applicable taxes. Offer not valid in Quebec. This offer is limited to one order per household. Books received may not be as shown. Not valid for current subscribers to Love Inspired Romance books. All orders subject to approval. Credit or debit balances in a customer's account(s) may be offset by any other outstanding balance owed by or to the customer. Please allow 4 to 6 weeks for delivery. Offer available while quantities last.

Your Privacy—The Reader Service is committed to protecting your privacy. Our Privacy Policy is available online at www.ReaderService.com or upon request from the Reader Service. We make a portion of our mailing list available to reputable third parties that offer products we believe may interest you. If you prefer that we not exchange your name with third parties, or if you wish to clarify or modify your communication preferences, please visit us at www.ReaderService.com/consumerchoice or write to us at Reader Service Preference Service, P.O. Box 9062, Buffalo, NY 14240-9062. Include your complete name and address.

LI19R

Get 4 FREE REWARDS!

We'll send you 2 FREE Books plus 2 FREE Mystery Gifts.

Love Inspired® Suspense books feature Christian characters facing challenges to their faith... and lives.

FREE Value Over $20

MUST ♥ DOGS COLLECTION

SAVE 30% AND GET A FREE GIFT!

Finding true love can be "ruff"— but not when adorable dogs help to play matchmaker in these inspiring romantic "tails."

YES! Please send me the first shipment of four books from the **Must ♥ Dogs Collection**. If I don't cancel, I will continue to receive four books a month for two additional months, and I will be billed at the same discount price of $18.20 U.S./$20.30 CAN., plus $1.99 for shipping and handling.* That's a 30% discount off the cover prices! Plus, I'll receive a FREE adorable, hand-painted dog figurine in every shipment (approx. retail value of $4.99)! I am under no obligation to purchase anything and I may cancel at any time by marking "cancel" on the shipping statement and returning the shipment. I may keep the FREE books no matter what I decide.

☐ 256 HCN 4331   ☐ 456 HCN 4331

Name (please print)

Address   Apt. #

City   State/Province   Zip/Postal Code

Mail to the **Reader Service:**
IN U.S.A.: P.O. Box 1867, Buffalo, NY. 14240-1867
IN CANADA: P.O. Box 609, Fort Erie, Ontario L2A 5X3

PETSBPA19

Get 4 FREE REWARDS!

We'll send you 2 FREE Books plus <u>plus</u> 2 FREE Mystery Gifts.

FREE
Value Over
$20

Both the **Romance** and **Suspense** collections feature compelling novels written by many of today's best-selling authors.

YES! Please send me 2 FREE novels from the Essential Romance or Essential Suspense Collection and my 2 FREE gifts (gifts are worth about $10 retail). After receiving them, if I don't wish to receive any more books, I can return the shipping statement marked "cancel." If I don't cancel, I will receive 4 brand-new novels every month and be billed just $6.74 each in the U.S. or $7.24 each in Canada. That's a savings of at least 16% off the cover price. It's quite a bargain! Shipping and handling is just 50¢ per book in the U.S. and 75¢ per book in Canada.* I understand that accepting the 2 free books and gifts places me under no obligation to buy anything. I can always return a shipment and cancel at any time. The free books and gifts are mine to keep no matter what I decide.

Choose one: ☐ **Essential Romance**   ☐ **Essential Suspense**
                (194/394 MDN GMY7)   (191/391 MDN GMY7)

Name (please print)

Address   Apt. #

City   State/Province   Zip/Postal Code

Mail to the **Reader Service:**
IN U.S.A.: P.O. Box 1341, Buffalo, NY 14240-8531
IN CANADA: P.O. Box 603, Fort Erie, Ontario L2A 5X3

Want to try 2 free books from another series! Call 1-800-873-8635 or visit www.ReaderService.com.

Get 4 FREE REWARDS!

We'll send you 2 FREE Books plus 2 FREE Mystery Gifts.

Harlequin® Special Edition books feature heroines finding the balance between their work life and personal life on the way to finding true love.

FREE
Value Over
$20

Get 4 FREE REWARDS!

We'll send you 2 FREE Books plus 2 FREE Mystery Gifts.

Harlequin® Romance Larger-Print books feature uplifting escapes that will warm your heart with the ultimate feel-good tales.

FREE
Value Over
$20